PRAISE FOR *THE IN*

'Jinks spins a feasible and fun story
irrational time, with a little unresolved sexual tension thrown in for good measure. Those rascally monks. The murder mystery is convincingly clever.' —*The Age*

'The most engaging Australian novel I have picked up this year . . . Jinks effectively creates a quite believable historical world which does not impede the wham-bam action and at the same time manages not to insult the intelligence . . . this book is a page-turner.' —*Sydney Morning Herald*

'Every bit as engrossing as Eco's ecclesiastical crime-adventure . . . It is a splendid display of insights into motives, grasp of historical forces, and the meticulous recording of social minutiae.' —*Australian Book Review*

PRAISE FOR *THE NOTARY*

'An astute eye for detail, both physical and emotional, and wry ear for conversational nuance . . . she peoples her tale with credible characters, stirring in just enough action, mystery, mischief and intellectual argument.' —*Weekend Australian*

'This splendidly subversive novel vividly imagines medieval ignorance, debauchery and prejudice in a world entirely in the grip of an implacable Church . . . Jinks combines bawdy Chaucerian humour with impressive religious learning and considerable knowledge of the period, all worn lightly: it's a popular and intelligent mystery to wallow in with complete abandon.' —*Sydney Morning Herald*

CATHERINE JINKS has won critical acclaim and a growing international audience for her literary talent, her versatility, and her compelling storytelling. Her medieval thrillers *The Inquisitor* (1999) and *The Notary* (2000) have earned favourable comparisons with *The Name of the Rose* and *The Da Vinci Code*. She has published more than thirty books across a wide range of genres; *The Secret Familiar* is her eighth novel for adults. Catherine lives in the Blue Mountains of New South Wales with her husband and daughter.

The SECRET FAMILIAR

(Confessions of an Inquisitor's Spy)

CATHERINE JINKS

ALLEN&UNWIN

First published in 2006

Allen & Unwin
83 Alexander Street
Crows Nest NSW 2065
Australia
Phone: (61 2) 8425 0100
Fax: (61 2) 9906 2218
Email: info@allenandunwin.com
Web: www.allenandunwin.com

National Library of Australia
Cataloguing-in-Publication entry:

Jinks, Catherine, 1963- .
The secret familiar.

ISBN 9781741750508.
ISBN 1 74175 050 4.

I. Title.

A823.4

Set in 12.25/18pt Requiem Text by Bookhouse, Sydney
Printed and bound in Australia by Griffin Press

10 9 8 7 6 5 4 3 2 1

To Sebastian Ritscher
without whom this book would not exist

Acknowledgements

With thanks to John O. Ward, Trish Graham, Andrew Hellen and Margaret Connolly.

Extracts from the journal of

Helié Bernier of Verdun-en-Lauragais

(alias Helié Seguier of Carcassonne)

1321

I.
Thursday after the Feast of the Epiphany

I am well placed, here. The site was carefully chosen. As long as I sit at this window, no one can approach my house unseen.

On each side I share a wall in common with my neighbours. At the rear, my courtyard abuts the wall of the Cité. And the western face of my house looks straight down a thoroughfare known as 'Stump Way', because it is cut off short like an amputated limb.

From my seat at this window I can see all of Stump Way, as well as a portion of the Rue de Sabatayre, which lies beyond. These streets are not much frequented by strangers. Pilgrims rarely pass through, for there are no hospices nearby. Sailors and fishermen favour the suburb of Villeneuve. The Old Market is not too close.

So I can recognise most of the faces that catch my eye throughout the day.

That face over there, for instance, belongs to my tenant, Hugues Moresi. He is heading off to buy wine; when he returns he will be drunk, and will beat his wife, and I shall have to pretend that I heard nothing. The woman by the well is my southern neighbour. Though I cannot see her face, I recognise her Genoa-red gown and the green trimming on her cloak. She is talking to her husband, who has just returned from a mill or a baker's shop. (There is flour on his boots.) The only stranger in sight is walking away, towards the Rue de Sabatayre. He walks like a man unaccustomed to crowds, his long peasant's stride breaking up into stuttering little steps as he tries to dodge the more nimble pedestrians. His undershirt is of Barchinone work, having one scarlet thread crossing one of rich cherry. So he must be from the west.

But he *is* a stranger. He is not Armand Sanche. I would recognise Armand Sanche even from behind. When I saw him today I knew him instantly, for all that his hair is now grey, and his nose is broken.

He knew me too. He started, and his eyes widened, and he turned his head away. Then he bolted like a hare down the nearest side street. I could not tell if he was merely a visitor to Narbonne or if he now resides here. Though his surcoat was made of the brown cloth for which this city is famous, it is easy enough to buy Narbonnaise cloth all over the world. You could be living in Sicily and still be dressing like a burgher of Narbonne.

What is he doing here? Hiding, no doubt. He was afraid of me, so he must be a fugitive. Perhaps he escaped from prison. Perhaps he was sentenced to wear a yellow cross, and has torn it off his clothes. Perhaps, in exchange for his freedom, he promised to track down and arrest some of his fellow heretics. If so, he has failed to keep his promise. That much was written on his face.

Perhaps he was able to avoid the inquisitors altogether.

I doubt it, though; he was always a fool. I remember the last time we met, twelve years ago. It was at Prunet, around Candlemas, and we were sleeping in a stable with the sheep and the oxen. This was partly for warmth, and partly because we were both in hiding. Armand was one of many gullible souls who had abandoned all reason to follow Pierre Autier, the famous priest of the heretical Cathars. And I was aping him as best I could.

'Helié,' he said, as we lay there in the straw, attempting to share a single threadbare blanket, 'have you heard the Good Men talk about evil spirits?'

'Many times,' I replied. And indeed, evil spirits are a favourite topic of the Cathar priests, who are also known as Good Men, or *perfecti*, because they eat no meat, and wear poor clothes, and live a chaste life that they describe as 'perfected'.

'Pierre Autier says that the air is full of evil spirits, which burn the good spirits,' Armand continued, in his plodding way. 'And that is why, when a good spirit leaves a dead body, it is anxious to find another body of flesh to dwell in. Because the evil spirits cannot burn or torment it there.'

'Yes, yes,' I said, yawning. 'What's your point?'

'Well—what if the weather is very cold, as it is today? If the good spirits can burn, can they freeze also?'

I was accustomed to such questions from Armand. I knew better than to laugh or to scoff. I refrained from pointing out that the lies of the Good Men would get him killed one day. All I said was: 'Next time you see Pierre Autier, you must ask him about the good spirits.' And I blew on my fingers, which were like ten icicles, without colour or feeling.

I do not think that Armand ever did see Pierre Autier again. The next morning he set off for Villemur, to find his cousin (who was also a fugitive *perfectus*), and I headed south, in search of Pierre Autier. He was my quarry that year; I was far less interested in humble believers like Armand Sanche. Armand was a minnow to Pierre's whale—and like a minnow, he may have slipped through the net. I do not know. Although I pursued the wily Pierre all the way to Belpech, and practically delivered him into the hands of my master, I was travelling towards the mountains that summer when he finally met his end. Pierre was burned, I know. But as to the fates of his many protectors and followers—that I was not told.

All I do know for certain is that Armand Sanche has come to Narbonne. He has come here, and he does not want to be found. That is well and good, for I do not want to be found either; he must think me a fugitive, much like himself. He would no more submit my name to the Archbishop than I would submit his. So I have nothing to fear from his intentions.

Alas, however, I have everything to fear from his lack of wit. Whatever he might have done to regain (or retain) his freedom, it will not be his for much longer, I feel sure. One day he will be caught, and then he will confess, and my own name is bound to surface during his interrogation. How not? Then my careful disguise may be stripped away, and if the hands that do it are clumsy enough, my plans might be overturned. I might have to move on, before I attract unwanted attention.

That is why I shall take note of every stranger in the street, and every odd request or unusual event that I might encounter henceforth. For my memory is not what it was, and I may need to refer back to the past some time in the future.

I must begin once again to plot the slow, small patterns that unfold before me.

II.
Friday before Septuagesima

I have just returned from the Capitol Tower, where I spent last night in the archiepiscopal prison.

It seems that my worst fears have been realised. That fool Armand Sanche has been spilling his guts to the Inquisitor of Carcassonne. And now I must pay for his stupidity.

When the summons arrived I was downstairs, lifting wet goat hides out of the biggest vat with a stick. So I heard my apprentice answer the front door, and knew at once that I was in trouble. Never before had I received a visit from any priest of St-Sebastien, for all that I make my confession there three times a year. My alms-giving is not generous enough to merit such condescension.

Yet I recognised instantly the voice of Anselm Guiraud, one of the canons, asking for me. And when my apprentice replied that I would have to be fetched, another voice broke in: a voice with a Catalan accent. 'Tell your master that he must come at once, on pain of excommunication,' it declared.

I am pleased to say that my skills have not entirely deserted me. My limbs moved even more quickly than my thoughts, and I made haste to bar the door separating my cellar from my shop. 'One moment, if you please!' I declared loudly, as I retrieved my master's letter. By a lucky chance, I was in the very room where it is normally concealed, and needed only to move the barrel, and lift the flagstone. 'Just let me hang this hide!' I said.

To look at that barrel, you might wonder that I could lift it at all. But it was constructed with a false bottom, high up near its mouth; though it seems to be full of lime water, it contains a mere bucketful. Therefore to move it is the work of a moment, even though I am a small man, and not in the first flush of my youth. The Catalan had barely uttered his protest before I was unbarring the door, my letter tucked safely into my clothes, my barrel returned to its customary position.

'Oh,' said the Catalan, when I appeared before him. 'Are you Helié Seguier, the parchment-maker?'

'I am,' was my response.

'Then you are wanted at the Capitol Tower,' declared the Catalan—who had once been a chandler, or perhaps a cooper, to judge from the little burn marks all over his face and hands. There were other scars too, one on each wrist: the scars of iron shackles. I am familiar with the marks. As clearly as any inscription within a register of sentences, they told me that the Catalan was a nuncio, or messenger, employed by his former gaoler. He was a reformed heretic turned inquisitorial lackey.

But I was a stranger to him. And for that I was grateful.

'This is a letter of peremptory summons from Brother Jean de Beaune, the Inquisitor of Carcassonne,' explained the canon, offering up a document composed in Latin. Since I cannot read Latin, I gave it straight back. 'As you see, it bears his seal.'

'You should tell your wife, and come directly,' said the Catalan, glancing at my apprentice, who is only a boy.

'I have no wife. Or children,' I countered, and turned to young Martin. It must be confessed that he looked as frightened as any son might have, on seeing his father arrested. For I had won his true allegiance by a very simple expedient.

Martin's father, you see, is Hugues Moresi. Hugues is a good tenant, being a skilled shoemaker, honest in his dealings. But he has a heavy hand within the confines of his own domain. And while the punishment that he metes out to his wife and his other children is no concern of mine, I will not tolerate any damage to my own apprentice, whom I have paid for. Generously.

I said as much three weeks ago. Whereupon Martin ceased to appear in my shop with split lips and blackened eyes, and my customers stopped looking at me askance—or making jocular remarks about sparing the rod to spoil the child.

The depth of Martin's gratitude for my intervention was evident in his sudden pallor, as the Catalan conducted me from my house.

'You must hang the other hides,' I said to Martin. 'And bar the door, and fasten the shutters.'

'Yes, Master.'

'Then you can go upstairs, and scrape that skin some more. But when the light fades, you should go home. Do you understand?'

'Yes, Master.'

'I shall return. Have no fear.'

Fruitless directive! Though I was confident in my own safety, I conveyed none of my assurance to Martin, who watched me leave as if he never expected to see me again.

It is not such a very great distance from my house to the Capitol Tower. On our way we passed St-Sebastien, where the canon bade me a muted farewell. The blessing that he bestowed on me was flustered, as if he knew not what to think. Once he had gone, the nuncio took my elbow. He was armed with a big knife, prominently displayed, and was blessed with a stronger grip than I would have anticipated.

But I had no thoughts of fleeing. I knew that I was safe enough—provided that Jean de Beaune did not keep me waiting for too long.

I had never met the man. He was appointed around the time that I left Toulouse, so our paths had not crossed. Nevertheless, I was aware of his presence in Narbonne—for it does not pay to lose sight of inquisitors. Even in my quiet corner of town, I had heard about the heresy trial taking place. It had caused some offence, because it should, by rights, have been convened and presided over by our Archbishop. Instead Jean de Beaune was in charge; he had come all the way from Carcassonne to trample upon the prerogatives of Narbonne's citizens, and offend the assembly of learned men who were summoned to help him pass judgement.

Knowing this, I was concerned that he might be too busy to question me in the immediate future.

'Where is Jean de Beaune today?' I asked. 'Is he at the Archbishop's palace? Or the Dominican priory?'

'How should I know?' the Catalan replied, and I saw at once that he was not clever. A clever turnkey is friendly with his charges, and learns much as a result. This Catalan was concerned about nothing but his own self-consequence.

So I abandoned all expectation of dialogue, and surrendered myself meekly to imprisonment.

The archiepiscopal *mur* was new to me. I suppose that I would describe the tower as a *murus largus*; being small and overcrowded, it offers few facilities for solitary confinement. Most prisoners wander about at will, sleeping where they can find an empty corner and receiving visitors at all hours. In Toulouse and Carcassonne, the inquisitorial prisons are different. They contain at least a few small cells in which certain prisoners are locked up and chained to the walls. In the Capitol Tower there are no cells of this description, and those inmates who *are* shackled can still shuffle about—albeit slowly and awkwardly. The gaoler and sergeants also strike me as being highly corruptible. While I was in their charge, I saw them take money not only for food and wine but for the admittance of women. Moreover, I had to pay for the privilege of avoiding heavy manacles.

Needless to say, I had come well furnished with coin, which I surrendered to the gaoler immediately. It is pointless trying to retain your money in prison. If the gaoler does not deprive you of it forcibly, the other prisoners will take it from you while you sleep. Understanding this, I provided the archbishop's gaoler with a handsome sum upon the very threshold of the *mur*, and was thenceforth treated with a precisely calibrated generosity.

I even received a blanket—for the *mur* was very cold. Fires are not encouraged there, and the thick stone walls are always damp. Bitter draughts penetrate them through every chink and arrow slit. Though circumscribed by no shackles or prohibitions, I found myself crouched in one spot, wrapped in my greasy blanket and blowing clouds of vapour into the fetid air. Like my fellow inmates, I sought out other warm bodies to huddle against. For solitude is not a favourable condition, if one's blood has turned to ice.

This is how I became acquainted with my first Beguin.

I have shared many cold nights with many frightened heretics. But in the past they were always Cathars, and had been hunted all their lives. Heresy is in the bloodline of most Cathars; they are raised from birth to regard priests as their enemies, and the Church as Hell's Gate. They are weaned on stories of martyrdom. So although they might be arrogant, they are also resigned. There is hardly a trace of reckless courage among them. The time for that is long gone, for the heresy is an ancient one, with deep roots in my country.

The Beguins are different—or so I deduced from the one I met. As we shivered together in a frigid stairwell, we began to exchange a few words. He gave me his name, and I gave him my alias. He was called Pons, and he talked incessantly. I thought him foolish beyond belief, for he knew nothing about me or my intentions. (For all he knew, I could have been a spy, planted there to learn his secrets.) But he was passionate, and frightened, and accustomed to declaiming; perhaps he wanted to distract himself from his miseries.

Whatever the cause, he furnished me with fresh news about the current heresy trial—which happens to be his own. Though such trials are normally held in secret, the events of this particular one are becoming well known in certain circles, owing to a bitter dispute that has arisen between the judges. Pons described it to me in detail. Apparently, he and several companions have been charged with spreading the doctrine that Christ and His Apostles owned no possessions, either separately or in common. Jean de Beaune has condemned this view as heretical. But one of the experts assembled to pass judgement on the captured Beguins—a lector at the Franciscan priory here in Narbonne—has begged to differ. He has declared that, far from being doubtful, such a belief was defined as orthodox in the decretal *Exiit qui seminat.*

'Now he has been ordered to recant by that devil, Jean de Beaune,' Pons lamented. 'Even though the truth of his position is manifest! It is beyond belief.'

'Perhaps,' I replied, though it all made perfect sense to me. I know little about the Beguin heresy, but a man would have to be blind and deaf not to have realised that Christ's poverty is now a subject to be avoided in public. Only three years ago, four Franciscan monks were burned at Marseilles for adhering too staunchly to their belief in holy poverty. Since then, three people have burned in Narbonne for much the same reason.

One can only assume that Jean de Beaune was planning some mischief by appointing a Franciscan to his judicial assembly. For there are many Franciscans who still nurse a fond regard for evangelical destitution, despite the Pope's unsympathetic stance. And what better way to sniff out a heretic than to have him condemn himself, on record, with his own tongue?

'Your Franciscan is a brave man,' I remarked tactfully. Whereupon I was treated to a harangue on the subject of honest Christians, and lying followers of the Antichrist, and why the monks of St Dominic are suckling at the teats of the Whore of Babylon. Once upon a time, I would have taken careful note of every word spoken, so that I might repeat them in a sworn statement. But Pons was a lucky man. Most of what he said I disregarded. In fact I drifted off to sleep while he was still rambling on about the Rule of St Francis, and how it is the same as the Gospel of Christ.

Hours later, I awoke to find that it was dark. Even Pons had fallen asleep by then. A *mur* at night is a dismal place, for every sigh and sob and groan is clearly audible in the silence. I remembered how once, long ago, I used to struggle with my rising sense of panic as I lay in the *murus largus* of Toulouse, imagining a tide of rats approaching me through the darkness. That was before my master's arrival, of course. But the memory did not make my night in the tower any more enjoyable.

In the morning it occurred to me that I was getting too old for prison. When I was younger, I never suffered from stiff limbs or aching joints, no matter how uncomfortably I was housed. During the last five years, however, I have grown accustomed to soft beds and good food. I have lost my endurance.

On reflection, I should perhaps make some attempt to strengthen my sinews again. Now that Jean de Beaune has found me out.

With regard to Jean de Beaune, he came that afternoon, just after nones. The bells were ringing at St-Sebastien when I was brought to the guard room. There I waited for some time, alone, quietly surveying the nutshells, fruit stones, old boots, piles of rags, empty casks and bits of broken furniture with which the gaoler's staff choose to surround themselves. I was beginning to wonder if I, too, had been left to moulder away like an apple core when Jean de Beaune suddenly appeared, accompanied by the selfsame nuncio who had fetched me the day before.

The Dominican arrived like a blast of wind, banging the door and sending discarded husks and straws whirling into the air. He is a very short man. Even *I* am taller, and my modest height has always worked to my advantage, since it is hard to see me as a threat. Imagine my surprise when I rose to find myself looking *down* at Jean de Beaune, who seems to be furnished with a short man's temper. He glowered at me, then looked around with a growing dissatisfaction that was engraved upon his face in many sharp lines.

'What is this?' he demanded of the nuncio. 'This is not suitable! Bring the gaoler. Now.'

'The gaoler?' said the Catalan. 'But—'

'*Now!*'

'Before you do . . .' I interrupted, and such was the shock occasioned by my daring that I was able to submit my letter without hindrance. 'Before you do, Father, you may want to read this.'

'Read what?' snapped Jean de Beaune, reaching out. 'What is it?'

As I surrendered the document, I pointed to its seal. Whereat the Dominican frowned and narrowed his eyes. They were small, bloodshot eyes, set a little too close together, but when he turned them on me I saw that they were not lacking in penetration.

He studied me for a moment, after which careful examination he scanned the letter with growing surprise. I watched his high colour fade, and his hostile, ill-natured expression yield to one far more open and intelligent. Suddenly he addressed the nuncio.

'Get out,' he said. 'Wait for me outside.'

'Father, are you sure?' The Catalan eyed me with suspicion. 'He may have a knife.'

'Are you deaf? I said *go!*' barked Jean de Beaune. Whereupon the nuncio withdrew in sullen obedience, closing the door behind him.

There was a long silence after he had gone. Jean de Beaune read the letter through once more, as if reluctant to trust his own vision. He peered very closely at my master's name, scrawled across the bottom of the parchment. He studied the seal again, chewing his bottom lip. At last he said: 'I know Bernard Gui. I know his script.'

I thought it better not to speak.

'Are you literate?' he went on. 'Can you read Latin?'

'Not Latin. No, Father,' I replied.

'So you know not what is written here?'

'Father Bernard told me. I was his servant for many years. He was afraid that my past might catch up with me, despite all my precautions. So he gave me this letter.' I nodded at the page in Jean de Beaune's hand. 'You see that he was right. My past *has* caught up with me.'

'Your name was mentioned by a heretic named Armand Sanche,' said the Dominican. 'Are you acquainted with him?'

'Yes.'

'He was captured near Quié last month, and brought to Carcassonne. He said that you were once a follower of Pierre Autier.'

I inclined my head, thinking: Armand Sanche. That fool. It was as I had suspected.

'I did follow Pierre Autier,' was my response. 'I followed him all the way to Belpech. Where I had him arrested.'

'So you were not a true disciple?'

'No, Father.'

'It would be hard to believe, without this letter.'

'Yes.'

'You are a faithful son of the Holy Roman Church? You believe that the bread and wine in the mass performed by the priests is changed into the body and blood of Christ by divine virtue?'

'Yes, Father.'

He chewed his lip again, very pensive. I could see that he was torn. There is nothing an inquisitor enjoys less than abandoning a fresh trail. On the other hand, he could not deny the letter. He knew my master's writing. He knew my master's seal.

He could not imprison me without offending my master.

'This is your real name?' he said abruptly, flicking the parchment with one finger. 'Helié Bernier of Verdun-en-Lauragais?'

'It is.'

'Yet you call yourself Seguier.'

'I have betrayed many heretics, Father. And there are some who know it, despite all my efforts. I could not stay in the mountains, or in the Toulousain. I had to come here, and pretend to be someone else.'

'If I were to ask Bernard Gui about Helié Bernier, what would he say?'

This was a clever and interesting question. It caused me to regard Jean de Beaune with more respect than I had felt hitherto.

It was the sort of question my master might have formulated.

'If you were to ask Father Bernard about Helié Bernier,' I replied, imagining my master's face and voice, 'he might perhaps say, "Why should you want to know such a thing?"'

I delivered this last remark in exactly my master's way, very mildly, with a blank face and a piercing look. By this means, I convinced Jean de Beaune. He blinked three times, and his breath caught in his throat for an instant.

'Ah—yes,' he said. 'I see. Yes.'

We regarded each other for another long stretch of time. Then, slowly and reluctantly, he relinquished the letter. I tucked it back into my clothes as he pursed his lips.

'You should not stir from this city until I have made inquiries of Bernard Gui,' he declared. 'I shall have you watched, be warned. You will not escape me.'

'No, Father.'

'You may have deceived the heretics, but you will not deceive the Holy Roman Church. Nor her loyal and devoted servants.'

I nodded, and Jean de Beaune seemed satisfied. He summoned the nuncio, who was ordered to release me. Then I was ejected onto the street—where I stood dazed for a moment in the noise and sunshine.

On my way home, I had to devise a convincing story. It was not difficult. In the mountains, I would have been hard pressed to explain away such a brief sojourn in the custody of an inquisitor. For after generations of betrayal, the men of the Pyrenees are highly suspicious. They know that an early release is generally bought at a price.

But the people of Narbonne are not so well acquainted with inquisitors and their habits. My tenants and neighbours seem content to believe that the whole affair was a case of mistaken identity. A Helié Seguet had been sought, and a Helié Seguier found: that, at least, is what I told them. And they appear to have accepted it, though they will not remain so complacent if I am too frequently and obviously watched.

God grant that Jean de Beaune receives confirmation of my claim very quickly. God grant also that Bernard Gui leaves me in peace. For I would rather not see him again.

He is my master, and a great man. Yet I would have preferred to escape his notice. 'Hide yourself,' he told me, and I obeyed—perhaps too well. No inquisitor likes to be outwitted.

I just want to be left alone. Is that too much to ask, after so many years of faithful service?

III.
Shrove Tuesday

I should have known when the order came. Normally it arrives every two months: a regular delivery of split-skin quires for the Dominican priory (one score). On this occasion, barely three weeks had elapsed since the last order. And it was for ten quires only.

I should have realised.

My suspicions were misdirected. I had been watching the street, as usual. I had been keeping alert when on my rounds, checking for patterns, putting names to faces, keeping clear of alleys. On my way to La Moyale, with my delivery of parchment, I doubled back twice before I reached the Old Bridge, and repeated this ploy in the Bourg, between Grain Square and the Lamourguier Gate. My mistake was to search for a *concealed* threat. After waiting five years for an unexpected attack, launched from behind, I was ill prepared to defend myself against a frontal assault.

I took the delivery myself, of course. Martin is too young to carry valuable loads beyond the walls of the Cité; I would be afraid for him, and for his parcel, were he to attempt it. By this time I knew that I would not be stopped at any of the city gates—that Jean de Beaune's threat had been an empty one. Had he *truly* been watching me, I would not have been permitted to set foot outside the walls of Narbonne. But I had done so on at least three occasions since our meeting, and for this reason, perhaps, was not as cautious as I should have been upon approaching the Dominican priory. Stupidly, I had begun to discount Jean de Beune. He seemed less dangerous to me than the unknown, unseen assailants who had haunted my dreams for years.

I left home shortly before midday, encountering few people after I had passed through the Lamourguier Gate and turned left towards the river. I saw four peasants ploughing. I saw two Dominicans—a preaching pair—deep in conversation as they headed for the Bourg. And I saw a dyer, whose hands were stained yellow with weld. This man I appraised cautiously, because he looked out of place. But then I noticed the boy with him, and realised that the dyer was almost certainly standing in his own vineyard, instructing his heir as to its management.

It was well before compline when I reached the priory, so there were no crowds milling about the door of the church—as there would have been at the start of the daily service. But I would not have been obliged to struggle through these crowds in any case, for the church was not my destination. Instead I knocked at the small portal that opens onto the cloister, its gardens and its offices. Then I waited, as I am always obliged to wait. For the Dominican priory (unlike its Franciscan counterpart across the river) is very difficult to penetrate.

The Franciscans have nothing like such high walls, nor such a dour porter to guard their seclusion. It is my custom to deliver my goods into the hands of the porter at the priory entrance, and I have never met with such morose discourtesy anywhere else. Admittedly, lay brothers are often prone to states of profound dissatisfaction, owing to their inferior status in the hierarchy of the church. Being low-born and poorly educated, they are sometimes treated with disdain by the clerics they serve, and have no means of improving their position. Nevertheless, it is rare to encounter a man so manifestly discontented with his lot as that Dominican porter—whose sour expression must have been carefully selected to repel frivolous inquiry. As a general rule he will scowl at my offering, snatch at my parcel, and slam the door in my face. If a word of any kind happens to pass his lips, I can count myself lucky indeed.

Imagine my surprise, therefore, when I was greeted today with a gesture of invitation.

'You are the parchment-maker?' he growled, in his thick and rasping voice. 'Helié Seguier?'

'I am. Yes.'

'Then you may come in.'

He stepped back. I gaped. Impatiently, he flapped his beefy hand.

'Come!' he insisted.

Even as I crossed the threshold, I knew that I was in error. Something was wrong. Jean de Beaune's voice flashed through my head; I looked for him nervously while attempting to keep up with the porter, who shuffled along, large and slope-shouldered, just ahead of me. In complete silence we skirted the kitchen garden, which had been sown with the spring crops, and plunged into a series of stone passages that linked dorter to kitchen to library. The arrangement of the buildings was almost identical to that employed in the priory at Toulouse. Even the smell was similar: a faintly sweet smell of herbs, incense and old books. The friars in their black-and-white robes could have been their brothers in Toulouse, transplanted. They moved about just as swiftly and silently, turning their faces in exactly the same way.

But none was Jean de Beaune. And none paid me the slightest attention until after I was ushered into a small whitewashed room lit by an open window. The porter then bade me sit on one of the wooden benches that lined the walls, and promptly withdrew. I heard his dragging footsteps growing fainter in the passage outside.

Clutching my quires of vellum, I waited fearfully. The silence was absolute. It occurred to me that I had waited in a small room not long before (albeit a darker, messier room) and I became more and more convinced that I was awaiting the same man on this second occasion. Jean de Beaune was back, I decided. Jean de Beaune had drawn me into his web.

After a while, the quiet padding of brisk, leather-clad feet became audible—as did the swish of long woollen robes. I recognised the sound of a monk in a hurry. Nothing prepared me, however, for the man who entered. I had been anticipating Jean de Beaune. His face was in the forefront of my mind.

Instead, I found myself staring at Bernard Gui.

'Helié, my dear son,' he said. 'What a long, long time it has been.'

I shall never forget the moment I first laid eyes on my master, in the *mur* of Toulouse. I was perhaps sixteen years old, small and thin and chained like an ox. My cell was dark and damp, slimy with growth and excretions. I had been starved, beaten and cruelly deserted by my next of kin. Even the last inquisitor had deserted me. He had gone off to Rome, to plead a case against some rich heretic with important friends—and had died in Perugia shortly afterwards, leaving my fate unresolved. I had not been tried. I had not been sentenced. I had been forgotten, it seemed to me. Forgotten even by my uncle and my cousins, who had paid nothing towards my keep in that terrible place. Having lured me into error, they had abandoned me, escaping into the Black Mountains before they, too, could be arrested.

For two endless years, I had suffered like a dumb animal. The gaoler had despised me. He had loaded me with heavy chains, because no one had bribed him to take them off. He had fed me crusts and offal, because my family cared nothing for my health. He had vented his frustrations on my unprotected limbs. And he had done all this without fear of reprisal, since there was no inquisitor to check him.

Then Bernard Gui became Inquisitor of Toulouse. I knew nothing of his appointment until he appeared before me, shining like a star in his dazzling black-and-white robes. He was about forty-five then, and still in his prime—tall, slim and vigorous. His long, pale face, somewhat blank in repose, was enlivened by a pair of large and piercing grey eyes. When he turned them on me, I knew at once that he was a man of immense learning and profound insight.

'Who is this?' he asked the gaoler. Upon being provided with my name the Dominican frowned, and his clear eyes flickered in a curious fashion, as if he was reviewing an invisible document. After becoming better acquainted with him, I realised that this is precisely what he *was* doing—for he had a remarkable memory, and seemed to keep an entire library of texts and lists inside his head.

'Helié Bernier has not been condemned to the *murus strictus*,' he declared. 'Remove those fetters. Release him from this cell. I shall review his case when I am able.'

And with those few simple words, Bernard Gui changed my life. Though he walked off immediately to inspect the rest of the prison, his influence continued to be felt. The whole place became invested with a sense of purpose and direction. No longer were its inmates dependent on the gaoler's whim. No longer did the guards wield their sticks without restraint. For they knew that Bernard Gui would only tolerate corporal punishment if he himself decreed that it should be inflicted.

He demanded utter obedience, and enforced his rule with iron resolve.

As for me, my life improved immeasurably. I could move about, and talk, and even perform various tasks in the hope of earning a few extra crusts. More importantly, I no longer despaired—for I had found a purpose to my existence. It seemed to me that Bernard Gui was my guardian angel. I watched for him always, and when he appeared, I tried to please him. My own father was long dead; perhaps I was seeking another. Whatever the reason, my thoughts were fixed on the black-and-white friar. I would hover in his vicinity. I would ask for his blessing. Nothing delighted me more than the sound of his mellifluous voice—unless it was the sight of his face, clear-cut and solemn, turned towards me.

Moved by such a passionate devotion, I would have done anything to win his approval. So when I overheard one of the prisoners speaking carelessly, I did not hesitate to betray her, though she had never done me any harm. By a lucky chance, Bernard Gui summoned me to appear before him only two days later. And I went to him dry-mouthed, bearing my gift, full of vague hopes and a desperate resolution.

He received me in an airy chamber, where a notary sat scribbling at a desk. The purpose of the meeting was simple; I was to be interrogated with a view to judging the extent of my guilt, so that I might be sentenced to a suitable punishment. The Dominican addressed me in the vernacular tongue. He asked me my name and birthplace. He consulted a register, and explained that a certain Cathar priest had identified me as the guide who had led him from one place to another, some five years previously.

'From this man,' said Bernard Gui, 'you received a blessing at the request of your uncle. Is this correct?'

I agreed that it was. I also confessed to having given some bread and fruit to the same Cathar priest on another occasion.

And I described my regret at having done so, though I was only a child at the time, and obeying my uncle's wishes.

'I was led astray, Father,' was my heartfelt plea. 'I know the Good Men are wrong. The earth is not the realm of Satan, and our spirits do not pass from one body to another on our deaths. It is not evil to kill animals, nor to eat meat or eggs or cheese. These are lies. I know that now. You have shown me the true path.'

Whereupon I offered up my gift of betrayal, recounting the exact words that I had heard three nights previously from the mouth of a Cathar believer who was sharing my corner of the prison. Bernard Gui listened in silence. His penetrating gaze never left my face as I spoke, and when I had finished he continued to regard me thoughtfully, his expression unreadable. At last he said: 'How old are you?'

I hazarded a guess (even now, I am not quite sure of my age), and he lifted an eyebrow.

'You look younger,' he remarked. 'Your term in prison has stunted your growth.'

'Oh no, Father. I was always small and weak,' I assured him. 'Good for nothing, my uncle used to say.'

'Indeed?' The grey eyes narrowed. 'I'm not so sure of that.' And he asked me further questions about my father, and my mother, and my life at home—which had never been particularly enjoyable—and by this means must have deduced that I was bound by no strong ties of loyalty to the people who had raised me, and that my parents, being dead, could exert no influence on me, for better or worse.

Then he dismissed me from his presence. But afterwards I felt myself the subject of his constant attention, for all that he did not single me out in any obvious way. I recall that he would send me to fetch things, and stop to inquire about events within the prison, and sometimes give me books to carry. Once or twice I was summoned to an interview. These were not recorded, however, and rarely addressed the subject of my heretical lapses. Instead, Bernard Gui would have me describe in great detail all the villages I had seen, and the people I had met, and the slights that I had endured. He would praise my memory, and explain to me how it should be exercised, like a weak limb. He would speak persuasively of religious faith, and explain that true piety must walk hand-in-hand with humility.

'Pride is the root of all error,' he expounded. 'Pride and vanity are the Devil's tools. Wherever there is heresy you will find proud men, who think themselves better than their fellows. Did not Christ wash the feet of his own disciples? How then can we set ourselves above all other men, each in our heart? Even where the whole world thinks a man great, if he shares this view, he will never find salvation.' And looking me straight in the eye, Bernard Gui added: 'Be always wary of the proud and headstrong nature, Helié Bernier. For it will lead you to hell.'

No one ever spoke a truer word, in my opinion. Every bad man in history has been eaten up with conceit, while there was never a saint not genuinely humble, and lowly in his own estimation. Bernard Gui himself was not proud. He did always as he was bid, whether by the Pope or by the

Master General of his own order. He worked ceaselessly and devotedly, without complaint. When false accusations were made, and people were imprisoned as a result, he was not too proud to admit openly that he had been mistaken. There are many inquisitors who would prefer it that innocent people should suffer, rather than that they should admit to an error of judgement. My master was not among them. Though greatly feared, he was neither vicious nor inconsistent. His reputation was founded on his formidable memory, his administrative skills, and his unswerving commitment to the Church of Rome. He pursued heresy with a devout and single-minded determination, sinning only perhaps in the extent of the wrath he felt against lapsed heretics. This was not so apparent in the early days, but became more evident as time went on.

'They have sought God's forgiveness and received it,' he once observed to me, in accents of deep frustration. 'Why would anyone reject Him again, after being welcomed back into the fold like a lost sheep? It defies all reason.'

Only after several years did he feel confident enough to express himself so freely in my presence. That was after I had proved my worth, and served him as loyally as he had served his own masters. By then we shared a unique bond, unknown to anyone but ourselves. Though we met only twice during the last five years of my service, we understood each other very well. And of all the rewards that I received, upon getting myself arrested and making my reports, I prized none so highly as my secret interviews with Bernard Gui, which always took place at night, in utter seclusion, over a modest repast of bread and wine. Then we would talk together as I have talked with no one else, before or since: not just about the heretics whom I had tracked down, but about the way their minds worked, and about the way all minds worked; about the labour with which Cathar *perfecti* earned their bread, and its influence on the wider question of trade and agriculture; about politics, and piety, and the latest gossip from Rome and Toulouse. We would talk until the bells rang for matins, whereupon my master would start, and blink, and smile his slow, lopsided smile, which was as rare (and therefore as precious to me) as sugar or cinnamon. 'Helié,' he would say, as we exchanged a farewell embrace, 'you have kept me from my duties again. Would that we had more time to discuss these things: to whom else can I open my heart, if not to my secret familiar? But duty calls. We are both its slaves. And I would not endanger your safety for all the world.'

Whereupon we would arrange very carefully the circumstances of my next mission, which would occupy me for months—if not years. Only on the occasion of our final meeting did the procedure vary. For by then we knew that I had come to the end of my usefulness; that I was too well known among the Cathar remnants to pass unmolested through their midst. At last, after ten years, I had nothing left to offer.

I cannot pretend that I was sorry. Certain changes had taken place within my soul. I was no longer the boy that I had once been, and Bernard Gui must have sensed it. Though he heaped praise upon my head, and bestowed on me all manner of riches, and kissed me like a father, his eyes never strayed from my face, as if he was looking for something that he could not find. Finally he remarked, 'I think it well that you have decided to abandon your former pursuits, Helié. Your face is no longer open and guileless. Once it was your greatest asset, but now it is shuttered, like a house full of secrets. You have built a wall between yourself and the world—and it is beginning to show, I fear.'

I should point out that this was the only time he ever reproached me during all my years in his service. Even when I was sentenced, in public, at one of his *sermones generales*, he passed over my crimes without comment. This was shortly after our first private talk together; I was condemned to wear yellow crosses, and to watch while three lapsed heretics burned at the stake. Afterwards, however, I was released with his blessing, and with a set of precise instructions that were engraved on my memory. And once I had completed *that* mission (which was the capture of Pierre Autier), I received nothing from my master but the most fulsome compliments. He respected me, I think. While he did not love me—I know that, now—he certainly respected my skills. He did not want to risk offending or frightening me: not, at least, until that final encounter, when he perhaps sensed that I was slipping away more quickly than he had anticipated.

But what can I truly know of his thoughts and feelings? If I have learned one thing over the last twenty years, it is that *no one* can be trusted. Though Bernard Gui has never betrayed me, what proof do I have that he would not, if given sufficient cause? No man is perfect. That is where so many heretics err; they look for perfection in man, when only God is perfect.

Once I confused God with Bernard Gui. Now I am older, and wiser—and more cautious, withal. While I might have bent my knee yet again, it was not through blind devotion. I did it because I had no choice. Because only a fool defies an inquisitor. And because I am getting too old for a fugitive's life, however expertly I might have pursued such a life in the past.

Besides which, when my master walked into that little room at the Dominican priory, I felt a sudden weakness that had nothing to do with fear or shock.

It was a weakness of the heart, which will always betray the head, no matter how well prepared one's defences.

IV.
First day of Lent

I had not the strength to finish my report yesterday, so must continue tonight. It is hard to sleep in any case. And if I must burn a candle to keep the shadows at bay, why not do something useful with the light?

I left myself in the Dominican priory, waiting in an empty room. When I heard Bernard Gui's footsteps approaching, I rose to meet my fate. On seeing him, however, my knees gave way, and I sat down abruptly. Then I began to tremble from an access of emotion.

My master noticed this, of course. He is a good inquisitor.

'Helié, my dear son,' he said, in his mild, musical voice. 'What a long time it has been.'

He is not much changed—in appearance, at least. Though all of sixty, he has worn well. A man with a tonsure does not age like other men, since any loss of hair is inconsequential; such hair as Bernard Gui is permitted has not turned white, but remained iron grey. He still holds himself erect, though his movements are not as swift and vigorous as they once were. His strength is perhaps retreating from his outer members, and concentrating itself in his eyes.

They have sharpened over the years; I saw no evidence of failing sight. From across the room he surveyed me, and I would be willing to swear that he missed nothing: not the state of my boots, not the chalk marks on my tunic, not the small scar near my mouth. In the last five years some grey hairs have appeared among the brown ones on my head, and I am quite sure that they were noted. So was my parchment-maker's stoop, no doubt, and the roughened tips of my fingers.

I am no earthly ornament. It is a burden that I came to accept many years ago. But I have never felt so small and pale and insignificant as I felt then, beneath Bernard Gui's searching appraisal.

'You look very thin,' he remarked. 'City air cannot agree with you.'

'I am well enough,' I croaked, having found my voice at last.

'Are you? I hope so. You have been in my prayers, Helié.'

He shut the door behind him, and advanced a few steps into the room. Overwhelmed by his presence, I was afraid that he might sit next to me—as he used to, during our long talks. But he knew me too well for that. Or perhaps he saw me flinch like a snail. Whatever the reason, he kept his distance, settling on a bench to my right.

'What have you there?' he asked. 'The parchment?'

'I suppose you have no real use for it,' was my reply.

'I most certainly do. The librarian here has shown me your parchment. It is of superb quality; you should be proud of your skill. To have mastered such a refined craft, after so many years as a cobbler . . . but it doesn't surprise me. I always said that you were a man of hidden talents.'

He lifted both eyebrows, to emphasise his little joke. My answering smile must have been a sickly one. For he cocked his head, and studied me in quite the old way, as if making a mental note of every lineament.

'Are you happy in your new life?' he inquired. 'Does it suit you, this existence?'

'Well enough,' I mumbled.

'You have no wife? No children?'

I shook my head. Though Allemande's face flashed into my mind, I quickly consigned it to the shadows.

'No,' said my master. 'I thought as much. No wife would have allowed you to wear that tunic. Not now that you occupy such a respected position. That tunic is long past its prime, my son—you should dispatch it. A mercy killing, I assure you.'

I fingered my skirts, but said nothing. He was right. My tunic was a disgrace to the city of Narbonne.

'You must forgive me for disturbing you, Helié,' he went on, without a trace of irony. 'It seems to me that you did not want to be disturbed. I can understand that. I can even sympathise. And I would not have troubled you, had I not been compelled by circumstance.'

'What circumstance would that be?' I said, forcing the issue. I did not want to exchange pleasantries with Bernard Gui. We were beyond such hollow etiquette, and had been for many years.

He nodded, as if conceding a point.

'Brother Jean told me about you,' he revealed. 'Jean de Beaune.'

'Yes.'

'He wrote to me after he left Narbonne, confirming all that he heard from you. He is very thorough in his methods. Very distrustful. Which is not a bad thing, in this deceitful age.'

I remained silent. What could I have said, after all? If it is a deceitful age, then my master and I have added generously to the sum of its deceit.

'Jean de Beaune has a great respect for the way I work,' my master went on. 'As a result, he has hired his own secret familiars.' He cut me a quick glance, as sharp as any steel blade. 'One of them is missing.'

At last we had come to the meat of the matter. I understood this immediately. And I looked up, waiting, as Bernard Gui began to choose his words with care.

'This familiar was formerly a member of the Third Order of St Francis, or the Poor Brethren of Penitence—whatever you wish to call them,' he began. 'A Beguin, in other words. By name Jacques Bonet, from Béziers. Have you heard of him?'

Again, I shook my head.

'No. Well. He was no heresiarch. Just a humble devotee, though he could be very persuasive.' Bernard Gui stopped suddenly, having heard the sound of approaching footsteps. To my immense surprise, the door creaked open and the sour-faced porter appeared, bearing a tray on which resided two goblets and a flask of wine. 'Ah, Henri. Thank you,' said my master, as Brother Henri slapped his burden down on the nearest bench. Then, with a cursory bow (more like a jerk of his chin), the porter left, his heavy gait emphasising how extra duties of this type were the most dreadful imposition.

Bernard Gui stared after him, blank-faced, until the door slammed shut. Then he turned to me.

'A little wine?' he suggested.

'No. Thank you.'

'I assumed that you would be thirsty, after such a long walk.' He fingered the neck of the pottery flask. 'We always used to drink wine when we met.'

'Please continue, Father,' was my blunt response. It surprised him, I think. But he was neither dismayed nor insulted. On the contrary, he may have been pleased that I no longer required so many kind remarks and proofs of abiding concern.

Without them, our business would be concluded all the more quickly.

'To avoid punishment for his heretical views, Jacques agreed to act for Jean de Beaune,' my master continued in a brisk fashion. 'It was felt that, as a known sympathiser, Jacques would have no difficulty in seeking out and discovering other Beguins. You may not realise that this part of the world is infested with such people. Jean de Beaune has uncovered them in Béziers, as well as the smaller towns and villages.'

I grunted.

'It is a recent heresy, of course,' he acknowledged. 'So you may not know much about it. Do you?'

'Hardly anything.' I marshalled the facts in my head, trying to recall what Pons had told me in prison, and what little I had learned during my years in Narbonne. 'They believe that Christ and the Apostles were the perfect poor, holding nothing personally or in common. And that the rule of St Francis is the very life of Jesus. And that the Pope, in allowing the monks of St Francis to wear long, full robes, and to keep wine and grain for future use, has fallen into heresy himself.'

Bernard Gui heard me out with obvious interest. When I had finished, he observed, with a glint in his eye: 'You still keep your ears wide open, Helié Bernier.'

'I know nothing else about the Beguins, Father. Except that they hate your order with a vengeance.'

My master shrugged. 'They hate all the Church, save for the friars of their own persuasion,' he replied. 'You must understand, they err at the root. They have come to believe that the Pope, cardinals and prelates are the Carnal Church, whereas the Spiritual Church comprises only the Poor Brethren of Penitence and those who serve the poor. They say that our lord Pope can no longer appoint bishops, or wield any power, because he has fallen into heresy. They say that in four years, or perhaps nine, the Carnal Church will be destroyed and cast down before the preaching of the Antichrist, and that there will remain only a few chosen men, spiritual, poor and evangelical—themselves, naturally.'

'Naturally,' I murmured.

'Then, after the collapse of the Carnal Church and the death of the Antichrist, the few remaining "spirituals" will convert all the world to their faith.' Bernard Gui uttered a weary sigh. 'Pride again. They think themselves greater tha all other men, save perhaps St Francis.'

'And where does Pierre Olivi fit into all this?' For I had remembered one other fact, which confused me. 'Were not his bones removed from their resting place at the Franciscan priory here? Because of the Beguins?'

'Yes.' Bernard Gui nodded. 'Friar Pierre Olivi was their prophet. His treatise on the Apocalypse is their Holy Scripture. They have used it to spin many fabrications. And they revere him as they revere St Francis.'

'Then he was a heretic?'

Bernard Gui hesitated. Again, he seemed to choose his words carefully.

'You must understand,' he said, 'that these Beguins have been led astray by their own imaginations. Much of what they attribute to Pierre Olivi may not have been his own words. Similarly, while *they* declare that he received his knowledge by direct revelation from God, there is no proof that he ever made the claim for himself.' My master tapped his mouth with one finger, reflecting, before he proceeded in a firmer, surer tone. 'But he had certain unreliable opinions, which were condemned by eight masters of theology at Avignon three years ago. So he *was* in error, though he did retract his views on at least one occasion before his death.'

'After which his bones were dug up.'

'And removed. Yes. They had become objects of pilgrimage. It was not thought wise to encourage such devotion.' Bernard Gui waved his hand. 'I cannot tell you where the bones were placed. But this is not important to you. Know only that

Narbonne, for various reasons, has been a source of Beguin error since the heresy first arose. And as a consequence, Jacques Bonet was sent here to befriend whatever Beguins he could find.'

'Whereupon he disappeared,' I concluded. Once again, I was anxious to discover what part I was to play in this business. 'Do you mean that he ran away? That he broke his promise, and relapsed?' It had happened before, as I knew only too well. Repentant Cathars are sometimes not as repentant as they appear.

My master winced. He has never liked to be reminded of his failures in judgement.

'It may be so,' he admitted. 'Jacques may have escaped. On the other hand, his secret may have been discovered by the Beguins, who may have killed him.' A measuring look. 'You know yourself that this also can happen.'

It was my turn to wince. I turned my face away, and studied the floor. For a moment there was silence. Then Bernard Gui proceeded with his narrative.

'Some thirty years ago, a woman called Rixende was tried for heresy in Narbonne,' he recounted. 'She was a Beguin, of sorts, and one of her followers, Jacquette Alegre, married a man named Guillaume Hulart. Though this man is now dead, his son, Vincent, is a merchant of the Bourg. Jacques was given Vincent Hulart's name as a starting point.'

I nodded.

'Jacques was told to make his confession at Christmas, to a priest of the church of St-Paul. During this confession, he was also expected to report on his activities. But he never approached the priest, who had been instructed by Jean de Beaune to watch out for him.' Another sigh. 'We need to find this missing familiar, Helié. We need you to hunt him down.'

'*If* he is in the city,' I amended. 'If he has left, I cannot help you. I am no longer a travelling cobbler.'

'I realise that. But his heretical friends may know where he went. For if he has escaped, it may have been with their connivance.' My master reached into the purse at his waist, drawing out a pair of little books. 'Here are some of the works that circulate among such people,' he explained. 'One is a portion of Pierre Olivi's *postilla* on the Apocalypse. The other is entitled *The Passing of the Holy Father*. It is an account of Pierre Olivi's death, and very short, as you see. The Beguins call him "The Holy Father who has not been canonised". They say that there has been none so great in sanctity and teaching.'

'I cannot read Latin,' I reminded him, eyeing the books doubtfully.

'They are translated into the vernacular. They have to be. Such people are not truly literate.' My master's crooked smile emerged for a fleeting instant. 'I would not distribute such texts to all and sundry, my son. One could argue that I was disseminating error. But your faith is strong, I know. You will not be led astray.'

'You want me to read them?'

'For your own protection.'

'And then approach Vincent Hulart?'

'Whatever your instinct tells you. It has never failed you before.'

I received the books, which felt slightly greasy to the touch, as if they had passed through many hands. I wondered which Beguins had been forced to surrender them.

'What does Jacques Bonet look like?' I asked. Whereupon my master's eyes flickered, as he reviewed his mental register.

'Rather a tall man,' he replied. 'Black hair. Green eyes. Big nose. Pockmarked face. One thick and crooked thumbnail on his right hand.'

'Has no corpse been found in the area that matches this description? Perhaps an unclaimed corpse buried in a field, or pulled out of the river?'

Bernard Gui shrugged. 'I shall make inquiries,' he promised. 'There is a fellow on the Archbishop's staff—by name Germain d'Alanh—who has served as an archiepiscopal inquisitor once or twice. I shall enlist his help. He can ask some of the hospitals and churches. Perhaps the city militia.'

'There is a brotherhood in Narbonne known as the Good Works of the Poor Dead of the Cité.'

'Then I shall have him ask this brotherhood as well. And report to you his findings.'

'Not directly.' I was alarmed at the very prospect. 'No archiepiscopal inquisitor must come anywhere *near* my house.'

'No. Of course not.'

'He must order some parchment. Then hide the report under the third folio, and send back the delivery. With some sort of complaint.'

Bernard Gui inclined his head. It has always been thus; despite his lofty rank and many talents, he has never once challenged my wishes on the subject of communication. For the preservation of my alias has always been paramount. And only *I* know how that should best be done.

'To whom should I make my report?' was my next question. 'To you? To Jean de Beaune?'

'To a priest, I think,' he replied. 'At your Easter confession.'

'No.' I shook my head. 'Easter is too soon.'

'Pentecost, then. Where do you normally go? St-Sebastien?'

'Yes.'

'Then I shall arrange it.'

'And after that, what will happen? A mass arrest?'

He fixed me with his cool, grey stare.

'That will depend on you,' he said.

My own gaze dropped before his. I felt breathless, as if I had been rushed along. It occurred to me that not once during our long exchange had the possibility even been considered that I would refuse to cooperate. Yet there would be inevitable consequences if I complied with my master's request. In the past, when I had served him as an informant, I had always been arrested along with my fellow heretics. An explanation had then been provided for my subsequent release; I might pretend that I had escaped, or bribed my way out, or even been let off with a light sentence—crosses, perhaps, or a pilgrimage. Increasingly, I had been forced to change my name and identity.

So I realised that, if the worst came to the worst, I might have to leave Narbonne. For I had no wish to become notorious in my neighbourhood as a traitor. Convicted heretics nearly always have relatives, and those relatives will invariably seek revenge on people like me.

Though it might be different in Narbonne. The Narbonnaise do not seem to have memories as long as those I used to encounter in my own country. Where I come from, the children of heretics are punished for their parents' crimes; they are forbidden to hold public office and deprived of their inheritance. In Narbonne, this is not so often the case—because there are laws against it. The citizens have many ancient rights, for reasons that I cannot fully comprehend. Perhaps it has something to do with the Archbishop? For Narbonne, after all, is this country's archiepiscopal seat. Although the Viscount of Narbonne rules part of the city, the Archbishop rules another part, so neither can do exactly as he wishes with the whole. They are always arguing, those two. And whenever the citizens want something, they can easily get it from one if the other is not amenable.

In a city such as Narbonne, whose people are so proud and defiant—whose Archbishop is so eager to win over the populace that he will sometimes turn a blind eye to heresy—in such a city, it may be easier to pretend that you have defied the inquisitors with money and power. It may be easier to stay on.

'Where will I go if I have to leave Narbonne?' I muttered, suddenly overcome by an immense weariness. 'If there is common talk of betrayal?'

'Montpellier would welcome you, I am sure,' remarked Bernard Gui, who had been watching me closely. 'With its university, it would always have a place for another parchment-maker. Or you could go further afield. To Marseilles. To Avignon.' He gave a little cough. 'If it becomes necessary,

I will of course provide you with sufficient funds to move. Have no fear of *that*, Helié.'

'Yes,' I said. But I was still tired. I looked down at the parchment in my lap. 'Do you want this?'

'Very much.' Bernard Gui rose, and produced from beneath his habit a little leather bag, heavy with coin. 'Take the price out of this sum, if you will.'

'Bribe money?'

'Bribe money. If any of these fools can be bought.' He gave me his little bag, receiving the parchment in return. By this time we were both standing, almost toe to toe. He smelled of lavender. 'Is there anything else you need to know?'

'You have no other names? Beguin names?'

'I fear not. Only Vincent Hulart.'

I nodded.

'You must be careful, Helié. If Jacques was indeed killed, then you could be risking the same fate. Do *not* put yourself in peril.' He placed his free hand on my shoulder, lowering his head so as to catch—and hold—my gaze. 'If you feel threatened, you must come here,' he instructed. 'Not to the Archbishop, or the Viscount, or any of the churches. You must come straight here. I shall have a word with the Prior, and he will speak to the porter, and these doors will always be open to you, day and night, for your protection.'

This seemed doubtful to me, if the surly porter had charge of them. But I said nothing. For a moment Bernard Gui seemed to scour the inside of my skull with his searching regard. Then he leaned forward, and kissed me on both cheeks.

'I'll not keep you any longer,' he said. 'It's good to see you again—to know that you are faring so well. I was concerned about you, Helié.' He squeezed my shoulder in a firm grip. 'Next time, when you disappear, you should not do it with such efficiency. Or how shall I watch over my most valued servant?'

His eyes remained fixed on my face for a long time. Then he straightened, muttered a quick blessing, and left the room. The graceless porter, Brother Henri, showed me out shortly afterwards, with a scowl and a grunt. Had he been tossing a bucket of nightsoil onto a dung heap, he could not have demonstrated less courtesy.

There may have been some rule concerning the outer door of the priory, and who should have ready access to it; the Dominicans, I know, follow many strict rules. But I am inclined to believe that my master did not accompany me to this door for another reason. Unless I am mistaken, he was signifying his disappointment in me. For no inquisitor likes to lose sight of anyone. He prides himself on his unsleeping eye.

He would not like his own familiar to escape him, as I myself had escaped for so many years.

V.
Last day of the first week of Lent

This morning a priest was fetched for the mother of Hugues Moresi, my tenant. But she did not die. Hugues himself never believed for one moment that she was in danger. He resented having to fetch the priest, who (he said) would undoubtedly want 'alms for the poor' as a consequence. I was surprised at the way Hugues expressed himself on the subject.

'Money, money, money,' he growled. 'All they want is money, those priests. And they wonder why so many people revere the Beguins!'

'But that money is for the poor,' his wife protested—perhaps with more courage than usual, since I was present. Whereupon Hugues snorted.

'That money goes into the bellies of priests, and the poor might perhaps eat their turds,' he rejoined. It is quite astonishing what people will say sometimes, in the presence of strangers. For what does he know about me, in all truth?

Only that I make parchment. And that I own this house. And that I have no wife or children.

His own wife and children were gathered by his mother's bed when I arrived. I was looking for my apprentice, and stumbled upon a deathwatch—or so it appeared at first. The old woman was very ill. Her daughter-in-law was weeping. The children had been enjoined to pray. And Hugues Moresi was refusing to fetch a priest.

'She will not die,' he insisted. 'Three times every winter, she thinks she is going to die, and she never does.'

When her breathing became stertorous, however, he agreed—with very bad grace—to send for a priest. He told Martin to hurry and ask at St-Sebastien. But I was firm. My apprentice, I said, had already been paid for his time. I needed him up in my workroom.

So Hugues sent his eldest daughter instead. Martin himself did not express any passionate inclination to remain at his grandmother's bedside. If he had done so, I might have allowed it—though on the whole I do not believe that children enjoy a deathwatch, nor profit much from the experience. One of my own most painful memories is that of attending the deathbed of my mother, who was blessed by a Cathar Good Man, and subsequently deprived of all food and water until she expired. This was considered a good death among the Cathars. In their minds, the blessing and the fast ensured that my mother would go straight to heaven. I must acknowledge that she would, in all likelihood, have been unable to eat or drink during those last hours in any case—since she was unconscious, and barely able to breathe, let alone swallow.

Nevertheless, it was a great sin. And being only seven at the time, I was much haunted and troubled by what I saw.

It seemed to me that Martin should be spared such a thing. For he is a delicate boy, who has clearly suffered under his father's blows. The other boys in that family are more stalwart, and take care to pass the blows on to their sisters and friends. In doing so, their fear is transformed into anger. Martin simply absorbs each beating—or at least, he used to. Before I intervened. Now he talks more freely, and what he says can sometimes be quite sensible.

He is not a child to be exposed to a lingering and painful death without consequence.

Therefore I took him back upstairs, where I made him scrape the greasy parchment with chalk, while I cut and marked. I had not visited my own kitchen in some time, and was feeling pleased at how neat and well-scrubbed it had looked. Hugues's wife is a good wife, for all the ill-treatment she endures. Perhaps the ill-treatment is at the root of her efficiency? Men like Hugues would certainly have one think so; there is always much talk among householders of how a wife must be beaten like an ox if a man is to get any work out of her. Myself, I can express no opinion on the matter—never having furnished myself with a wife.

One thing is certain: had I married Allemande, I would not have beaten her. She had been too much beaten already, and it had done her no good at all.

But this is of little consequence. More important was the priest's visit. After we settled down to our work, my apprentice and I were silent for a long period. I saw the priest arrive from my window, and identified him as Anselm Guiraud, the canon of St-Sebastien. But Hugues's daughter led him through the front door, so I said nothing to my apprentice. I did not want to disturb Martin in his labour; I thought it best that he should get lost in his task, rather than that he should become careless through keeping one ear cocked for wails of distress from downstairs. Although he works well, and can be trusted to concentrate on the task at hand, death is a great distraction.

Only later, when he was resting his tired arms, did I open my mouth to speak. And this was in response to a question that he voiced. For Martin had seen our neighbour Adhemar returning home. He wondered aloud where Adhemar might have been.

'To church, perhaps?' Martin suggested. 'Or to the Rue Aludiere, to buy leather?'

'No.' I had noticed Adhemar's passage myself. 'He went to the wool-carders' quarter. There was fluff all over the hem of his surcoat.' Wielding my scissors, I cut one large folio into two smaller pieces. 'If he *must* go to visit Astruga Ruffi, he should do it in shorter skirts.'

'Astruga Ruffi?' Martin stared at me in surprise. 'Why should he visit her?'

'Why do you think?'

'But he is married!'

'So is she. To a wool-carder.'

'But—'

'I have been watching them for years, Martin. In and out of each other's houses at all hours. Now that she has wed, the situation has become more difficult for them. One day, Adhemar will return with a missing nose or ear. I guarantee it.'

Martin gazed at me in awe. 'You know everything,' he said.

'I most certainly do not.'

'Not everything,' he amended. 'Not Latin. But you know what people do. And where they come from. And where they go.'

'Because I watch them closely. As a farmer might watch the sky or the crops. It is simply a matter of watching and remembering.'

'*I* have good eyes. My father says so.'

'You have your mother's eyes,' I remarked, for it is true; of all her children, Martin is the one who most resembles his mother. He has her dark colouring: the brown eyes, the black hair, the olive skin. 'But you need more than acute vision,' I explained. 'You need to understand what you see.'

At that moment, I heard footsteps on the stairs. And I rose to meet my visitor, who soon revealed himself to be Anselm Guiraud, the priest. He was panting from the exertion of his climb, and I wondered why he had not sent one of the children to fetch us.

Naturally I assumed that the end must be fast approaching for my tenant's mother.

'No, no,' he panted, when I asked him if Martin was required downstairs. 'No, her time is not yet come. I could see it at a glance—I have some experience in these matters, as you must realise.' He steadied himself against the wall, still puffing heavily, as he looked about him. 'This is a good house you have here, Master Helié. Very big. Do you eat with your tenants?'

'They bring me my food,' I replied, calmly waiting. 'They pay rent for the kitchen.'

'That is a good arrangement. Since you yourself have no wife.'

'Yes.'

He nodded. It occurred to me that he might have climbed my stairs in search of more alms, and I prepared—with an inward sigh—to give him money. For it is never wise to annoy a priest. I have made a point of buying the good opinion of most priests in my neighbourhood, and many monks as well. My purse has only been shut to the Franciscans, who have not been endearing themselves to the rest of the Church lately.

Not that *all* Franciscans have been courting disaster. I refer only to the Spiritual faction, and most of them left Narbonne long ago. The very year after I arrived here, forty-five of them were summoned to Avignon by the Pope, and afterwards dispersed to many far-flung prisons and abbeys. (Those, at least, who chose to recant rather than burn.) But even now there is a Spiritual taint to the Narbonne priory—and I would be reluctant to become associated with it.

In any event, if the Franciscans are so attached to the notion of Holy Poverty, they will not be wanting *my* money, I feel sure.

'It is good to see you back in your house,' said the priest, whereupon I revised my opinion. He did not want alms. He was simply curious about our last meeting, when he had witnessed my arrest and surrendered me into the hands of

Jean de Beaune. 'Hugues tells me that you were mistaken for somebody else by the Inquisitor of Carcassonne,' he observed. 'Is that true?'

I nodded.

'Though it was your own name inscribed upon the summons?'

'In error,' I replied. 'The scribe wrote "Seguier" instead of "Seguet".'

'And who is Helié Seguet?'

'I have no idea, Father.'

'Whoever he is, he must be a Beguin,' the priest remarked. 'For the Inquisitor of Carcassonne has been hunting Beguins most diligently.'

'Yes,' I said.

'He intends to burn some very soon, I have heard.' The priest seemed to be studying me with more interest than I perhaps merited, and I became wary. No doubt he was simply wondering if I had bribed my way out of prison, but I am always wary when I attract anyone's interest. 'There is talk of a *sermo generalis* in a few weeks. On the Feast of St Benedict,' he concluded. 'You were fortunate indeed that the Inquisitor was mistaken.'

'Utterly mistaken,' I declared firmly. 'For I am a faithful son of the Holy Roman Church, Father, as you well know.' And to prove my point, I gave him some money. Just a few copper coins, but they served to get rid of him.

The news was worth the fee, in any case. For I could not have been better pleased to hear about the *sermo generalis*. If Jean de Beaune has decided to burn some Beguins, then other

Beguins will be lured into the open. This is inevitable. Wherever a heretic is burned, you will find some of his friends in the crowd. Therefore I have more than once recommended to my master that he patrol most carefully the sites of his *sermones generales*, and take note of anyone behaving oddly. I do not mean to imply that people who weep or pray at these spectacles are invariably heretics. There are pious men who weep with pity at the sight of an unrepentant soul on its way to hell. There are good Catholics who pray fervently that dying sinners will see the light of Truth. Nevertheless, one should always take note of spectators who linger at the site afterwards; who abuse those soldiers charged with breaking up the charred corpses; who even attempt to retrieve scraps of partly incinerated hair and clothing, before the remains are utterly consumed. Such conduct seems highly suspicious, and worthy of investigation.

I should confess that my advice on this matter was never much heeded. The problem, perhaps, lies in that curious custom of 'relaxing' condemned heretics into the custody of the secular authorities. It is not the inquisitor's role to kill, any more than it is the job of the Church. That responsibility must fall to the local lord or king, whose interest in pursuing heretics, or even keeping a close eye on the execution grounds, is often lukewarm. God knows, it is hard to blame the secular arm for this lack of dedication. There are few sane men who would remain within sight of a burned corpse for longer than is absolutely necessary—and I can sympathise with the desire of every guard involved in a *sermo* to retreat to a quiet corner with a large jug of wine as soon as the event is over.

All the same, I truly believe that I am right. And I shall demonstrate the wisdom of my view on the feast of St Benedict, when I shall witness the spectacle of Jean de Beaune's *sermo*. By watching the crowd gathered in attendance, I might perhaps flush out a possible Beguin. I certainly hope that I might. Because so far, my efforts have turned up nothing.

You might argue that I have shown a lack of enthusiasm for my appointed task. And it is true that I approach it with a certain weariness of spirit. The Beguins have done me no wrong. They are not my enemies, as the Cathars were. Nor, in hunting them down, am I assisting my master in his daily rounds. For the Beguins of Narbonne are Jean de Beaune's meat, and I owe nothing to Jean de Beaune.

On the other hand, I owe even less to the Beguins, who seem cursed with the same wilful arrogance as any other heretical group. Furthermore, I know how to protect myself. I know that my safety depends not only on obliging the inquisitors, but on proceeding with the greatest caution. I would rather be slow and secure than quick and clumsy. If I have made little headway in the last week or so, it is not because I am reluctant to act. It is because I am reluctant to act in a careless and ill-considered fashion.

To begin with, I could have made inquiries of the priest at St-Paul. I chose not to, however. For that priest knew about Jacques. He was instructed to receive Jacques's report. And now Jacques himself has disappeared. Does this fact alone not merit a cautious approach? Though I doubt very much that the priest was involved in Jacques's disappearance, one cannot be too careful in such matters.

Nevertheless, I went to the Bourg a few days ago, and visited the church of St-Paul. I went there to see if anything struck me as odd or unexpected. I went to listen for the names Hulart or Bonet as I wandered the streets in that area. It is sometimes through overhearing prayers in church, or conversations around a well, that one collects the most valuable information. I half expected to encounter Jacques himself, slinking out of the hospice of St-Paul or ducking into a baker's shop.

But I was unfortunate. There was nothing to be learned in that part of town—not in such a short time, on such a miserable day. For it was rather wet, and people do not stop in the street to gossip when it is raining. They hurry along, heads down, anxious to return to their hearthsides.

On my way back to the Cité I also went to the House of Merchant Exchange. Here it is easy enough to linger, as long as you are dressed well; there are any number of merchants, notaries, brokers and seamen who will stand or sit in its vaulted halls for hours at a time, discussing trade, forging agreements, investing money and drawing up contracts. The high stone rooms ring with talk and laughter and the chink of coin. Pale men scribble furiously in giant communal registers of transaction, which are chained to the wall like prisoners. Money-changers flaunt their wealth with crimson-draped tables and tooled-leather cartularies. There is so much to occupy the eye and the ear that one can pass unheeded through the noisy throng, even when asking questions.

It is not so unusual to be seeking a debtor or creditor at the House of Merchant Exchange. All I had to do was approach some of the busier notaries. 'I am looking for Vincent Hulart,' was my simple inquiry. 'Can you tell me where I might find Vincent Hulart?' Without looking up, the notaries furnished me with a variety of useful answers: the location of his house, the name of his cousin, the details of his business. Vincent Hulart is a spice merchant. He lives on the Rue de la Parerie Neuve. His cousin, Berengar Blanchi, lives with him.

Neither of them were at the House of Merchant Exchange yesterday. And if Vincent Hulart was at home, I did not see him. Though I passed his house before returning to the Cité, it was as quiet as a grave. So was the street outside it. There was no opportunity to stand and stare—not without arousing suspicion.

It will be very hard indeed to investigate Vincent Hulart. I have no legitimate reason for approaching him; what interests can a parchment-maker share with a spice merchant, after all? We have no common friends or relatives. We do not attend the same church. We live in different quarters of the city, separated by a river and two thicknesses of city wall.

The only possible course open to me is a risky one. I must wait two weeks for the anniversary of Pierre Olivi's death. I seem to recall that, when Olivi's bones were still buried near the altar of the Franciscan church, many people used to congregate there in the middle of March. If Vincent

Hulart is a Beguin—or if he knows any Beguins—he will surely do something to commemorate the passing of Pierre Olivi. There will surely be some sort of activity at his house on that day. The question is: how shall I watch the house without attracting unwanted attention?

I must give the matter some thought.

VI.

Monday, anniversary of the death of Pierre Olivi

Today, after much preparation, I kept watch outside the house of Vincent Hulart from dawn till dusk.

I told Martin that I would be visiting certain cloisters beyond the city walls: those of St-Felix, St-Etienne, St-Martin, St-Vincent. I told him that I would take samples to show the canons of each church, who might decide to patronise my shop. By this means, I neatly forestalled any questions about the length of my absence. And I was able to pass off my bundle of clothes as a bundle of parchment.

I promised that I would return before the gates closed

It is many years since I disguised myself. I was concerned that my gums and oils and gall waxes might have dried up in their little glass vessels; that my alternative wardrobe might have rotted away under the flagstone in the cellar. But I need not have worried. Such garments as I kept have not deteriorated. Even if they had, it would hardly have mattered, since a beggar's rags should never look well preserved.

I took with me to the Bourg my old green hooded cloak, my short grey tunic and my rope girdle. All these garments are so encrusted with food stains and bodily excretions, so frayed and rent and reeking, that they offer nearly as much protection as a leper's bell; no one dares approach them who has any desire to remain in good health. To add to their effect, I took my coloured gums, some dirty rags, and a few torn fragments of split-skin parchment. All of these things I rolled into a length of soiled blanket, which I tied with a leather thong. I also took a wineskin filled with water, a steel mirror, and the stick that I use in the vats.

I reached the Old Bridge at daybreak, just as the gates were opening. From there I crossed the river into the Bourg, where the streets were largely deserted. Even so, I was careful. When it comes to privacy, one has very little choice in a place like Narbonne. I would have assumed my disguise in one of the vineyards or ditches outside the city walls if I had been confident that a diseased beggar would be welcomed back in again. Instead, I had to take my chances in the graveyard of St-Paul.

Normally, one does not find people drifting around a graveyard at sunrise on a chilly March morning. There might be dogs, and rats, and perhaps one or two unconscious drunkards. But even beggars tend to avoid burial grounds. According to popular prejudice, they are places of ill omen.

Therefore I was fairly confident of having the place to myself. The canons, I knew, would not be bothering me; I had heard the bells ringing for prime when I crossed the bridge. Nor would the graveyard walls stop me, for I had examined them when I was last in the area, and knew that they were full of holes. My only concern was the possibility of illicit lovers. Privacy being in such short supply, and lust being such an overwhelming force, I knew that lovers were the most likely threat to my peace.

I was lucky, however. No unclad couples were surprised among the graves by my incursion. No snoring sots had tumbled into any open pits. I found myself a sheltered spot without hindrance, and proceeded to change my clothes. I pissed in the dirt, then rubbed it into my skin and hair. I began to apply my various coloured gums.

This delicate procedure took me back to my first lesson on the art of deceitful ointments. I was in Aragon, on the route to Compostella, when the beggar Abril confessed to me that he earned his keep by imitating serious illness, and wringing the hearts of gullible pilgrims. This man had learned his mastery from the Moors; I wish I could remember half of what he told me. Nevertheless, I still recall how to create open sores filled with pus that can be washed off at the end of the day. And how scraps of parchment can be made to look like shredded skin. And how a tincture of brazil-wood, applied to the tongue and teeth, can mimic inflamed and bleeding flesh.

Having brought a mirror, I accomplished my own transformation without too much difficulty. I favoured scars above sores, because sores can be counterproductive. (A leper will find no welcome inside the walls of Narbonne.) I darkened my brows with gall, and bound my feet with rags. The final touch was a plaster of wax around my eyes. By covering one entirely, and embedding the other in a gleaming eruption, I contrived to look as if I must surely be blind.

Then, with my respectable clothes hidden in my bundle, I shuffled into the street again, stumbling occasionally to convince the few onlookers who passed me that I was, indeed, sightless. The beggar Abril once told me that the trick to passing oneself off as a blind man is to lift one's chin, and to use one's stick. By swinging the stick in front of me, from side to side, I not only appeared to be plotting a course around any obstacles, but kept others from coming too close.

It is a little-known fact, by the by, that most people are recognised by their gait alone. Hence, when assuming another identity, it is important to change the way one walks. A stone in the shoe is the best method. That is another thing Abril taught me.

When I finally reached the Rue de la Parerie Neuve, it was later than I would have wished. The sun was quite high and the street was noisy. I took up a position opposite the house of Vincent Hulart, which is narrow but tall, with two storeys built over the recessed shop on ground level. In point of fact, this seems more a warehouse than a shop, for not once during the day were its big shutters pulled back to reveal tables or shelves. People came and went—using a small door cut in the larger one—but not as frequently as I had expected. Nor were these people the kind of matrons and maidservants who frequented many neighbouring shops, like the bakery down the street. Visitors to the house of Vincent Hulart were generally labourers carrying loads, or well-dressed merchants carrying nothing.

I shall now describe the men I saw visiting Vincent Hulart.

There was a balding man of middle age dressed in blue Champagne toile, who must have been a notary. (I say this because his hands were stained with ink, and his shoulders were stooped, yet he was not wearing a clerical habit.) He brought with him a register, and left with it also, even more ink-stained than before. That he had come on business was evident to me.

There was a squat, bare-legged, well-muscled man in a tunic of coarse grey stamin, who carried a wooden cask. His companion was probably a seaman, and recently disembarked, to judge from his curious rolling gait; he had unusually long grey hair, yet his face was relatively unlined. These two men were undertaking a delivery of some sort. They left without the cask.

There was a fat man who came with his servant. The wealth of this man was clear for all to see: he wore boots of cordwain, robes of embroidered Elne silk, and a cloak that looked like Chalons cameline, lined with more silk. His buttons were made of pearl, and his face was highly coloured from many good meals replete with rich food and fine wine. His servant, in contrast, was thin and pale. Left on the doorstep to wait for his master, this servant gazed at me dully at first, before venting his frustration by pulling a series of grotesque faces. Undoubtedly he assumed that, being blind, I would be oblivious to his crossed eyes and bared teeth. I was not, however, and had to struggle with my own expression. (One smile would have unmasked me.)

When the rich man emerged, he was attended by Vincent Hulart. I know this because the rich man spoke loudly, and addressed the spice merchant by name. Vincent Hulart was a slight, fair-skinned, curly-haired man, whose grave expression made him look older than he probably was. He was neatly dressed in solemn colours—grey, black and purple—but I doubt that he is a true Beguin, for there was a silver clasp on his belt.

I barely glimpsed him before he went back inside, leaving the rich man with a little leather bag of something that he sniffed at appreciatively, on his way to the Grain Market. (Nutmeg, perhaps. Or saffron.)

Another visitor was an elderly man whose face looked vaguely familiar to me. Ever since I saw it I have been racking my brain, but I cannot place those sunken cheeks or that square jaw. His eyebrows were grey and bushy; he was slightly lame, but solidly built. Despite the gold ring on the middle finger of his left hand, he wore brown worsted clothes of the very simplest cut, and a leather thong around his waist. When he reached the house of Vincent Hulart, a serving-girl answered his knock.

I heard him ask for Berengar Blanchi, whereupon she requested his name. 'Imbert Rubei,' he answered—yet still I was at a loss. (The name Imbert Rubei means nothing to me, alas.) The girl withdrew; there was a short wait; then a man emerged from the house who bore little resemblance to Vincent Hulart. He was taller and darker, with a vivid and mobile face, all nose and mouth and large, dark eyes. He flung wide his long arms when he saw his elderly visitor.

'Blessed be the name of Jesus Christ!' he exclaimed, embracing Imbert Rubei. Who immediately responded with an identical salutation: 'Blessed be the name of Jesus Christ.'

This is worthy of remark, I think. It had almost the quality of a recitation, or formula.

'Will you break bread with us today?' Imbert inquired of Berengar Blanchi.

'I should be honoured,' was the reply.

Whereupon the two of them walked off, arm in arm. I should have liked to have followed them, but I could not—not as a blind beggar, in any case. Besides, I had set myself a task. I had determined to watch the house from dawn till dusk, in the hope of identifying any unusual activity that might relate to the anniversary of Pierre Olivi's death.

By the end of the day, I had determined that Vincent Hulart's mind was not on dead Franciscans. He was a busy man—prosperous, respectable and preoccupied. His wife was pregnant, and wore fur trimming on her cloak. She already had three young children. The household also consisted of a wet nurse, a maid, and a witless-looking manservant. I saw the maid several times, scuttling out to buy bread and fish and fetch water. I saw the wife only once, when she emerged to pay someone a visit. The youngest child was all over the street. He kept escaping the custody of his wet nurse; he even pushed open a first-floor shutter, and might have fallen if someone had not pulled him back inside. I have no doubt that the piercing screams I sometimes heard were his. Nor was I surprised when, during one of his forays into the wider world, he came to stand before me, his thumb in his mouth, his eyes wide with curiosity.

I was concerned that he might prod at one of my scars. But the wet nurse soon discovered him, and whisked him off before he could do any damage.

I was approached on only three other occasions during the day. Even in a city the size of Narbonne, a newcomer cannot remain utterly unremarked—especially in a quarter full of respectable burghers and guildsmen. The Rue de la Parerie Neuve is not the sort of thoroughfare where dead dogs, heaps of excrement or expiring beggars are roundly ignored. At one point, an angry matron approached me with a broom, and urged me in no uncertain terms to stop spoiling the look of the street. The hospice of St-Paul, she said, was the proper place for someone like me. In response, I mumbled the Lord's Prayer in Saxon (having learned it from a mercenary guard in Toulouse), and convinced her that I could not understand. Then she pushed at me with her broom, causing another woman to scold her from across the street. 'Is this street your very own, that you would decide who uses it?' my defender snapped. I was forgotten in the ensuing argument.

Towards the middle of the day, a man passed me who stopped, turned, and retraced his steps. He wore the robes of an Augustinian canon. He said: 'Can you hear me, Blind Man? Do you need guidance?'

I knew that Saxon would not avail me, since there was every chance he might have some acquaintance with it. So I simply held out my hand, and was much relieved when my female defender from across the street—who was sewing in the good light to be had upon her doorstep—remarked: 'He cannot understand you, Father, he is foreign.'

'Foreign?' said the canon.

'Only a foreigner would try to beg here,' she joked. 'There are much better pickings near St-Sebastien.'

'If he is still here at nightfall, you should take him to St-Paul,' the canon suggested.

'*I?*'

'You will serve God in doing so.' The canon traced a cross over my head, then went hurriedly about his business.

I resolved that I would make my escape long before any attempt was made to succour me.

The third person who approached me was Berengar Blanchi. He returned to the house not long before I departed, and his appearance was curious; his eyes had a damp sheen, his cheeks were flushed, and he seemed to be somewhere else in his mind—to judge from the way he walked straight through a pile of horse dung. He noticed *me*, though. Just as he reached his cousin's front door, he hesitated, swung around, and came up to me, fumbling in his purse as he did so. From a closer vantage point, his expression was even more peculiar: wildly exultant, yet at the same time deeply troubled.

He dropped a silver *livre* into my hand, and did not stay to receive my mumbled blessing.

I have my suspicions about Berengar Blanchi. His long, dark robes had a vaguely clerical cut to them. He wore a scrubby beard and very short hair. His fervent gaze and uncontrolled movements hinted at a mystical nature of the kind that is better walled up in a monastery than set free to roam unchecked through the streets. I wish I knew where he went. Of all the people I saw today, moving in or out of Vincent Hulart's house, he was the one who most resembled the Beguin I met in the Capitol Tower.

So far, he is my most likely suspect.

The sun was sinking towards the horizon when I finally left the Rue de la Parerie Neuve. I did not return to the graveyard of St-Paul. Instead I went straight to the church of St-Nazaire, which is small and very dark inside. Here I wedged myself between a corner and a column, and washed myself as best I could with the water from my wineskin. I would have done so at a city well, or on the bank of the Aude, had I been careless of my privacy. Such a transformation, however, was not one to be effected in public if I wished to avoid notice.

I had to change my clothes, too. This was a more difficult task. At one point I was interrupted by the passing of a priest very close to my hiding place, and had to freeze with one arm held aloft, thrust halfway into a dangling sleeve. Fortunately, the priest was old and half-blind. I heard him trip over a stair, and mutter something most unpriestly as a consequence.

I would not have attempted such a mad undertaking if any daily office had been in progress. But with the choir empty, I was confident that I would not be disturbed.

It was impossible to wash my hair. Instead I hid it under my hood, resolving to attend to it when I was at home. I also abandoned my stick, which can easily be replaced. And on my way out of the church, I left my beggar's takings for the poor.

I was one of the last back into the Cité, before the gates closed.

Martin must have been waiting in my workroom. He came scampering downstairs as I entered the shop, even though it was twilight and he should have been with his parents. His presence annoyed me. I was concerned that he might question the state of my hair, or wonder why I still carried a heavy load when I claimed to have been distributing samples all day. Though it was dark down in the shop, with every shutter closed and no candles lit, I would have preferred an unseen arrival.

'What are you doing here?' I snapped, and he faltered on the stairs. I could not see his face very well in the poor light, but I am quite sure that it assumed a stricken look.

'I—I—'

'There was no work for you today. I told you not to touch any of the skins.'

'Master, I did not . . .'

'Then you had no business here. Go home.'

I was eager to conceal all the secret things in my bundle. I was anxious to reach the barrel in my cellar, and lift the flagstone beneath it. But Martin's whispered apology, and the way he fumbled at the wall for support as he turned from me, had a chastening effect on my conscience.

'Martin,' I said, in a gentler tone, 'these are my quarters. You should not make free of them as if they were your own.'

'No, Master.'

'Of course you are welcome. More so than anyone else. But you must not come in if I tell you to stay out.'

'Master,' he objected—albeit in a very small voice—'you told me not to touch the skins. You did not tell me to stay out.'

Surprised, I peered through the gathering shadows. Was he being insolent? Even now, I cannot decide. Yet there was no trace of disrespect in his stance or his manner. Just an earnest desire to avoid condemnation.

'You have the mind of a legist, my friend,' I said dryly. 'Very well. You have me there. Do not presume on my goodwill, however.'

He assured me that he would not. All the same, I have my doubts.

He will continue to presume on my goodwill, I feel sure. Because he knows quite well that he has it.

VII.
Monday, Feast of St Benedict

Today I went to the *sermo generalis* of Jean de Beaune. The Inquisitor himself was present, as was the Archbishop, the Viscount, and many priests and friars. I did not see my master. But I did see Pons the Beguin.

He was burned, along with sixteen others.

I cannot imagine the expense of such an undertaking. In Toulouse, I remember, there was always much bickering about the exorbitant cost of an execution: of the stakes, the ropes, the wood, the straw—even the executioners. (One is appointed to each heretic, and they cost twenty *sols* apiece.) To burn one heretic, it is necessary to spend something in the region of three *livres* a head. Multiply that by seventeen, and marvel at the threat posed by these Beguins—whose confiscated possessions cannot be *that* much of a prize, if they truly believe in Holy Poverty.

Proceedings began yesterday, in the cathedral. They took place on a high platform under the makeshift roof. The crowds were not so great in there, and I had an excellent view of the heretics, and of Jean de Beaune as he delivered his sermon. It was not a good sermon. The Inquisitor scoffed at those who would 'die for no good reason'. 'These men wish to be burned for barley and for the colour brown!' he proclaimed, leaving all to think: then why kill them? Bernard Gui would not have made such an error.

After the sermon came the oath of obedience, and the solemn decree of excommunication against all impeding the Inquisitor in his work. To my surprise, no confessions were read aloud; only the charges. Some were very minor, and the accused in these cases all agreed to repent. They were given terms of imprisonment, and in one instance a pilgrimage with crosses. Seventeen Beguins, however, refused to abjure their heresies. Some of them tried to explain why—Pons among them. They were immediately silenced, by the simple expedient of removing them from the cathedral with great force and speed.

All were returned to the Capitol Tower for one more night's reflection, before their sentences were carried out.

None changed his mind. Seventeen stakes had been raised in Caularia Square, next to the gate, and each of them was used today. There was hardly room in the square to accommodate so many piles of faggots, let alone every person who turned out to watch the Beguins meet their fiery ends. The crowd at the execution site was far bigger than that in the cathedral. Indeed, it was so great that I despaired of spotting a hidden Beguin among all the good Catholics. Nevertheless, I scanned the hundreds of faces with great concentration, and was finally rewarded after most of them had gone.

The execution itself was particularly unpleasant. As ever, the fault lay in a lack of proper organisation, such as my master would never tolerate; I suspect that the root of the problem was money. It costs money to buy ropes and kindling, as I have said. In Toulouse, heretics are always tied at the ankles, below the knee, above the knee, at the groin, at the waist, and under the arms. A chain is also secured around the neck, and faggots mixed with straw piled up almost to the chin. By this means, the fire is quick and fierce, and the possibility of an unexpected release, through the burning of any one ligature, exceedingly remote.

Today, no chains were used. The heretics were tied only twice, around the ankles and chest. Most dreadfully, the fuel was insufficient, and some of it must have been a little damp. (Even as Jean de Beaune was asking the Beguins to recant, I was thinking to myself: 'These pyres are not finished, surely?') When lit, the wood emitted a lot of smoke and very little flame. There were hacking coughs, and pitiful cries, and more wood and straw had to be rushed into the square as people fled from the stinking pall that hung over the cathedral and palace. Even some of the clerics departed, looking pale and sick.

This made matters a good deal easier for me. Only the most fervent souls felt constrained to hold their ground—whether they were for or against the Beguins. While covering my mouth and nose with a piece of cloth, I peered through the smoke with streaming eyes at those who remained.

There was no point looking for tears. In that smoke, *everyone* was weeping. People who covered their faces were not necessarily overcome with horror, though it must be confessed that one of the heretics had dropped from his stake; owing to the unevenness of his pyre, his bonds had burned through while he was still alive (if unconscious), and the panic-stricken guards were heaving more vine branches onto his twitching body. I cannot think such a spectacle worthy of the Church. I was glad that the smoke obscured much of the initial conflagration, though a wind sprang up soon after the bells of St-Just began tolling, and dispersed some of that noxious cloud.

I was also glad that Martin did not attend. Though his father and eldest brother were present, Martin himself had been left in my workroom, with firm instructions about finishing a parchment. It was the first time I had ever let him finish a parchment (that is, scrape it for the second time), and I was worried that he might ruin it. But I am so very, very glad that he did not witness what I witnessed today. It was a disgraceful exhibition of greed and incompetence. No doubt the Viscount was to blame—or perhaps the Royal *Viguier*. I hope that Jean de Beaune calls him to task for it.

Despite the confusion, however, I can testify that there were some who died most bravely. Pons was among them. My wandering gaze was drawn back repeatedly to his pyre, where he prayed aloud in a firm voice until the smoke billowed up to choke him. I was not close enough to hear any final pleas, nor to witness his death agonies—for which I am grateful. The smoke obscured much of what I preferred to avoid seeing. Nevertheless, I observed that he died well.

And this was noted, as it is always noted. I was watching a group of muttering Franciscans when I heard a voice remark, just behind me: 'He died a good death. He must be a holy martyr.' Looking around, I perceived a man of about my own age, addressing his older companion. The younger man was tall and swarthy, with a scrubby jaw, a tumbling thatch of thick black hair, and eyebrows as dark and threatening as thunderclouds. His distinguishing features were his missing front tooth and the hard calluses on his right thumb and forefinger, which marked him as a tailor. (Shoemakers have similar calluses, but in slightly different locations on the hand.)

His companion was shorter, fatter and half-bald. He had small features clustered together in the middle of his round, red face: a button nose, a pursed-up mouth like a cat's fundament, and a pair of little, watering eyes the colour of the Aude after heavy rain. I was at a loss when it came to *his* livelihood, until I saw him roll his right shoulder in a certain way, and wince as he rubbed his elbow.

A weaver, I thought. And my senses were suddenly alert. For of all the trades, in all parts of the world, weaving is the most prone to errors of belief. I do not know why. Perhaps it is because a weaver must sit rooted to the spot, day after day, making the same motion over and over and over again. Perhaps, in the circumstances, anyone would take leave of his senses, and start pondering questions that should rightly be left to people with more education.

Whatever the cause, you should never lose sight of a weaver if you can possibly help it. I kept my eyes on this one, and was pleased that he did not leave the site of the execution. Instead he and the tailor remained in the square, sometimes praying, sometimes solemnly watching, as the heretics died and the flames guttered. I should mention that Imbert Rubei was nowhere in evidence. This surprised me, because I had thought that such a pious-seeming man, in such humble brown worsted, would certainly attend this most solemn of occasions. But I did see Berengar Blanchi, Imbert's friend and Vincent Hulart's cousin. He was red-eyed and white-faced, swaying back and forth at the edge of the crowd, praying fervently.

I myself prayed, of course. I grieved and I prayed. How not? At such a solemn and awful event, it is imperative that one pray for the souls of those condemned to the Eternal Flames, however one might deplore their blind arrogance. I find it hard sometimes to understand why a man like Pons, who might have been argued into a more submissive frame of mind by St Dominic, or St Francis—or even by Bernard Gui—must suffer so frightfully both before and after his death, simply because he was not exposed to the sort of enlightened teaching that would have put him on the right path. For though proud and wrong-headed, he was not vicious, I am sure. A good example might have made all the difference. What these people fail to understand is that one *cannot* look to the priests and friars for perfection. While many of them are indeed grievous sinners, it is unreasonable to expect anything else—here on earth, at least.

Thoughts such as this sometimes occupied me as I waited patiently in that blighted square. By God's mercy, the smoke eventually cleared. But as the afternoon advanced, the wind picked up even more, and the embers began to fly about in a most disconcerting fashion. It was at this point that Jean de Beaune withdrew, together with his entourage. The Archbishop had long since disappeared into his palace. The Viscount had become engaged in a protracted and intense dispute with a couple of consuls; from what I could hear of it, carried on fitful gusts of wind, this dispute concerned the supervision of grain weights. Meanwhile, the crowd slowly dispersed. Those left were either grief-stricken relatives, or secret sympathisers, or old women with nothing else to do, or people of that very peculiar disposition which enjoys the dismemberment of half-consumed corpses.

I myself am not equipped with such a disposition. Few men are, in my experience. It was evident that many of the guards had made themselves scarce for that very reason: they had no wish to take part in such a disgusting ritual, however necessary it might have been. I have been informed by Bernard Gui that the true purpose of breaking up the remains, and consigning the charred pieces to a fresh pile of burning logs, is to ensure that the bodies are reduced to ashes, which can then be cast into a river in order that no blasphemers shall ever find an earthly resting place (least of all in the home of another heretic). God grant that *I* am never the object of such implacable resentment, however logical or reasonable it might be. Yet almost as dreadful as this fate is the fate of those who must throw water on the smoking embers, and then walk about on them, hewing at blackened joints with their axes, smashing bones with their spades, and stoking the flames of the last remaining pyre with shrivelled viscera.

The men who do this must be seasoned soldiers. They must be accustomed to severed limbs and scattered guts. Nevertheless, I pity them. The stench alone is enough to turn even the strongest stomach—as I witnessed today. Of the few men brave enough to undertake so grisly a task, several were taken ill before they could finish, and staggered away to recover.

Therefore many of the seventeen corpses were left unattended for long periods of time.

I had expected something of the sort, and was prepared for it. In my vivid scarlet cloak I hovered near one of the extinguished pyres, which was now a sodden heap of charcoal, ashes and charred bone. Though I cannot be sure, I believe that the Beguin on this particular pyre had been female; it must be admitted that I took care to avoid the site of Pons's death, owing to a culpable weakness of the heart. For a while I seemed to pray, though I was in fact keeping a close watch on the weaver, the tailor and Berengar Blanchi from beneath my hood. Then, when I saw that they were observing me, I stepped forward to retrieve a fragment of the woman's burned finger, holding my breath as I did so.

It was more difficult than I had expected. The sinews were not burned through, and I found myself wrenching the joints apart as if trying to suck the marrow from a knuckle of roast pork, God forgive me. I wish never to attempt such a thing in all my life henceforth, so help me God. But I remembered everything that I have learned, and stayed calm (though gravely concerned that the guards might see if I fumbled about for too long), and at last the finger came away, and I was able to wrap it up in my piece of linen cloth. Even as I tucked it into my purse, I saw Berengar approaching another pyre nearby. But I knew better than to join him there.

For I had devised a more subtle way of stalking my quarry: namely, by allowing him to stalk me.

Sure enough, it worked. I was reciting another prayer when someone tapped me on the shoulder. Turning, I found myself face to face with the swarthy tailor, who employed the informal 'you' when addressing me—though I had never met him before in my life.

'Did you know this woman?' he inquired, nodding towards the fragmentary corpse that I had plundered. His voice trembled; he seemed greatly moved.

I myself, being hoarse and red-eyed from the smoke, must have seemed just as distraught.

'No,' I replied. 'But I would have wished to, God rest her soul.'

I said nothing more. I certainly did not ask any questions. That is the first rule of a successful disguise: do not ask questions. Especially leading questions. For there is nothing more likely to arouse concern among those with a reason to be suspicious.

The tailor must have shared my opinion, for he too fell silent. Then he nodded, and moved away. It was at this point that an old man hailed me from a shop doorway. He had keener vision than I would have given him credit for.

'If you are hungry, Redback,' he cackled, 'there is better meat to be had than the meat off *those* bones! For they were Beguins, and starved themselves in the name of God.'

Immediately he was instructed to hold his tongue—by as many people as heard him, I am pleased to say. I thought it a good time to withdraw, and did so. But I marked that the tailor watched me go, his dark eyes speculative under his thick black brows.

And now, alas, I have a piece of burned Beguin sitting downstairs. I hid it in my special place of concealment, under the cellar flagstone, with my beggar's clothes and my special cloak and the little Beguin books my master gave me. Even so, I am concerned that it might start to smell—for all that I wrapped it in leather, and put it in a pot, and sealed the pot with wax. God help me if anyone sniffs *that* out. For they will find the books, and the gums, and Bernard Gui's letter, and I shall be thoroughly unmasked. Perhaps I did the wrong thing. Perhaps I should conquer my revulsion, and boil up the digit, and scrub it clean, and make of it something like an ivory trinket—as harmless and inoffensive as a pair of horn dice.

But the Beguins may not desecrate their relics in such a fashion. And I should not like to cause offence if I am ever again obliged to produce the finger. It preys on my mind, though. It should not; I should be accustomed to having bits of people concealed around the house. My aunt used to keep her children's umbilical cords—I know not why. And I have many times come across the hair and fingernails of the dead, in homes where retaining them is regarded as a sop to good fortune.

Nevertheless, it preys on my mind.

My clothes and skin and hair still smell of smoke—even, faintly, of burned flesh. Or am I imagining that stink? Is it part of the memory that I must put aside, though the picture remains so vivid: the picture of sooty skin, spotted with pink blisters, splitting over oozing, swollen fat.

I have the most terrible headache.

Martin did well today. His work on that parchment was flawless. I told him so, and he was greatly pleased. He asked me about the execution, and I put him off.

I need not have bothered, however. His father has been talking of nothing else, to judge from what I have since overheard. He was out in the courtyard earlier, describing the grisly event to his wife in great detail. According to Hugues Moresi, no man among the crowd in the square today was half as staunch as he; while others voided their bellies to his left and right, he stood firm in the face of so much suffering. He was no weakling, like those others. He was strong enough to bear witness, and saw everything that befell the unfortunate condemned—whose sins, he said, were no worse than the sins of the gluttonous priests come to watch them die.

If he *was* so staunch, it surprises me that he did not offer to join the soldiers, and merrily assist them in the task of dismemberment. Indeed, I am astonished that he has exhibited any sympathy at all for the dead Beguins. I have always thought him rather brutal in his relations with those who are younger, weaker, and more unfortunate—like most men who pride themselves on the strength of their character.

But I doubt that he was as resolute as he claims. If he had stayed to the end, I would have seen him. The crowd had thinned so much, I would never have missed such a familiar face. I would be willing to wager money that he repaired to the nearest inn as soon as the first belly burst.

God help me. I cannot sit here any longer.

My poor head.

VIII.
Tuesday before Holy Week

At last I have hooked my fish.

It has been difficult, I must confess—largely owing to the heavy burden of my work, which has increased greatly with the approach of Easter. I do not know why. The notaries seem to be especially busy; perhaps the prospect of Holy Week has been causing people to rethink their wills. Perhaps merchants are trying to draw up contracts before Palm Sunday brings all business grinding to a halt. Whatever the reason, it has certainly complicated *my* life. I must try to fill many new orders, while at the same time weaving my net across the city.

But I should not complain. In the end, I made only two passes through the Bourg, and one through the Cité. I was expecting to find my Beguins in the Bourg, if only because Berengar Blanchi lives there. Imagine my surprise, therefore, when I picked up my horsefly in the Cité.

It was the fat weaver. I recognised his balding pate even from the rear.

My scarlet cloak must have caught his eye. I had worn it on every trip since the *sermo generalis*, hoping that its vivid colour—and the distinctive black stain on its back—would jog someone's memory. Specifically, I had hoped to jog Berengar Blanchi's memory, because he was my chief target. His demeanour at the execution had marked him out, as had his garb, and the fervent glint in his eye. Hence the amount of time that I had lavished on the neighbourhood of his cousin's house—despite the fact that I had already dismissed Vincent Hulart from my list of suspects. Vincent Hulart is not a Beguin, I feel sure. No Beguin would have filled his day with business on the anniversary of Pierre Olivi's death.

But the fat weaver must live in the Cité, not the Bourg. I saw him first as I was entering the Fursteria, or carpenters' quarter; he was carrying a wooden shuttle and arguing a price with one of the wood merchants. Since there are carpenters enough in the Bourg capable of building or repairing a weaver's shuttle, I am convinced that he lives much closer than that.

Hoping to catch his attention, I stopped to admire a carved chest. When at last I moved on again, he moved on with me, just a few steps behind. Name of a name, but he was clumsy! At one point I had to double back—since I wanted to show him where I lived—and he lost me after only two left-hand turns. I looked around and he was gone. So I had to stay where I was, pretending to count coins in my palm, until he found me again. After that, I walked more slowly. I walked so slowly that I was almost going backwards.

But I reached my house at last.

Had I been following him, I would not have stood openly watching his house after he had entered it. Nor would I have hailed his neighbour across the street, and inquired as to his name and occupation—as the fat weaver did, in his search for my identity. I watched him from behind a half-open shutter, and I saw him *pointing at this house*. Not only that, but he described me to my neighbour. He measured my height against his own with his hand; then he pushed both hands together ('thin'), drew them down on either side of his face ('long, straight hair'), and traced rough circles in front of his eyes. ('Green eyes'? 'Dark lashes'? I know not.)

My neighbour nodded. His reply must have satisfied the weaver: perhaps it was my name, or my situation. Whatever it was, the weaver thanked him for it, and went away looking both pleased and anxious. Now all I have to do is wait. I must wait for the weaver and his friends to approach me as a fellow heretic, or heretical sympathiser.

Unless they are suspicious of my motives?

Surely not. I have given no cause for alarm. I have asked no questions, nor sought anyone out. I have been going about my business like a good citizen—as anyone can testify who might have been pursuing me.

Not that anyone has been pursuing me. Of that I am convinced. I have not relaxed my vigilance for a moment since I first saw Armand Sanche, and I have grave doubts that any Narbonnaise Beguin could outfox a man trained up in the mountains, among Cathars. Among the forts built long ago by Cathar lords, against the Church and the northern invaders.

Of course, following someone on a crowded city street is different from following someone over a mountain. It is both easier and more difficult. As a pursuer, it is easier to conceal oneself in a crowd—just as it is easier to lose one's quarry among all the people. On a lonely mountain, every man is clearly visible to a trained eye. Even if he attempts to hide himself, he will leave telltale signs and tracks behind him. He will leave wisps of smoke and warm ashes; spit and ordure; footprints and broken branches. Most importantly, he will leave a clear portrait in the memories of those who see few strangers from one year to the next.

Sometimes, when following a man over a mountain, it is easy to forget that you are leaving your own traces.

I have learned this lesson well, God knows. I have learned not to forget the road behind me, even when I am watching the road ahead. When I was following Guillaume Autier (this was after his brother, Pierre, was arrested in Belpech), I asked too many questions, and left too many traces. I became an object of suspicion among Guillaume Autier's Cathar friends. Had I not been so alert, I would have ended up dead, like all the other men murdered at around the same time, in Junac and Montaillou and Ax-les-Thermes, simply because they were regarded as potential informers.

It happened nine years ago. Nine years! I must have been heading for San Mateo, in Tarragona, where many of the most faithful Cathars had found a home. Yes, on reflection—I was. Because the shepherd's cabane in which I found refuge was on Mount Vezian. And the men there welcomed me cheerfully, since it can be lonely work tending the pastures. Besides which, in those days I did more than mend shoes; I sold needles and thread, and collected news from the lowlands. I made myself a welcome guest. I worked hard at it.

But one of the five shepherds was a friend of Raymond Issaura de Larnat, the heretical believer. And at Larnat there is a long history of intolerance when it comes to dealing with inquisitorial agents. I have heard tell that, somewhere up in the ravines near town, there lies the body of a Franciscan lay brother who went there to arrest Guillaume Autier twenty years ago.

At any rate, I was stupid. I was lulled by the wine and the fire and the merry company. When we were eating, I saw Raymond Issaura's friend bless his bread in the heretical manner—and asked him one too many questions as a result. He must have lain awake thinking about me all night, while I snored. (What a fool I was!) The next morning, he and his friend offered to guide me to Morella, where—they said—Guillaume Autier could be found. And I believed them. At least, I believed them until I saw one of them take up an axe. He said that he was a woodcutter, and that the axe was his own.

Though I might have been a fool, however, I was not *that* foolish. I had seen woodcutters before—many of them. And the one thing they all share is a massive set of shoulders.

Whereas this fellow was built like a shepherd's staff.

To my credit, I acted at once. Claiming that I needed to empty my bladder, I went off into the rocks. I knew better than to waste a moment. Instead I abandoned my possessions and ran, before anyone understood that *I* had understood. Moreover, because I had left all my things, I bought myself some time. The men could not believe that I would relinquish my tools. They waited just long enough to give me an advantage.

I needed it, too. For they were good trackers. I had thought I might outwit them by abandoning my quest and heading back towards Lérida. They split up, however, in anticipation of this very ruse. I had one of them on my trail all the way to the Vicdessos Valley, because I carried nothing but money, and had to buy or beg assistance along the way. By this means I left traces, which led my pursuer to the cave of La Vache. Where I was waiting for him.

It must be understood that when a man follows you for such a long distance, he does so with good cause. I knew what his reason must be: I knew his name, after all, and had seen him bless his bread with a heretical sign. In the circumstances, I had no choice. I saw him enter that cave with his axe raised. Had he found me at rest by the fire inside (which was still smoking), he would have knocked my head from my shoulders.

So I struck him with a rock when he emerged. It was an act of self-defence, as I will attest to this day. My master agreed with me. He said that I had no cause for shame; that I was assured of God's forgiveness. He said that, being small and weak, I had owed my tall pursuer no chance to make his peace with God—since he would not, in all certainty, have taken it. When I persisted in doubting, my master brought me a priest, in order that I might make my confession. And the priest confirmed all that my master had said.

I feel that I cannot have been wrong. For I would have died up there in the mountains, and the crows would have eaten me. I was exhausted by that time. I was penniless. Had I stayed my hand, it would have been suicide. And suicide is a mortal sin.

To this day, I regret nothing—save the skills that were lost. For the man who followed me was a hunter of unparalleled knowledge and experience. He taught me many things, even as I fled from him. He taught me that covering shit with a rock is better than burying it, since turned earth is clearly visible; but that it is impossible to disguise the smell unless you leave rotten meat nearby. He taught me to scatter ashes, so that they will cool more quickly. He taught me to avoid pasture at all cost, since you beat out your own path every time you cross it.

And he taught me never, ever to ask questions.

That is why, when I saw the fat weaver asking questions today, I shook my head. And I went upstairs wondering at the significance of such a clumsy pursuit. The fat weaver is either very stupid or extremely intelligent. Could he be trying to influence me as I have tried to influence him? It seems doubtful. A Cathar might have the wit for such a plan, but a Beguin?

When I reached my workroom, Martin was there. He was standing at the window, peering down at the street. Upon hearing my step, he swung around.

'Master,' he said, through a mouthful of bread and garlic, 'someone followed you.'

For a moment I was speechless. I looked at him, slowly removing my scarlet cloak, as I tried to formulate a response.

'I saw him,' Martin went on eagerly. 'He was walking behind you, and when you came into the house, he stopped outside. Then he went over to Adhemar, across the road, and spoke to him. He pointed at this house.'

'Indeed?' I said. 'How odd.'

'He wanted to know who you were. He was asking about you. I saw him show Adhemar how tall you are.'

'And what were you doing staring out the window?' I asked, recovering my composure. 'When there is so much work to be done?'

'Master, I was eating. You told me never to eat while I work, in case I stain the parchment.'

'True.' I laid my cloak carefully on the linen chest. 'Is he still there, this man?'

'No. He walked away down the street.'

'What did he look like?'

I was interested—genuinely interested—in how attentive Martin had been. I wanted to know if he had drawn any conclusions.

'He was fat,' the boy declared—inevitably. (He himself, being as thin as a reed, would consider anyone fat who could not slide himself into a length of worsted hose.) 'Fat and bald, with a red face.'

'Anything else?'

'He wore a blue surcoat over a brown tunic.'

'Long or short?'

'Knee-length.'

'Anything else?'

'Um . . .' Martin's smooth brow puckered. He was trying very hard. 'His belt was brown . . .'

'Did he wear a cloak? A purse? A knife? Did he carry anything?'

'He carried a wooden thing, like a big comb with no teeth.'

This was hardly an adequate description. So I tried again.

'What did he do?' I queried.

'Do?'

'With his body. How did he stand? How did he move? Show me.'

Martin's imitation of a fat man waddling caused me to smile. When he grinned back, however, I refused to indulge him with a word of approval.

For I was still not satisfied.

'What else?' I pressed. 'Show me his hands. Show me what he did with them. *Exactly* what he did.'

Martin hesitated. Tentatively, he pointed one finger.

I waited.

He measured a height against his own, brushing his fingertips across one cheekbone. He pushed both hands together. He drew them down on either side of his face. He traced two circles over his eyes.

Then he rolled his shoulder, wincing, and kneaded his right elbow with his left hand.

'Do that again,' I said.

He obeyed, watching me intently. I could read the question in his dark and solemn gaze.

'Unless I am mistaken, child, your man is a weaver,' I declared, putting the boy out of his misery. 'If you watch a weaver for any length of time, you will see him make a movement like the one you just imitated. It is the sign of someone who spends too much time at his loom. When you are next in church, you should look for the weavers.'

Martin's jaw dropped in astonishment.

'In the meantime, you should tell me if you happen to see him again,' I recommended, moving over to the frame on which was strung Martin's latest hide. 'Now, what have I told you about pressing too hard? You are still using too much force, here. You are stretching the skin.'

'Master, why would a weaver follow you home? And then go away without speaking to you?'

'Perhaps he has need of a parchment-maker. Perhaps he saw the chalk on my sleeves.'

But Martin shook his head.

'Master, no one else sees such things,' he objected. 'Only you.'

'And you,' I said, whereat he flushed, and looked pleased. Nevertheless, he would not be distracted from his purpose.

'Master, it makes no sense.'

'Perhaps not to you or to me,' I replied. 'But there must be a reasonable explanation.'

'What, though?'

I decided that such persistence, though admirable in some ways, should not be encouraged where it related to my affairs. And I fixed upon my apprentice a cold, unwavering look.

'The weaver was following *me*,' I said. 'So whatever his intentions, they can hardly be any of your business. Can they?'

Again Martin coloured. I thought him offended, at first. When he mumbled an apology, however, it became apparent that he was merely crushed.

It takes very little to crush that boy. After enduring so many blows, he should have developed a thicker skin. Yet it remains as thin as my best parchment, with every change of mood written clearly upon it, as if inscribed there by a thick-cut quill dipped in the most expensive black ink.

He must learn to dissemble. He *must*. Or what will become of him?

IX.
Wednesday before Holy Week

I have yet to start reading those Beguin books.

Alas, I have been very remiss. In putting off such an unwelcome task, I have condemned myself to a sleepless night. For if I have not mastered their contents by tomorrow, I shall find myself in the gravest peril.

I should have known that the Beguins would not wait.

They came to my shop this morning: two of them, both women. I was stitching quires when they entered, and looked up to see a matron standing over me, very tall and well dressed. She had a long nose, high cheekbones and an ardent gaze. Her firm jaw enclosed a full, soft mouth, while her hair was concealed by an abundance of plainly coloured but finely woven silk.

The girl with her could not have been older than seventeen. Though her clothing was simple—even poor—she challenged me with a gaze that was oddly proud and fierce for someone so thin and pale. She had the long neck of a goose, and the stooped shoulders that you often see on weavers and seamstresses and nuns.

By her appearance, I did not judge her to be a relative of the matron. Nor did she impress me as being a maidservant. Her demeanour was something between that of a favoured friend and a poor dependant.

'Blessed be the name of Jesus Christ,' the matron declared, fixing me with a bright and expectant look. For one instant I was at a loss. Then, almost before I had drawn breath, I remembered that Berengar Blanchi had used the same phrase when greeting Imbert Rubei—who had responded with an identical salutation.

Like the sun emerging from behind a cloud, understanding dawned in my mind. I realised that the Beguins must use 'Blessed be the name of Jesus Christ' much as the Cathars use 'Can we do something for our betterment?'. Both are greetings that distinguish the heretics from all others. They are like passwords into a besieged city.

'Blessed be the name of Jesus Christ,' I therefore replied, noticing as I did so that the women's gowns were covered with an unusual number of stray threads from other cloth. There were drifting strands of gold silk, and thick lengths of dull-coloured wool, and fibres that might have linen or even cotton—I could not tell. All I *could* tell was that these women were either weavers, drapers, or the wives of tailors (though not tailors themselves, to judge from their hands).

When I spoke, the matron nodded. My response had evidently satisfied her.

'You are Helié Seguier?' she inquired.

'I am.'

'Then I wish to buy parchment.'

'Yes.' I rose, thankful that Martin was upstairs, at work. 'For an account book, perhaps? A register?'

'For a holy book,' the matron replied, still watching my face. 'I wish to have a copy made of a book written by Pierre Olivi. His *postilla* on the Apocalypse. Have you read this work?'

I could not have been more surprised. Her recklessness astonished me; I had been expecting a far subtler approach.

Indeed, she was so blatant that I became cautious. No genuine Beguin, I felt, would reply frankly to such a question. Surely even the witless heretics of Narbonne would suspect a trap?

'That book has been condemned,' I said.

'But did you read it *before* it was condemned?' she pressed me. 'If not, then you should read it now. For that book is a wonder. If all the heads of all the men in the world were one, they could not have written that book unless through the agency of the Holy Spirit.'

Amazed, I glanced from the woman to the girl, and back again. Both wore eager expressions, though the girl's eagerness had an edge to it, while the woman's was altogether more serene.

'I have read the book,' I lied, praying that Martin was not listening at the top of the stairs (as he frequently does). 'I shall be honoured to provide parchment for another copy.'

The two Beguins glanced at each other. Then the matron turned back to me, smiling. Her teeth were beautiful.

'If you have read the book, then you must know how long it is,' she said. 'Bring me as much parchment as I shall need, tomorrow, directly after the first meal of the day. Bring it to my house. It is the draper's shop near the Inn of the Star. You know the Inn of the Star?'

'Yes.'

'Bring it to the shop, and I shall pay you a fair price.'

'What name shall I give when I get there?' was my next question, put to her quickly, before she could leave. 'Your own?'

'I am Berengaria, wife of Pierre Donas the draper,' she replied. Then she glanced around the shop, wrinkling her nose a trifle as she sniffed the tainted air. 'Make sure the parchment is good. Brother Pierre Olivi's *postilla* should not be desecrated by inferior parchment.'

'I do not sell inferior parchment.' Quietly but firmly, I defended my reputation. 'All of my stock is good.'

'An honest labourer will never want for custom,' Na Berengaria observed, in approving tones. 'I will see you tomorrow, then. You yourself. In person. Is that understood?'

'Of course.'

'Blessed be the name of Jesus Christ.'

With a swish of her heavy gown she departed, taking the girl with her. It was some time before I recovered from the shock. I had anticipated nothing so abrupt, and felt almost as if I had suffered a blow to the head.

At last, however, my jumbled thoughts settled themselves into a more orderly arrangement. I began to consider the implications of Berengaria's visit, weighing all the probabilities in my mind.

Is she a genuine Beguin? It would seem so. Does she truly regard me as another convert? Perhaps. Is she acquainted with Jacques Bonet? Ah—now *that* is the most important question.

If she does know Jacques, she must know him as a fugitive—if not as an agent of Jean de Beaune. In which case, why this open and reckless behaviour? I cannot believe that someone who has either aided or killed a fugitive tertiary would go about merrily asking complete strangers if they have read Pierre Olivi's *postilla*. Not without a hidden purpose. Unless the woman is a fool?

She could be, I suppose. On the other hand, she could be suspicious of my motives. If she knows Jacques Bonet as an inquisitor's agent, then she might be concerned that I am one also. In which case she might be attempting to lure me into her lair. To kill me just as she killed Jacques.

It must be confessed, I find it hard to imagine her killing anybody. That girl, now—*she* might kill, in a fit of passion. But not Berengaria. I have yet to meet a murderer distinguished by such an air of fulfilment. And I have met several murderers in my time.

There are four possibilities. One is that she does not know Jacques Bonet, and is simply eager to share the teachings of Pierre Olivi despite the dangers involved. Another is that she knows Jacques as an escaped Beguin, yet persists in naïvely taking risks. A third is that she has killed Jacques, and now wants to kill me. A fourth is that Jacques revealed his deadly secret, and threw himself on her mercy. Perhaps she is the sort of woman who would be only too pleased to help someone in Jacques's position escape the clutches of Jean de Beaune.

I cannot decide which of these alternatives is the most likely. I am not sufficiently well acquainted with the woman to make an informed choice. Nevertheless, it would be stupid to walk, all unprotected, into a trap. So when I visit her house tomorrow, I shall take a knife with me. Concealed in my boot. And I shall avoid entering any darkened rooms—especially if there is someone directly behind me.

This, then, is my plan. I judged it a good one earlier today. Whereupon, having decided on a course of action, I went to my shelves and gathered together a number of quires. These I wrapped in a cloth, setting them aside for Na Berengaria. But as I did so, something occurred to me.

She had stated that she was buying parchment so as to make a copy of a heretical book.

Could it be possible, I wondered, that other such purchases had been made from my shop in the past? Not by scribes or notaries or priests or monks, but by weavers and drapers and other people not renowned for their interest in the written word? Of course, such people *might* require some form of register or account book in their business. But the folios in that case are generally quite large, and their purpose clearly specified.

A heretical codex, on the other hand, would have to be small—for ease of concealment. Moreover, if I were a heretic buying parchment for a prohibited text, I would take care to patronise a shop where I was a complete stranger. And be sure never to return there.

After all, who knows what transactions the inquisitors might decide to investigate, in their pursuit of forbidden books?

Moved by a sudden curiosity, I went upstairs to check my own register. This I keep from force of habit, though it is of little use for the most part; it is a record of all orders and purchases made from my shop, together with details of the individuals concerned. Sometimes I am given a name. Sometimes the name is withheld. But always, in the left-hand column, I make a special mark if the customer is unknown to me. And in these cases, I take care to describe the stranger as fully as possible. It is mere habit, I suppose—though not without purpose for a man in hiding. I have found that even a good memory needs some assistance.

Upstairs in my workroom, Martin was busily scraping away with his chalk. He seemed quite happy to mind the shop for a while; I told him to call me if anyone came in. He said: 'Who were those ladies?'

I looked at him. 'Were you listening?' I asked.

'No, Master.' He shook his head. 'I saw them enter. And leave. From the window.'

'Then you should have drawn your own conclusions,' I declared, and sent him downstairs. He could sweep out the shop, I said, and tidy the shelves. Meanwhile, I had work to do.

My register is kept within easy reach, beside my bed. There is no need to conceal it by locking it away in the linen chest, as I do with this journal. Consequently, it was the work of a moment to retrieve the unbound volume, which—being a collection of ragged offcuts and inferior samples, stitched together—has a somewhat scrappy appearance.

I scanned the pages hurriedly, looking for the special mark. Whenever I found it, I checked for a name. Then I read the description. (Some were quite detailed, especially where no name or profession had been supplied.) In disregarding all priests, monks and notaries, I was left with a very much reduced list of customers. This I shortened further by winnowing out various merchants who have become familiar to me since their first visit to my shop.

Then all at once, a name seemed to leap from the surface of one yellowing folio. It had been inscribed there some three years before, beside a special mark.

It was the name Imbert Rubei.

I believe that I hissed as I caught sight of it. Imbert Rubei! Sure enough, it was the same man. The description matched. I had described him as elderly and slightly lame, with bushy grey eyebrows and a square jaw. I had also described him as a silk merchant. He had ordered three quires of pricked parchment, and had provided me with an address in the Bourg, as well as his name.

Beneath this entry I had scribbled another, in different ink, using a slightly narrower quill.

I remember this name, was the entry. *It was affixed to a letter sent to the Pope by the consuls of the Bourg. They were protesting against the excommunication of Narbonne's Spiritual friars. This must have been just after I arrived in Narbonne, when I was still living in the Bourg—for the letter was read out in the church of Notre-Dame Lamourguier. The consuls were concerned that many burghers who worshipped at the Franciscan priory would be unable to do so any longer.*

Imbert Rubei must have been a consul, once.

I was astonished—and disgusted. How could I have forgotten such an important fact? In a flood it all came back to me: the high stone vault of the church roof, the toneless delivery of the priest, the six names of the consuls, who—it had seemed to me at the time—were running a terrible risk. I had made a mental note of their names for that very reason, wondering if I would soon see these same men recanting heresy at a *sermo generalis.* Already, in those days, I could sense the gathering storm that would soon engulf so many Spiritual Franciscans.

And being new to Narbonne, I was not accustomed to the brazen self-confidence of its people.

My memory of Imbert Rubei's visit to the shop is not so clear. His face has remained with me; I recognised it instantly, upon first sighting him outside the house of Vincent Hulart. But I cannot place him in my shop, no matter how hard I try. I cannot recall what he wore, nor what he said. It is maddening.

If nothing else, this demonstrates why my register—and this journal—are so necessary. Without them, my memory is a weak and imperfect thing.

Imbert Rubei's name appears only once in the pages of my register. Having bought his three quires of parchment, he promptly disappeared, and never returned to my shop. Could he have been buying parchment for a heretical text? Perhaps. If this was the case, however, why did he identify himself? Such a purchase would have been better made anonymously, or under an assumed name.

Perhaps the parchment was intended for a legitimate purpose. After all, a silk merchant is a man of many financial transactions, which must be recorded somewhere. I have no way of knowing what his intentions really were.

The only thing I *do* know, now, is the location of his house. This is very fortunate, since he must be a Beguin. Only consider the facts: firstly, he used the phrase 'Blessed be the name of Jesus Christ' in greeting; secondly, he protested the excommunication of the Spiritual Franciscans; thirdly, he is a silk merchant who wears a brown worsted tunic.

Furthermore, he is a friend of Berengar Blanchi. The pair of them spent a long time together on the anniversary of Pierre Olivi's death. And Berengar Blanchi is the cousin of Vincent Hulart. And Vincent Hulart was the only name given to Jacques Bonet, before he vanished.

It seems to me that I should pay a visit to the house of Imbert Rubei. Though not before I visit the house of Berengaria Donas.

All at once, I feel as if I am surrounded by Beguins.

X.
Thursday before Holy Week

Today I went to the draper's shop near the Inn of the Star, my head full of Pierre Olivi's *postilla*.

I was unable to finish it last night, because it is a long and difficult work. Nevertheless, I read enough to understand why my master finds it alarming. According to Olivi's interpretation of the Holy Scriptures, there are seven eras of the Church, and the sixth was founded by St Francis. In the writer's opinion, St Francis was, after Christ and His mother, the chief observer of the evangelical life. His evangelical rule will be crucified at the end of the sixth era, as Christ was once crucified. The seventh era will then begin with the death of the Antichrist, and the bodily resurrection of St Francis. It will also see the founding of a new Church.

If I were a Dominican, I would be *very* concerned to read such things.

My master once gave me some advice that I have never forgotten. He had discovered a Cathar book called *The Secret*

Supper, which he asked me to read—for it had been translated into the vernacular. This book was full of lies. It claimed, among other errors, that Satan had made all living things; that he had fashioned man out of clay in his own image, and had thereafter imprisoned the spirits of angels in each clay body.

Before giving me this book, Bernard Gui told me a great truth. He told me that many people will believe a lie when it is written down, simply because they regard script of any sort as somehow holy. He warned me that uneducated men will often be led astray in this manner. For they will read or hear only vernacular translations, of which there are very few; since Latin is the only language that can be understood throughout the world, most of the wisdom available to us is in Latin.

'Heretics draw their own conclusions even where their knowledge is incomplete, and therefore imperfect,' he said to me. 'If they had read everything that I have read—if they were familiar with the words of St Augustine, and St Jerome, and St Anselm, and all the other great writers who have defended both God and the Church with their pens—they would know better than to accept as the truth any lie that they happen to read, simply because it is written.'

Now, I myself have discovered that lies seem to have more substance when they are written down. Even *The Secret Supper* impressed me as being remarkable, despite its many absurdities. Had I read it without my master's guidance, I might have been moved to believe it. For I am not an educated man. I am unfamiliar with the words of St Augustine, and St Jerome, and St Anselm.

But I *have* been exposed to a number of heretical texts. And the more you read of such works, the less you are inclined to believe them. For they all have something different to say, and none of it seems proven or confirmed by what I have seen of the world around me. I ask myself: if these heretics are so right, then why are their various truths not manifest? And why, if I must choose between heresies, should I choose any one above another?

My master is correct when he says that pride is at the root of all heresy. How, in good conscience, can a man like me—so small and weak and uneducated—set himself against the Church, with all its earthly glory and its ancient wisdom? This is something that I frequently ask myself. Yet heretics fail to do so, and fall into error as a consequence.

In many cases, such pride is their only fault. While some heretics are murderers, and liars, and hypocrites, and men without conscience, others are in many ways worthy of admiration. They live modest lives, replete with good works and severe self-denial. Even Bernard Gui has admitted as much. 'The school of the devil, with its appearance of good, seems, in monkey fashion, to imitate the school of Christ in some ways,' he once remarked.

I wish that it were not so. I wish that the Beguins, for instance, were venal and vicious. If they were, it would be easier to betray them. It would be easier to think: 'They are a canker in the heart of Christendom, and must be cauterised immediately, lest they infect and corrupt the body of the Church.'

But I fear that Berengaria Donas is neither vicious nor venal. She strikes me as being fervent, generous, warm-hearted, overconfident, somewhat strident, and just a little bit stupid. Yet she is also a heretic, alas. And as such, she is a danger to us all.

If only there was some way to make her see reason, before she brings ruin down upon her friends and family!

The problem, as I see it, is her self-assurance. And the reason for *that* becomes clear when you visit her house. She lives off the Rue Droite, in a large and handsome stone building which is open to the street on the ground floor. Here I saw roll upon roll of the very finest cloth: *biffe* of Provins, *sarge* of Beaucaire, toile of Reims, brocade and samite and damask. The spotty youth watching over this valuable stock cannot have been more than twenty years old, yet he was dressed with the sombre dignity of a middle-aged consul, in long and full garments, beautifully cut.

I did wonder if he was Berengaria's son. It seemed likely. He was tall and thin, and his face was long. Yet when I greeted him with the words 'Blessed be the name of Jesus Christ', he gave a snort, and jerked his head towards the back of the shop.

'My stepmother is in the kitchen,' he said.

It would be impossible to convey his exact tone, which was at the same time impatient, dismissive, subdued, hostile, haughty and disillusioned. It surprised me, I must confess. So did the richness of his apparel, and the lavish furnishings of the shop. (I counted at least three pairs of scissors, and there might have been more.) No expense had been spared to demonstrate that Pierre Donas the draper was a man of the most immense wealth, taste and importance.

But this illusion ended at the kitchen door. In the Donas kitchen, there was no trace of excess or indulgence. Everything was simple and unadorned; even the few pieces of furniture were as humble as anything you might see in the passes of the Pyrenees. Aside from this furniture, and a meagre amount of food, the kitchen contained only a couple of iron pots, one sharp knife, some wooden spoons, an axe, a hook and a small collection of plain terracotta, none of it decorated in any way.

The room's sole adornment was Berengaria Donas, who whirled around in shock when I burst in. My entry was deliberately abrupt; I wanted no one prepared for my coming. Since the spotty youth had not announced my arrival, I felt that I would be safe enough if I slammed through the kitchen door (hard enough to make it bounce off the wall beside me), before closing and barring it, so as to guard my back. Naturally, I had kept close watch on Berengaria's stepson, who did not attempt to follow me in.

There were two other doors leading out of the kitchen. One opened into a courtyard, and stood ajar; the second was shut. No fire was burning. I counted three people in the room: Berengaria Donas, the swarthy tailor, and the long-necked girl. The man and the girl were sitting at a table, eating.

'What—what—' the matron stammered. 'Is that you, Helié Seguier?'

'Yes.'

With her hand to her breast, Na Berengaria sank onto a stool. 'Why such haste?' she said. 'You startled me.'

'I brought your parchment.' Crossing the room, I flung open the closed door without taking my eyes off the tailor, who was large and well built and posed the greatest threat. 'You asked me to come.'

'You're early,' said the tailor. And it was true. I had timed my visit so as to surprise those awaiting me—in case they wished me ill.

The adjoining room was a kind of cellar, filled with casks and sacks. No one appeared to be hiding in its shadowy recesses. So I shut the door on it, and moved to the next—which I closed and barred.

'Are you afraid of something?' asked the tailor.

'Of many things,' I rejoined. 'This parchment is valuable.'

The tailor scowled. 'Are you calling us thieves?' he demanded, whereupon Berengaria placed a reproving hand on his arm.

'Master Helié has good reason to be nervous,' she said. 'As do we all. He has seen what befalls those who remain faithful.' And her eyes filled with tears. 'May we ourselves prove as steadfast in the face of such terrible suffering and persecution.'

The pale girl crossed herself. The tailor rose abruptly. I must admit that I fell back in alarm, for he was—as I have said—a large man, with long limbs and a broad frame. But he offered no violence. Instead he placed a hand on each of my shoulders.

'We saw you at the field of martyrdom,' he announced. 'We saw you gather up holy relics of our brothers and sisters in Christ.'

'You are mistaken,' I said, wriggling out of his grasp. The tailor, however, would not be denied.

'I saw you,' he insisted. 'I was there, to bear witness.'

'We have our own holy relics,' Berengaria added. She too rose, and held out her hand. 'Come. Let me show you.'

I hesitated.

'You have nothing to fear from us.' Her eyes were still wet, yet she offered me a smile of entreaty. 'We embrace you as a brother, Master Helié. What makes you so afraid?'

'I come from Carcassonne,' was my carefully thought-out reply. 'The home of Jean de Beaune.'

'That devil!' spat the pale girl. 'He will burn in hell!'

'We must pray for the soul of Jean de Beaune, that he may become enlightened,' said Berengaria. 'But we are not his friends. We are *your* friends, Master Helié.'

She then introduced the tailor as Blaise Bouer, and the girl as Guillelma Roger. Blaise appears to be a customer of the Donas family, while Guillelma's father—according to the matron—is unsympathetic to his daughter's spiritual needs. Therefore she spends most of her time at the Donas house, where she helps to cook and clean and cut wood.

'We are all of us good Christians, dedicated to serving the poor,' Na Berengaria informed me. 'On Sundays we gather here, with some other good people, and pray, and read from certain holy texts, and collect alms for those whom the Carnal Church would condemn—such as the poor and the weak, and fugitives from unjust persecution.'

You may be sure I was interested to hear *that*. Yet I asked no questions, and remained wary, standing with my wrapped parchment clasped to my chest.

'We would welcome you into our midst, on those days,' Berengaria continued. 'We are overjoyed to have found you, Helié Seguier.'

'You will draw strength from our faith,' said Guillelma. 'This is a house of poverty, and we all believe in the evangelical life, such as was described by the blessed Pierre.'

'You must bring your relics with you,' Berengaria instructed, 'that we may venerate them along with our own.'

I looked from one guileless face to another. Though Blaise had a slightly forbidding aspect, his brown eyes were clear and keen. Na Berengaria smiled serenely, like the Blessed Virgin. Guillelma's countenance shone in a way that boded ill for the lot of them; she had about her the appearance of someone moved by an incandescent rage against the rich and the powerful.

'You are mistaken,' I repeated, stalling. Whereupon Berengaria took my hand, and led me into the cellar. I must confess that I was reluctant to follow, since Blaise was practically treading on my heels. But I could not with any justification have refused to go; I had already shown myself suspicious enough, and was afraid that any further show of resistance would cause them to wonder at the extent of my distrust.

So I put my faith in the knife that I had concealed in my boot. And I went into the cellar, where I met with no rough handling. On the contrary, the mood of my companions was subdued and reverent. And I saw why when Blaise opened one of the casks.

Concealed inside this cask was a large wooden box, almost as big as a linen chest. Though the light was poor, I could see that it was finely carved. Gently lifting its lid, Blaise revealed a bundle of white silk, rather bulky and evil-smelling. Then Na Berengaria knelt down. With the practised ease of a woman accustomed to manipulating rich fabrics, she unwrapped the bundle rapidly and gracefully, to expose one of the grisliest objects that I have ever encountered.

'This is the head of Esclaramonde Serrallerii,' Berengaria murmured. 'And this is her shoulder, and part of her chest.'

'Amen,' said Guillelma.

'And this is the kidney of Jean Egleysa. And *this* is the shin of Brother Pierre de Frayssenet, holy martyr of God.'

Solemnly they all three crossed themselves, apparently unmoved by the unpleasant odour. I followed their lead. There was a moment of devout silence, after which Berengaria leaned forward and gently kissed the blackened, grinning teeth of Esclaramonde Serrallerii.

When she looked up at me, I knew what I had to do.

God knows, I have done worse in my life. Once I hid in a dung heap. Once, while starving in the *mur* at Toulouse, I ate bread that the gaoler had pissed on. Once, outside the cave of La Vache, I killed a man, striking him with a rock and then finishing him off with his own axe.

Once I abandoned a girl who loved me.

Always, in life, there are acts that must be performed, and suffering that must be endured. God has willed it so. Therefore I dropped to one knee, and planted a lingering kiss upon the shin of Brother Pierre de Frayssenet, which looked like nothing so much as a piece of splintered charcoal.

By this simple display of veneration, I won Na Berengaria's entire sympathy and trust. Even Blaise was convinced—as well he might be. Having passed such a challenging test of devotion, I was embraced by all, one after the other. Then, while Blaise returned the relics to their hiding place, I was gently questioned by Berengaria. When had I come to Narbonne, and why? Was it in pursuit of enlightenment? Or had I been fleeing persecution?

I explained that my family had been active supporters of the Franciscan Bernard Delicieux, who for so long had fought the Dominican inquisitors at Carcassonne, and who had died in prison as a consequence, only the year before. Jean de Beaune was suspicious of everyone who bore my name, I said. Therefore I had left Carcassonne some five years previously, and had found peace in Narbonne.

'But I live in constant fear,' was my earnest—and truthful—declaration. 'Jean de Beaune seems to be everywhere, nowadays. If I were to raise my head, he would surely chop it off. I have kept myself to myself, for how can I trust anyone?'

'You can trust us,' Berengaria insisted.

'You have given me no choice,' I replied. 'You know me now, and I know you. We must trust each other.'

'Have no fear, Helié Seguier,' said the matron, with a confidence that seemed ill-founded to me. 'You should understand that we are not required to take oath before prelates and inquisitors in regard to anything but the faith and the articles of faith. Are you aware of that? If we are questioned about our brothers and sisters, we are not obliged to speak, even if under oath, because in doing so we would not be loving our neighbour in the way of Christ. Also, if we are excommunicated for refusing to tell the truth before any court, such excommunication is unjust, and does not bind us. Since the prelates and inquisitors themselves are heretics.' She smiled at me, in a reassuring fashion. 'Therefore you need not fear that we shall betray you. Even if one of us is arrested, there is no risk. We have all agreed not to speak of each other to our enemies.'

'We would die, rather!' Guillelma exclaimed, and Blaise nodded. I hardly knew where to look. The naïvety of these people is astounding.

Do they truly believe that inquisitors extract information purely by the imposition of solemn oaths?

'So do not abandon us through fear,' said Berengaria, in a tone almost of command. 'You are the lost sheep in the wilderness. You must return to the fold, where you will find strength in your faith, and where you can do good for the poor. Come to us on Sunday. Come and join us in our prayers, after Mass.'

'This Sunday is Palm Sunday,' I pointed out.

'All the more reason to come. Better to worship Christ among the humble and devoted, in a house of poverty, than before wicked priests hung about with gold.'

There was a murmur of agreement. I felt constrained to join in, and when I did so, was rewarded with Na Berengaria's approving smile. This widened when I agreed that my parchment should be donated, free of charge, to the holy cause of spreading Pierre Olivi's wisdom. 'For the money that you have saved me,' Berengaria observed, as she conducted me from her kitchen, 'I shall be able to feed an entire hospice full of lepers for a month.' And she patted my cheek, with a kind of brisk and motherly indulgence, before turning me loose on her doorstep.

She is somewhat overbearing. It makes me wonder about her husband, whom I did not see before I left. Is he also a heretic? Or is he too weak to prevent his wife from worshipping in his house with her heretical friends?

No doubt I shall have my answer on Sunday. For I have agreed to return then, with my Beguin finger and my heretical books. If I do, perhaps, I shall discover more about the 'fugitives from unjust persecution' referred to by Berengaria Donas. Could one of them be Jacques Bonet? Will he appear at her house on Sunday?

Or has he been reduced to a collection of burned bones concealed in an empty cask?

When I first saw the contents of that cask, it did occur to me that they might be the earthly remains of Jean de Beaune's missing familiar. What better way to hide a corpse, after all, than by disguising it as another corpse? I thought: Perhaps he was chopped up and thrown on the kitchen fire.

Almost at once, however, I discounted the possibility. There are better ways to dispose of old bones than to keep them in your cellar. You can feed them to a dog. You can throw them in the Aude, weighted down. You can bury them under your dung heap.

No: if Jacques Bonet is indeed dead, Berengaria's house is the last place I shall find him. (Why invite a stranger to one's house, if it contains a murdered corpse?) My only hope is that Jacques might have left traces. Signs. Perhaps some hint of his presence still lingers there, even if he himself is long gone.

God grant that, if dead, he was indeed killed in that house, by those people. It would make me feel more resigned to my task.

XI.
Friday before Holy Week

Poor Martin is very unhappy. He came to work this morning with red eyes and a persistent sniff, but would not provide any sort of explanation. When I asked him if Hugues had been twisting his ears, or otherwise inflicting injuries upon him that would not leave a mark, he denied it.

Perhaps he was distressed at the sufferings of his mother. Or perhaps his brothers have been doing the damage.

I wish he were not so small and thin.

It seems to me that he is not fed enough. In the Moresi household, Lent is simply an excuse to starve the children. I gave Martin some bread before I left for the Bourg, saying that I had no use for it, and he bolted it down as if he were afraid it might grow legs and run away. He also told me that his father 'does not believe in' eating too much, since gluttony is a terrible sin, which will lead even the youngest child straight to hell. According to Hugues Moresi, real saints eat boiled nettles and stale crusts, because God does not love those who eat pies and roast meats and spiced eggs and loaf sugar.

My heart sank when I heard this. For it has been the refrain of every Cathar *perfectus* in existence, and appears to be an opinion shared by many Beguins, also. Though a man might be a liar, a cheat, a hypocrite, and an idle, bloodthirsty parasite, so long as he is on a perpetual fast, and wears simple clothes, he is considered holy. Among the Cathar heretics, even eggs and meat and milk are sinful, because they are the product of fornication. I recall being denied a scrap of bacon rind when I was a boy, on the grounds that it would be bad for my soul.

Needless to say, my soul was of little real consequence to the girl who deprived me of that bacon, which she herself was eager to consume. It was ever so. There are few Cathar believers who follow wholeheartedly those tenets governing the lives of their priests. I have seen believers eat lamb and pork, eggs, cheese, game, and fowl of every description. Yet they will often forbid such fare to children, and to anyone else of low degree, because they want it all for themselves.

Perhaps Hugues Moresi is of a similar disposition. Perhaps his views are not as heretical as they seem. Yet this is the third time he has taken a sympathetic stance towards the Beguins and their doctrines.

Surely I have not opened my house to a secret Beguin? It would be *most* disconcerting if I have.

I must keep a more watchful eye on my tenants. A clean kitchen and regular payments are all very well, but not if they are accompanied by unwelcome spiritual beliefs. Furthermore, it troubles me that Martin might have been affected. If his father *is* unorthodox, can it be my responsibility to counter the paternal influence? That is certainly my inclination. When I heard the poor child spouting nonsense about pies and nettles, my response was very sharp. I said: 'Why would God have created pies, if not to be eaten? For what other purpose do pies exist?'

To which he responded, with a furrowed brow: 'But *God* does not make pies, Master. People do.'

'People make pies because there is flour and butter with which to make them. Without wheat, there would be no flour. Without beasts, there would be no butter. God made all of these things. And he made them in a certain way—so that wheat could be milled, and milk churned.' I was quoting Bernard Gui, who explained these matters to me a long, long time ago—when I was still under the impression that meat and milk were somehow wicked. 'To believe in the sinfulness of butter is to believe in the sinfulness of God's creation. Is that what you believe, in your heart?'

'No!' Martin shook his head. 'No, Master, I would never believe such a thing!'

'Gluttony is a sin, but the sin lies in excessive quantities. To consume too much of anything is bad, whether it be an excess of sugar or of stale bread. And I doubt that *your* belly is large enough to accommodate very much of either. You have not the look of a glutton, child. You are not fat enough.'

Having delivered myself of this homily, I told my apprentice to attend the shop while I was out. He had my permission to take orders, but not to sell parchment off the shelves, since he does not know all the prices.

I also instructed him to study carefully each customer who walked through the door. Upon my return, I would be expecting a full report on the appearance, speech and possible livelihood of every stranger he served. This would give him something to do, and would provide me with information that I need for my register.

Martin is proving to be an observer of some skill. It must be confessed that I never would have considered training him up as an extra pair of eyes, had he not started asking me questions. I thought myself sufficiently burdened; to educate an apprentice is hard enough, and three years ago Martin could barely read, let alone write. For all of twelve months I spent a good portion of every evening guiding him through his letters, so that he would be literate enough to take down orders and find his way through a book of accounts. At the same time I was showing him how to soak, scrape, split, hang, cut and mark skins.

It never crossed my mind that I should be employing him in other ways.

But I have certain foibles, which become evident if I am not constantly on guard. Martin soon noticed them. So would anyone sharing my house for the greater part of each day; that is one reason (among many) why I spend my nights alone. A few careless comments were all that it took to demonstrate my abiding interest in hands, boots, clothes, scars, accents and habits. I had only to remark that butchers are inclined to have more missing digits than professional soldiers, or that the fingers of shoemakers are calloused in a certain unmistakeable way, to find myself bombarded with questions from my apprentice. Were saddlers callused like shoemakers? Were soldiers missing more ears and eyes than butchers? And what about a peasant who killed his own beasts—would not he and a butcher bear similar scars?

In answering these questions, I became once more an instructor, and Martin my student. He is a bright boy in many ways. He also has a sharp eye, and an intense desire to please. Perhaps he hopes to be my heir, since I have no children. Perhaps his father has instructed him to win my favour by whatever means possible. If so, he has carried out his father's bidding with dedicated efficiency. For I have been *more* than generous. I have, in fact, been indulgent.

God grant that I do not come to regret my weakness. A man in my position cannot afford even the tiniest breach in his defences. Yet I am unable to believe that the boy's regard for me is false. No one so young could present such a perfect, undetectable mask, day after day after day.

Only consider what happened this morning, when I took my leave. He looked crestfallen, and asked if I would return soon. He did not say: Can I come? He did not say: Where are you going?

He said exactly what I would have expected him to say, asking if I would return soon.

'Perhaps,' I replied. 'If my business is concluded quickly.'

In fact, I was not engaged in any form of business. I was visiting the Bourg once again, in order that I might see for myself the house of Imbert Rubei. Had I been less busy,

I might have expended a whole day on the task, disguising myself as a beggar to keep watch. Alas; I had not the time to spare for such activities. With Palm Sunday fast approaching, I was unable to do more than pass the house—twice but not thrice—and perhaps make a purchase in the neighbourhood.

As you may imagine, I did not wear my scarlet cloak on this ramble. Instead I donned my customary dull colours and unmemorable garments, not wishing to attract anyone's attention. Though I am small, I am not so small as to engender pity or shock. My shoulders are not distinctively narrow, nor my legs startlingly thin. My teeth are in reasonable but unremarkable condition. Excepting perhaps in the east, where (I have heard) everyone is dusky and black-haired, I am the sort of man who tends to escape notice because I am in no way imposing to look at. People do not recall my face, unless I choose to arouse their interest deliberately—and even then I rarely make much of an impression.

This is as it should be. I would have it no other way. And though I admire great beauty, I also fear it. A man or a woman with a beautiful face has nowhere to hide, any more than has a cripple, or a leper, or a giant. If you have a beautiful face, you will be watched, pursued and appropriated just as if you were a treasure of gleaming gold.

Bernard Gui once said that my eyes could, on occasion, be arresting. He did not know exactly why, though he thought it had something to do with the way I stare when my guard is down. Mostly I try not to stare. A piercing stare has the same effect as too many questions; it causes alarm and consternation. But it is a habit that I fell into as a very young child, and one that is hard to break, especially when I am tired or distracted.

That is why, wherever possible, I favour hoods. They are commonly worn, they are as efficient as hats, and they shade the eyes. If I had scarred hands, I would favour worsted gloves or long, dangling sleeves for the very same reason.

Needless to say, I scrupulously avoid jewellery, sandals, rich fabrics, vivid colours and foreign cuts—unless I am out fishing for attention.

Today I was not. Today I wanted to move unseen along the Rue Aquitaine, where Imbert Rubei dwells. I am still not sure exactly what I was hoping to achieve. I believe that I had some vague idea of approaching one or two neighbours—of pretending to look for Imbert Rubei, or Jacques Bonet, and 'mistaking' the address. But I was in luck. When I approached the vicinity of Imbert's house, I was delighted to observe that he lives almost directly opposite an inn, of all things.

An inn!

I could have asked for nothing better. An inn is the perfect vantage point. You cannot outstay your welcome at an inn, unless you start swinging an axe at the patrons. What's more, a stranger at an inn is like a bunch of grapes in a summer vineyard: wholly welcome but entirely unmemorable.

I offered up a prayer of thanks to St Paul, whose parish I was then occupying, and headed straight for the inn. At the same time, I studied Imbert's house—a fine and venerable building which has been sadly neglected. It is, in fact, a study in dissolution. Someone very wealthy erected that house, which is practically a palace; the present occupants, however, are apparently too poor to replace the missing shutters, or repair the stonework.

I discovered this after spending some time at the inn, which is called the Crescent Moon. Having started life as a warehouse, the hall of this hostelry is dark and airless, with a faint but lingering smell of wool-grease discernible through the strong odour of wine. Nevertheless, it seems to be a popular destination. Even in the middle of the day there were enough people slumped around its long wooden tables to allow me some concealment. A few were travellers, on their way to Minervois and the west, but the majority were local residents, seeking company and forgetfulness. It was this latter group that interested me. Among them I hoped to find someone acquainted with Imbert Rubei, or at least with his history. I was sure that a man who had once been so rich, and was now so poor, must have attracted at least a minimum of speculation around the quarter.

And I was right. Having planted myself among the tipplers lined up against the front wall of the hostelry, I became privy to a long conversation about Imbert Rubei that *I did not initiate*. By a lucky chance, I sat down beside two of Imbert's neighbours—who were soaking up the sun on a bench placed near the inn's front door—and overheard them discussing the woman who had suddenly emerged from Imbert's house.

She was small and thin, and advanced in years: her hair was mostly grey, and her back was slightly bent. Noting that she carried a basket, I assumed, correctly, that she was on her way to make a purchase. Her clothes were coarse and plain.

According to the men beside me, she was Imbert Rubei's sister-in-law.

Their interest in her was limited to one thing: the question of whether or not she was sharing her brother-in-law's bed. The younger man—a barber, to judge from the hair adhering to his clothes—was sure that she was. The older man, whose burned hands and floury sleeves marked him as a baker, defended her stoutly. Na Maria, he said, was a pious woman.

'It is a sin for a man to take his brother's wife,' the baker declared. 'Though both be widowed, it is still a sin. And Na Maria would not sin in such a way.'

'What would *you* know?' the barber retorted. 'Why live together, if they are not lying together?'

'Because he has no choice,' said the baker, and began to recount the tale of Imbert's ill fortune. I deduced from his remarks that Imbert was once very rich, and a consul of the Bourg, but that he lost most of his wealth some thirty years ago. Apparently, when three officers of the Archbishop were charged with murder, Imbert Rubei and nine other prominent citizens sanctioned their hanging—despite their appeal to the Royal Court. As a result, Imbert was fined a monstrous sum by the King, and had his goods confiscated by the Archbishop.

His current residence was left to him by his brother, on the condition that he look after his brother's wife.

'Yes, yes, I see,' said the barber. 'That makes sense. But after such a long time, why has he not restored his fortunes?

He trades in silk, after all. Surely he can afford more than one miserable maid?'

'He had a manservant at one point,' the baker remarked, to my intense interest. 'About six months ago. I don't know what happened to him. He disappeared.'

'Perhaps it is wise to feign poverty,' the barber observed. 'If you are rich, people will try to fleece you.'

'Yes, indeed. Only consider what happened to Imbert Rubei when he was rich! If he had been poor, I doubt that the King or the Archbishop would have bothered with him.'

There followed a long discussion on taxes and tolls, while I pretended to fall asleep—and by this means disguise the fact that I was listening. But nothing more was said of a revelatory nature. No one again referred to Imbert's mysterious, disappearing manservant. Nor did the baker or his companion propose that Imbert's poverty (which they both considered to be partly assumed) might have had any cause other than a desire to avoid paying taxes or tithes.

The word 'Beguin' never crossed their lips.

At last I was forced to leave, the sun having moved some considerable distance across the sky. I waited only until Imbert's sister-in-law returned, her basket heaped with bread and root vegetables. Then I stretched and yawned, and did my best to imitate a man aroused from the deepest slumber. Before departing, however, I returned my goblet to the innkeeper—and took a huge risk by asking one question, carefully phrased in a heavy Gascon accent.

'Your inn was recommended to me,' I said, 'by a tall fellow with black hair and pockmarks, who called himself Jacques.

Said he worked in a house nearby. I was hoping to meet with him again. Does he drink here still?'

'He never did,' replied the innkeeper, who was oddly liverish and uncongenial for a man in his line of work. I thought that perhaps he was ill, for his complexion was yellow, and his brow damp. 'If you mean Imbert Rubei's manservant.'

'Long nose? Crooked thumbnail?'

'I was never close enough to see his thumbnail. I hardly ever laid eyes on him. He certainly never set foot in here.'

'Oh.'

'He moved on, in any case. Before Christmas. Why did you want to meet him? Does he owe you money?'

'No, no. But he was an interesting man, with a lot to say. And since I was in the neighbourhood . . .' I shrugged. 'Never mind.'

'Imbert Rubei would not have allowed him in *here*,' the innkeeper growled. 'Not in *this* den of vice, oh no.' And he moved away to serve another patron, having supplied me with more information than I could reasonably have hoped for.

As I walked home, I reviewed what I had learned, and was pleased. There can be no doubt that Jacques Bonet made his way to the house of Imbert Rubei. He stayed there for a while, but departed before Christmas. Where exactly he went at that point is still a matter for conjecture.

Did he leave Narbonne of his own accord, under a false name? Was he murdered? Or is he still hiding in the city somewhere, with the connivance of Beguins like Berengaria Donas?

Perhaps tomorrow I shall find out.

Martin was pleased to welcome me back. He said that business was suddenly very quiet, though he had received two visitors, one regular and one secular canon.

'Can you tell me anything about them?' I asked. 'Aside from their station in life?'

'One was tall and one was short. Both were thin. The tall one was quite old.' Martin pondered for a moment. 'I think he might have been a master from the cathedral school.'

'What makes you say that?'

'Because of the way he spoke to me, and looked at me.' A reluctant grin stole across the boy's face. 'As if he suspected that I would squirt ink on him the moment his back was turned.'

I had to laugh.

'But did he box your ears when you could not sell him his parchment?' I queried, and Martin shook his head.

'It was an order. For St-Just.'

'Then it was probably the Subtreasurer, or the Master of the Common Funds. Only a very few canons are permitted to make purchases for the chapter—especially costly purchases like this.' Seeing Martin's face fall, I tried to reassure him. 'Which is not to deny that a Treasurer might once have been a Grammar Master. Nothing is more probable. Always remember that *past* experience can inform the present. It is something I often forget myself.'

Martin nodded eagerly. I almost wish that he were not so keen; it unnerves me. He is even beginning to copy the way I crack my neck after a long day's work at the frames.

'What about the other canon?' I inquired. 'What can you tell me about him?'

At this Martin frowned.

'He was covered in ink. There were even smudges on his face. When I said that you were not here, he became angry. He became even angrier when I would not sell him the parchment.'

'Did he place an order?'

'Yes. For the Archbishop's palace.'

'Indeed?' This was important news. 'Did he give a name?'

'No.'

'Have you packed the order?' I demanded, and Martin gave a nod. He could provide me with very little more that was of any use. The Archbishop's representative had been short and thin, with large ears and a close-cropped, strangely shaped head. The ink all over his face, hands and clothes had served to distract Martin from the man's more permanent features.

'*There* is a lesson for you,' I said. 'Sometimes a stink, or a stain, can serve as a shield. Your memory will fasten on this one characteristic, and discard all others.'

'It is good that the Archbishop wants your parchment,' was Martin's response. 'For he must use a *very great deal* of it. Perhaps he will ask for more!'

'Perhaps,' I said, though I was not so sanguine.

I fully expect to receive the parchment back soon after it is delivered—with a complaint attached, and a report on unidentified corpses tucked between the folios.

XII.
Palm Sunday

What fools these Beguins are. Do they know nothing? If they were wise, they would not gather together in such large groups. Under Roman canon law it is very, very difficult to convict a man on the evidence of one witness. Even two witnesses are easily discredited. But with three or four or five, there is little hope of extenuation.

I felt tempted to say as much, today at Na Berengaria's house. In the end, however, I held my tongue. For my master taught me that 'whoso keepeth his mouth and his tongue keepeth his soul from troubles'. And I have taken the lesson to heart.

I was a little late in arriving because Martin detained me. Not in the shop, mind you; Sunday is meant to be a day of worship, not a day of toil. I did not expect to see Martin at all, and was startled when I caught a glimpse of him ducking behind a pillar on the Rue Droite as I made my way towards the Inn of the Star.

He was following me.

For an instant my head swam, and my heart pounded against my ribs. I thought: who has sent him to spy on me? After a brief period of reflection, however, I realised that there was a far less ominous explanation. Martin, I decided, wanted to know more about me for his own sake. I had trained him to be curious, and he was curious about his master.

Moreover, since my quarters were today closed to him, he was undoubtedly looking for amusement far away from his own quarrelsome family.

Though I write this now in a tranquil spirit, at the time I was not amused. On the contrary, my irritation was so profound that it verged on anger. Quickly I accomplished a very simple ruse that I call the Foursquare, ducking down an alley and pelting at top speed around the next three right-hand corners. This brought me back almost to the point at which I had begun, having circled an entire building. I therefore came up behind Martin, who was hesitating at the alley's first junction, not knowing whether to turn left or right.

Such a ploy will only succeed if you know the terrain, of course.

'Martin Moresi,' I said, and he jumped. His face, when he saw me, was a picture of consternation.

'M-master . . .' he stammered.

'You will have to do better than this, my friend. I never lose sight of the road behind me.'

He had the grace to look ashamed. Moreover, he did not attempt to deny that he had been in pursuit. Many would have, but he did not; rather he hung his head, and mumbled an apology.

'What were you hoping to achieve?' I asked, for I was curious. 'Today is God's day, Martin. Did you think I would be devoting it to any purpose other than His praise and glorification?'

'No,' said the boy.

'Or perhaps you were hoping to find out whether I would spot you?'

This, I think, was the truth. Martin had been practising certain skills that I may have mentioned to him, carelessly, during our time together—though in doing so I'd had no intention of encouraging him to acquire them.

I said: 'You should be with your family. You should not be wandering the streets like a beggar's child. Your mother will be worried.'

'No, she will not,' Martin replied, glumly and with resignation. 'She has too many other concerns.'

'Then you must take care not to add to them,' I advised. 'You are a good boy, Martin. Go back home. It will set my own mind at rest, as well as your mother's.'

I spoke with more kindness than he perhaps merited, but it worked. I have found that, with Martin, a soft voice and a warm smile will exact instant obedience (derived from an odd mixture of guilt and gratitude), whereas sharp words will only paralyse his will, and muddle his thinking. In this instance, I did not even warn him that I would surely detect his presence if he continued to defy me. He knew it well enough. So I was not required to accompany him back to my house.

I only stood and watched until he was out of sight. Then I resumed my journey to Na Berengaria's residence.

There were five Beguins waiting in her kitchen when I arrived. Berengaria was there, of course. Blaise Bouer the tailor was also in attendance, as was the goose-necked Guillelma, and the fat weaver with the red face—who was introduced as Guillaume Ademar. With him was a young man who has almost the look of a monk: his pale, refined features, dreamy gaze and attenuated frame give him the appearance of someone who has been raised in dark cloisters and kept up all night singing psalms as a child. His name is Pierre Espere-en-Dius, but he is known to his friends as Perrin.

It did not entirely surprise me to learn that, like Guillaume, he is a weaver. For I have already commented on the heretical tendencies of weavers.

Though I had taken care to dress as simply and dully as possible, I saw at once that I had underestimated the asceticism of certain devout Beguins. Perrin and Guillelma, in particular, wore clothes made of stuff that I would hesitate even to call sacking: it looked almost as if it had been woven out of chaff and nettles, and I did wonder, for an instant, if this was indeed the case. Since Perrin is a weaver, a tunic made with thorns or willow-canes would presumably not be beyond him.

Na Berengaria was dressed in garments of a somewhat finer weave, though still very plain. She herself answered my knock;

the downstairs shutters were closed, and her husband's shop was in almost total darkness. 'Blessed be the name of Jesus Christ,' she said, as she ushered me through the shop to the kitchen. Here her associates echoed her in chorus, and their faces showed not one hint of suspicion or anger.

Naturally, I had brought a knife in my boot. But by this time I was convinced that I was in no immediate peril. Not from Berengaria, at any rate.

No food or drink were offered me, once I had been welcomed. Instead the whole group immediately began to pray, at which point I was almost caught out. For Beguins, I discovered, do not pray like other men and women. Rather than falling to their knees with clasped hands, they cover their heads and sit bending over, turning their faces towards the ground or an opposite wall. In this position they recite the *Salve regina* and *Gloria in excelsis Deo.*

It was fortunate that I was wearing my hood. It was also fortunate that my companions shrouded their own heads before praying; if they had not, they would have seen me commencing to kneel, and then stopping halfway to the floor as I observed that no one else was imitating my actions.

I quickly sat down again, copying Berengaria. She led the prayers, as well as the discussion afterwards, which was chiefly concerned with identifying specific people who merited our prayers. One of the names suggested was that of Pons, whom I had met in the Archbishop's prison. We prayed for his immortal soul, and for the souls of his sixteen fellow Beguins, burned in front of St-Just not long ago. We also prayed for the souls of those friars burned at Marseilles, and for every true martyr who had died on the stake since.

Then Berengaria proposed that we pray for 'our fugitive brethren Pierre Dominici, Pierre Trencavel and Jacques Bonet'. I pricked up my cars at this, and was hoping that more might be said on the subject. But Berengaria moved on, soliciting more names from the rest of us. She turned to me with a maternal smile, and asked if there was no one *I* might choose to nominate.

I replied that I should like to pray for my tenant's sick mother. As well, I submitted the name of Brother Bernard Delicieux, who had perished in Jean de Beaune's prison at Carcassonne.

This suggestion was well received. There followed a few more prayers, and no further mention of Jacques Bonet. I should have liked to ask after him, but knew that it would be unwise to exhibit too much curiosity. Instead I sat humbly and silently through the subsequent debate on charitable works, which greatly increased my understanding of Blaise and Guillelma.

The purpose of the debate was simple. Having collected from each of us a *denier* or two as alms for the poor, Na Berengaria wanted to know which institution should receive these alms. Obviously she was not about to place them in the hands of a priest, who like as not would spend them on the satisfaction of his own appetites.

'For they are most of them heretics, drunk with the blood of martyrs, and they accumulate grain and wine in abundance,' she remarked, at which Blaise nodded vigorously.

'Yes, indeed!' he exclaimed. 'Give money to a priest, and he will not succour the poor. He will buy superfluous clothing, or rich viands, or costly books full of wicked lies.'

There was a murmur of agreement. Guillelma even went so far as to throw her hands in the air. 'They are servants of the great Whore of Babylon,' she said, 'who persecutes the poor and the ministers of Christ, and they will be condemned and rejected as was the synagogue of the Jews.'

Another 'Amen' to that. Blaise went on to rail bitterly against bishops, and cardinals, and the Pope, and the Dominicans, and all those Franciscans who had betrayed the rule of St Francis. He accused the Cistercians of Fontfroide of avarice, because these monks had acquired more than a quarter of the right of measuring and weighing all the grain brought into Narbonne. 'They care for nothing but their own bellies!' he ranted, and it became clear to me that he belonged to a certain category of heretic that is quite common in every part of the world.

You will find such people embracing many different kinds of error, simply because they stand in opposition to men who are wealthier or more powerful than they are. The Church, being both wealthy and powerful, is a natural target for their resentment. They feel perpetually ill used, and their anger is never far from the surface. If at any time they decide that their heretical associates have treated them unjustly, or are insufficiently grateful to them, there is every chance that they will change allegiance. My master, Bernard Gui, was fully aware of this. He sought out such people diligently, asking me always to keep alert for them.

And here, I saw, was another example.

Guillelma was of a different ilk. Though she, too, was passionate in her condemnation of the Carnal Church, it was not on account of her own wounded vanity. She was genuinely outraged at the injustices of the world—as the young so often are—and, being young, she found it hard to be patient, or to control her anger. She seemed to feel that wrongs must be righted at once; to refrain from doing so was to demonstrate an utter disdain for Christ's commandments, which disdain must be punished at all costs. Her inclination was to act, rather than to reflect.

She will, I am quite sure, end up on a stake before she grows much older.

I need hardly add that Blaise and Guillelma were very difficult to please when it came to the distribution of alms. The hospital of St-Just was an unacceptable recipient, in their eyes, because it was run by the cathedral chapter. The leper hospices were equally suspect, because so many of the rich merchants associated with their management were less interested in helping the poor than they were in promoting their own high repute. Even the Franciscans were frowned upon, now that their Narbonnaise establishment had been practically emptied of Spiritual brethren.

At last, after much bickering, it was agreed that the money should be given to the House of the Repentants, near the Royal Gate. This would enable more prostitutes to escape sinful pursuits, and devote themselves to acts of piety. Even the men conceded that many females of this description were driven by poverty to abase themselves like the Magdalene.

'And now,' said Na Berengaria, at the conclusion of all business relating to alms for the poor, 'let us venerate our holy relics. Master Helié, have you brought your own with you today?'

I had, as it happened. And I produced it to the accompaniment of many sighs and groans—for it was, indeed, a pitiful remnant. Guillelma shed tears of sorrow over it, before passing it along to Perrin, who kissed it fervently. After each Beguin had venerated the finger in his or her own fashion, and the relic had been returned to me, Berengaria extracted a familiar, silk-wrapped bundle from the concealed chest in her cellar.

Once again, I was obliged to press my lips to a half-cooked human shin bone.

'You do great honour to these holy martyrs,' I observed carefully, upon completing my act of homage, 'by wrapping their relics in such fine and beautiful silk. My humble linen cloth is put to shame.'

'Not at all!' Berengaria responded. 'Wealthy trappings are of no account, Master Helié. I happened to have this scrap of silk, and could think of no more fitting a use for it. It is wonderfully figured, is it not?'

'Wonderfully,' I agreed.

'All of our silk comes from a devout and honest trader called Imbert Rubei,' the matron continued. 'He has an eye for good damask, in particular. But he would as soon wear garments of human skin as don silken clothes.' As I absorbed this unexpected announcement, Berengaria placed a hand on my arm. 'Your own relic *is* deserving of a more glorious shroud,' she conceded. 'If you wish, I can ask my husband for a silk offcut. He would not begrudge it, I feel sure.'

More fool he, I thought. But I simply smiled and expressed my gratitude, wondering at the same time if Berengar Blanchi, or his friend Imbert Rubei, had ever graced Na Berengaria's Sunday gathering with their presence. Jacques Bonet probably did, so why not they?

'Now let us reflect on our blessed teacher, Brother Pierre Jean Olivi,' said Berengaria, once her relics had been restored to their proper place in the empty cask. It soon became clear to me that she herself enjoys sole custody of the Beguins' holy books; only two were circulated among us, to be reverently kissed, before the matron began to read from one, very slowly, as if intoning a psalm. This book was none other than *The Passing of the Holy Father* and concluded with a description of Pierre Olivi's deathbed.

There followed a general 'Amen', whereupon I was asked to read from my copy of the *postilla.* This I did until told to stop. Then there was another prayer (recited at the floor or wall), after which the gathering broke up. It was the master of the house, Berengaria's husband, who dispersed our company. He appeared suddenly at the door with his son, looking irritated but resigned; his son, in contrast, seemed very much put out to find so many unwelcome guests on the premises. While the father merely sighed, the son glowered. Perhaps the difference could be attributed to their age, since Na Berengaria's husband was much older than I had expected. Though solidly built, he had the gnarled appearance of an old tree root, and had lost most of his hair.

He watched his wife's friends glumly as, one by one, we made our escape.

It was upon leaving the house that I first became properly aware of the man in the dirty clothes. He had been squatting in the alley beside the house when I first arrived—apparently relieving his bowels in a very public manner. And because this is not an unusual sight in Narbonne, I had paid him little attention.

Surely, however, no dose of the flux is so serious as to keep a man voiding his bowels from late morning until mid afternoon?

My suspicions were instantly aroused. And they deepened when, having yanked up his drawers as I passed, he set off for the Rue Droite just a few paces behind me. There was no mistaking his intention—for his pursuit was clumsy. He followed me all the way home, and once I arrived, he did not linger. Instead he took to his heels before I could reach the upstairs window. I do not know where he went.

But I do know, in detail, what he looked like. Thanks to a few well-tested tricks, I was able to study him quite closely. He was a gangly fellow with stringy brown hair and a nose like a tuber. His eyes were almost triangular, like arrowheads, but were not in the least flinty or sharp; instead they were of a soft and smoky grey. His teeth were poor. He had two burns on his hands, probably from lamp oil or candle wax. And he smelled strongly of urine.

Normally, when a man smells of urine, and is not so ancient as to raise the question of incontinence, I am inclined to dub him a fuller. But I never knew a fuller who was not covered in fuller's earth, and this man bore not a trace of the stuff. Though filthy, his clothes were stained with splashes of food and vomit, rather than with fuller's earth. The smell of that vomit was almost as strong as the smell of urine; a faint underlying whiff of smoke told me that he must spend a lot of time indoors, and I did wonder if he might be employed at an inn.

No self-respecting innkeeper, however, would be so foolish as to allow his servants to walk around looking—and smelling—so repellent. Moreover, when I doubled back under the pretence of changing my route, and brushed past him, I detected the scent of comfrey and aniseed. So, unless I am mistaken, I have been followed by someone closely associated with a hospital.

My task now is to discover why.

XIII.
Monday of Holy Week

I wish now that I had followed the man in the dirty clothes. Had I made more of an effort, I may have caught up with him. As it is, I have been most of the day in fruitless speculation.

Who was he?

Perhaps I should visit all the hospitals, and find out. It would be an expensive exercise, since my excuse would have to be the general distribution of alms. Nevertheless, it could be worthwhile. And it would arouse no suspicion—not during Holy Week. I must give the matter some thought.

The fact that he knew enough to be waiting outside Na Berengaria's house when I arrived indicates that he might be an acquaintance of hers. Can she be suspicious of me after all? Did she hire someone to follow me, and make sure that I did not head straight for the Archbishop's palace to make a report?

If so, then I have been thoroughly fooled. I was quite convinced that the Beguins had accepted me. I was even starting to believe that Berengaria was innocent of Jacques Bonet's death. Only consider what I discovered yesterday, at the meeting. I heard Berengaria mention Jacques Bonet, in a very particular context. She led a prayer for him. She described him as one of her fugitive brethren, and seemed well-disposed towards him. This does not suggest that she killed him, or arranged to have him murdered. This suggests that she believes him to be in hiding somewhere—perhaps that she had a hand in his escape.

If so, then there are two possibilities. Either Jacques Bonet used his Beguin friends to effect an escape without telling them his secret, or he *did* tell them about Jean de Beaune, and they helped him despite the danger. If the latter is true, then Berengaria would naturally be suspicious of me. And she would almost certainly employ a spy to make sure that all my claims are true.

Yet I sensed nothing of this at her house yesterday. Nothing! They deceived me utterly; I thought them guileless in the extreme. How could this have happened? Am I really so gullible?

Perhaps only one or two of them were suspicious. Perhaps Blaise and Guillaume were responsible for the spy, and the rest were kept ignorant. I cannot believe that Perrin, for example, is anything but a fool or an innocent; probably the latter. He spoke not a word that I can remember; his child-like gaze was as artless as that of a nun immured in a hermitage. Manifestly, he has been sheltered from the harsher realities all his life, and is living in a pious dream. I remember thinking to myself at the time: Stay clear of *that* one. For a holy innocent is the greatest of all threats, and should be avoided wherever possible. In the Garden of Eden such people might be harmless enough, but not in this sinful world, where they see no evil, and have no understanding of either subtleties or compromise. When led into heresy—on account of their own simple natures—they arouse such pity among the orthodox as to be the occasion of endless doubt and despair. Even Bernard Gui was affected by cases of this kind. I remember how, on one occasion, he was greatly troubled by the predicament of a man whose error was not rooted in self-conceit, but in a fatal lack of discrimination. This man was devoted to poverty and lived like a hermit, sometimes begging and sometimes labouring, but always in search of God. Though he followed no particular heretical creed, he seemed incapable of distinguishing between true priests and Cathar *perfecti*, or Waldensian brethren. When he encountered wandering preachers of any description, he would succour them in all humility, seeming to think them worthy of regard because they preached poverty, lived in a simple manner, and proclaimed their devotion to Christ.

'You know the falsity of so many heretics,' my master observed, at one of our rare meetings. 'If by their wily astuteness they escape punishment, they glory in having eluded learned men through their sly cunning and tortuous ambiguities. With people of this kind, their pride has been their downfall.' My master sighed. 'It is so much harder to condemn a man for abject humility. This man of whom I speak is like a simpleton in his thinking, and a saint in his habits. Yet in many ways he is more dangerous than the most rabid Pseudo-

Apostle. Because I look at him and I think: can such innocence be truly sinful?'

'Can it?' I asked, to which Bernard Gui replied: 'It must be. How not? The Devil is as cunning as any of his minions.' But all the same, my master looked melancholy, and touched on the troubling topic many times before we parted, quoting various authorities and referring to himself repeatedly as a physician of souls.

I would claim no such distinction for myself. Yet I understood his unhappiness, for I have shared it. Confronted by a youth like Perrin—or a girl like Allemande—I am always affected by a kind of dull and impotent dismay. It is frankly a punishment to condemn such people, and my master acknowledged this. 'It is our cross,' he said. 'Perhaps it is God's way of ensuring that we do not enjoy our work, which, though necessary, is contrary to every natural human inclination. Like a surgeon cutting into flesh, we must gird our loins, fix our thoughts on God, and think of the future good.'

Wise words from a learned man. I wish that I was able to follow his advice. But my own method is not so praiseworthy. Rather than think of the future good, I concentrate on small things that serve to occupy all my thoughts. Small things like the connection between Berengaria Donas and Imbert Rubei.

That was a useful discovery. Not only is she accustomed to doing business with him, but she respects him. She admires his ascetic habits. The question is: how often do they meet? Does he ever attend gatherings at her house? Certainly they must have spoken together at some point during the last six months, or she would not have known about Jacques Bonet, his one-time servant.

I am less and less inclined to believe that Jacques Bonet is dead. The Archbishop's report on unidentified cadavers told me nothing to the contrary. It arrived today, buried among my rejected parchment, and could not have been more unexpected. *My* shop is never open during Holy Week; to conduct business at this time seems to me impious and improper, especially among clerics. No doubt I am naïve, but I was under the impression that every priest, monk, deacon and lay brother in Narbonne must be wholly occupied with preparations for Easter. I assumed that, when one is under the obligation of celebrating the Last Supper, our Lord's Crucifixion and His Resurrection all within the space of a few days, one must set aside one's usual activities in favour of the many rituals that transform Christendom for an entire week every year.

It seems that I was wrong, however. For the report was delivered to me this morning, practically at first light. I was still dressing when I heard a knock, and was forced to scurry downstairs bootless, my shirt all untied, my hair uncombed. When I unbarred the front door, and pulled it open, I found myself nose-to-nose with an ink-stained priest. I recognised him instantly, thanks to Martin's careful description; it was the secular canon who came to my shop last week.

I recognised him instantly, if only on account of his ink-stains. As Martin had pointed out, his ears were large, and his close-cropped head was shaped rather like a knuckle-bone. When he saw me he started, his small eyes widening in shock. Beneath its ink stains, his face lost some of its colour.

'Yes?' I said, and he swallowed.

'Uh—are you—am I speaking to Helié Seguier?'

'Yes.'

He extended the wrapped parcel that he had been clasping to his chest.

'This is not of suitable quality,' he said, licking his dry lips. 'I have been instructed to return it.'

'By whom?'

'By—by Germain d'Alanh. Of the Archbishop's Chancellery.'

'Ah.' I received the parcel, but before I could add anything the priest turned, as if to leave. I had to call him back. 'Father,' I said, 'if you return my parchment, I must return your money. Your *depositum*.'

He stopped. 'Oh—ah—yes . . .' he stammered.

'Come in. Please.'

It was true that I had to retrieve a half-payment from my chest upstairs. But it was also true that his apprehensive behaviour intrigued me. I could not account for it. And I wanted to see whether he would accept my invitation.

He did, it transpired. He even answered a few of my questions about the parchment, which I put to him more in a spirit of mischief than in a spirit of honest inquiry. For it had occurred to me that his unease might lie in a full awareness of what lay hidden in the parcel. And if this were the case, then he must know, at the very least, that I was interested in corpses.

Hence his jittery demeanour.

'In what way did my goods fail to satisfy?' I asked, picking at the cord that bound them. 'You did not order a quire of the very *best* split skins. If you had, you would have received what you undertook payment for.'

'It was not my decision,' the priest mumbled. 'I am only the messenger.'

'For Germain d'Alanh?'

'Um . . . yes.'

'Would he care to view a sample of my most expensive parchment?'

'No. I don't know. Not now. I need to get back.'

'Very well.' Having counted the folios, I saw that not one was missing. There was, in fact, an inclusion. As I had anticipated. 'I shall fetch your money, if you would wait here an instant. Forgive me . . .' I waved my hand. 'But as you can see, my shop is not open for business during Holy Week. I did not expect to receive any patronage. Especially from the Archbishop's Chancellery.'

The priest coloured beneath his ink stains. I left him blushing, and went to retrieve a few *sols* from my chest upstairs. If the floor of my workroom had not been so creaky, I would have attempted to surprise the priest with my sudden return—and by this means, perhaps, catch him pawing through the parcel that he had just surrendered to me. But I decided against this plan. I knew that my every footstep would be clearly audible above his head, announcing my approach like a herald's trumpet. Wooden floors are always noisy.

Stone or earth floors, in contrast, give nothing away. That is why I was startled to hear the creak of a hinge while I was counting out money in my workroom; no footsteps had prepared me for the fact that someone downstairs was opening doors. This was most unexpected. It was also unwelcome. So I completed my task as hurriedly as I could, and descended the stairs at a brisk pace—only to find that Martin was in my shop. He had obviously come through from the kitchen (where he sleeps) to investigate the sound of voices.

I concluded that the squeaky door must have announced his arrival, and thought no more about it.

'Your *depositum,*' I announced, restoring the Archbishop's money to his agent. 'And now I should like you to sign a receipt, if you would do me the honour.'

'A receipt?' the priest echoed, in evident perplexity.

'Forgive me, Father, but I must protect myself. What if you were to say that I did not return the money? Who would your masters believe?'

I have, on occasion, resorted to safeguards of this type—but in fact the request was simply a stratagem, which allowed me to discover the priest's name. He conceded to my request in a dazed fashion, transcribing a short avowal on a scrap of torn parchment and affixing a signature to it.

He is called Sejan Alegre.

The name is familiar, though I cannot for the life of me remember why. I was racking my brain when Father Sejan departed; even now, the vague sense of past association is driving me mad. I have checked my register, but can find no record of a 'Sejan Alegre' in its pages. Perhaps I should read back through this journal.

As my apprentice barred the door behind Father Sejan, I quickly extracted Germain d'Alanh's report from the pile of unused parchment. This single folio (of rather inferior goatskin) was concealed in the folds of my shirt long before Martin turned back to me, eager for instructions. I told him to tidy away the returned stock before he went home.

'It is Holy Week,' I said, ignoring the unspoken plea in his eyes. 'You should be with your family.'

Then I went upstairs to read the report.

One glance informed me that it must have been transcribed—if not actually composed—by Father Sejan Alegre. The style of script used for my report was very similar to that employed on my receipt; close examination revealed, in each case, cramped and ungenerous proportions, an identical use of contractions, an inconsistency in the use of *t* and *c*, and a tendency to slip into Latin occasionally, though the texts were both written in the vernacular.

It is therefore probable that Father Sejan was aware of the true contents of the parcel he delivered.

The report itself told me almost nothing. It merely announced that of the five unclaimed corpses found in Narbonne and its vicinity during the past six months, none had been identified as fitting the description submitted to Germain d'Alanh. Two had been fished out of the Aude in such poor condition that little had been gleaned from the remains—excepting that one was female, and the other a child. A foreign pilgrim who had died unmourned in the hospital of St-Jacques had been neither tall, black-haired nor pockmarked; his eyes had been blue, not green, and his thumbnails intact. Another man, a possible beggar, found beaten to death in the fields outside the city, had been too old to fit the description. The baby abandoned on the doorstep of St-Felix one bitter night during Advent had been too young.

I observed that no names were mentioned and no conclusions drawn. There was not even a seal attached anywhere. All in all, I was disappointed.

Nevertheless, I decided to keep the report—along with the receipt. And I went downstairs to hide them beneath the barrel in my cellar. Having moved this vessel aside, I lifted the loose flagstone, and was about to deposit my latest incriminating documents into the cavity underneath when I noticed something.

My secret possessions seemed to be in slight disarray.

It is my habit to place each item in a very particular order. So when I saw that the two Beguin books were out of alignment, I felt a growing sense of unease. Had I been careless during my last consultation? Or had someone else been examining my hoard—someone like Sejan Alegre, for instance? Had the squeaky door that I'd heard from upstairs been the door to my cellar?

But Sejan Alegre could not have known where to look. Nor, indeed, could anyone else. I have always been so careful: how could my secret have been discovered? Not even the Hugues family has free access to my cellar. And they are certainly not permitted anywhere near it when I am lifting the flagstone, or moving the barrel.

Perhaps I am being overly vigilant. Perhaps I am jumping at shadows.

As a safeguard, however, I realigned the books, and positioned a single straw where any attempt to move them will surely disturb it. Then I carefully replaced the flagstone, moved the barrel back onto it, and went looking for Martin.

He was chopping wood in the courtyard, with such an absence of skill that I feared for his wellbeing. When I called, he came running, his face alight. But my expression must have alarmed him.

His pace slowed. He began to look anxious.

'Have you been moving anything in the cellar?' I asked. 'Without my permission?'

He blinked.

'No, Master,' he said.

'Are you sure?'

'Yes, Master.'

'Has any of your family been in there?'

'I—I think not.' His tone was nervous—but then it always is, when he senses even the slightest hint of disapproval. Like a deer or a rabbit, he can sniff a threat in the air. 'You always told us to stay away. Because of the bad smell.'

'When you entered the shop, just now,' I continued, 'what was the priest doing? Was he emerging from the cellar?'

'No, Master, he was just standing there.'

'In the middle of the room?'

'Yes, why?'

'Have you let anyone else go into the cellar, during my absence? Within the last few days? Any customers or visitors?'

He shook his head, frowning. 'Oh no, Master.'

'Think. Think hard. Have you left *anyone* alone there for even a short time? Have you walked into the street and left the door open?'

By this time he seemed really scared. 'Master, what's happened?' he exclaimed. 'Is something missing?'

'No, no.' I was already regretting my decision to question him. By doing so, I was only alerting him to the cellar's importance. 'It is of no consequence. Thank you, Martin. You may go back to work now.'

And so the mystery remains unsolved. It seems logical to conclude that a moment's absent-mindedness must account for the displaced books. For who besides myself has ever seen the exposed cavity in which they rest? I *always* close the cellar door when I lift the flagstone. I *always* make sure that the shop is empty, and that no one is listening from the room above. Therefore, if no other explanation is possible, I must blame my own carelessness.

Even so, I am no longer at ease.

I feel as if I have missed something.

XIV.
Tuesday of Holy Week

I hardly know where to begin. With my journal, perhaps. It has proven its worth beyond all doubt.

Having checked my previous entries in this journal, I now know why the name 'Alegre' is so familiar. It was my master who mentioned it during our last meeting. Alegre was the maiden name of Guillaume Hulart's wife, Jacquette. Jacquette Alegre was a follower of the Beguin Rixende, some thirty years ago. Her husband was Vincent Hulart's father—and Berengar Blanchi's uncle.

So the priest from the Archbishop's Chancellery may very well be related to Berengar Blanchi.

I cannot tell how important this connection might be. In my own native land, I have known Cistercian abbots and Cathar *perfecti* who have sprung from the same stock. I have known cousins who would happily kill each other, and cousins who would die for each other. In a city such as Narbonne, moreover, it is easy enough to avoid one's relatives, as long as one lives in a different quarter and parish.

Besides, the connection between the priest and the heretic might be too remote to count as a connection at all.

It is worth keeping in mind, though. Sejan Alegre interests me. If he works for the Archbishop's Chancellery, then he cannot live far from the Archbishop's palace. In which case he might very well have a benefice at the cathedral of St-Just, next door. And if Sejan Alegre *is* attached to the cathedral, there could be a link between him and the man I finally found this morning, in the Hospital of St-Just for the Poor of Narbonne. Who knows? Nothing can be disregarded—not at this stage.

Happily, the search was not as long as it could have been. Though I was absent from my shop for an entire morning, it could easily have been a whole day; visiting all the hospitals in Narbonne would be a full day's work. I had decided to disregard the city's leprosaria, at least for the time being. Since they occupy sites outside the walls, I thought it more likely that my quarry would be working elsewhere. It must also be confessed that I was reluctant to visit a leprosarium, unless absolutely necessary. Such places are not for the faint of heart.

I began my search near the northernmost gate of Narbonne, at the hospital of St-Jacques, with the intention of moving southwards and ending at St-Paul. St-Jacques was an alarming sight. It had not occurred to me that Easter would fill it to bursting point; only when I reached it, and saw the mass of people spilling from its doors and silting up its rooms, did I recollect that St-Jacques is above all a place of lodging for pilgrims, and that pilgrims tend to be very much in evidence during Holy Week.

I cannot give the vaguest estimate of how many people were seeking shelter there. Had I tried to count them, the ceaseless movement would have defeated me. In the hall every bench and table was occupied by shrouded, sleeping forms. Whole families—some with children—were encamped in corners. One or two of the guests inhabiting this room seemed poorly; there was a grey-faced old woman slumped wearily against the wall with her mouth hanging open, and a man shivering with fever. But for the most part I saw only healthy travellers in the hall.

The ill and dying had been relegated to a couple of long, rush-strewn dormitories. It was in the largest of these chambers that most of the attendants were concentrated—among them many lay brethren. I recognised two members of the charitable group known as the Good Works of the Whites. There was also a man carrying a water jug who was dressed rather like a Franciscan tertiary, though I doubt that he could have been one (since Franciscan tertiaries often end up on the stake, these days) and another man clad in the robes of the order of St-Esprit. A priest of St-Sebastien murmured prayers over one deathbed, while a dishevelled but handsomely attired layman was bloodletting with grim efficiency, stopping every once in a while to scold the queasy-looking boy who held the basin.

But none of these attendants was the man who followed me yesterday. Nor did I find him in the courtyard, where more weary pilgrims clustered around the well and the entrance to the latrines. Though I spent some time picking my way across crowded floors, and scanning all the dazed, fretful, flustered, pinched, tired and unhappy faces, I saw no trace of the man I sought. Neither was I challenged by anyone in authority, though one of the guests did ask me for food. Since the demand was made in French, however, I pretended that I did not understand it. And I left without making a donation, having identified no one of official status to whom I might safely entrust my money.

My next stop was the House of the Repentants, which lies very close to the hospital of St-Jacques. In contrast to the latter, this foundation would not admit me. After inquiring as to my name and business, a portress allowed me to make my donation through a hatch in the front door. Though baulked, however, I was not much dismayed. Being a refuge for reformed prostitutes, the House of the Repentants is no doubt inhabited by a large number of healthy young women, and is almost certainly staffed by lay sisters and nuns. It is not the sort of place you would expect to find a large, shambling young man covered in vomit and urine.

So I moved on, passing St-Sebastien, crossing the Old Market, and following the Rue Droite all the way to Caularia Square. Here, just before the street meets the square, the Hospital of St-Just for the Poor of Narbonne stands directly opposite the cathedral. It is, in fact, more a chapter hospital than anything else, as I saw when I gained entry. The place is full of impoverished, incontinent, toothless old clerics. Having never in my life paused to wonder what might happen to the world's senile priests, my visit to the Hospital of St-Just was quite a revelation.

Though freely admitted, I discovered that I could not simply wander in off the street, as I had at St-Jacques. The fat and jovial porter (who could not have been more different from that surly porter at the Dominican priory) had me wait inside the door after I had explained my business—under a false name, of course. I should perhaps mention that this same porter happened to let slip the term 'crooked stick' during his brief conversation with me. I believe that his exact words were: 'Come in, come in. Sit yourself down and be at ease. You will find no crooked stick among our brethren, for we are happy to welcome all who seek admittance.'

At first I was startled, but quickly realised that he had meant nothing by it. Certainly he did not recognise me, any more than I recognised him. I wonder if he even realised what he had said. As I watched him swagger away, I thought to myself: You are luckier than you deserve, my friend. And I made a mental note.

He is the second former Cathar that I have identified in the last four months.

Within the time it would take to recite a dozen paternosters, I was joined by a lay brother who described himself as the 'Lieutenant of the Procureur'. My promise of alms must have drawn him to me as dung draws a fly. I explained that I had not been impressed with St-Jacques, and wanted to inspect his own foundation before parting with my money.

'For the remission of my sins at Eastertide,' I said, 'it seems fitting that I should bestow a generous sum on the poor. But I do not want my money squandered. I want it put to good use.'

This seemed reasonable to Brother Bongratia, who conducted me through the hospital so briskly and assiduously that I hardly had time to catch my breath. As I have already observed, a great part of the hospital's population comprises aged men whose former occupation could be deduced from the number of them moved to bless me when I passed, or to mumble vacantly in Latin when asked how they were. They could not really be distinguished by their clothes, since *all* the brothers and sisters, no matter what their origins, wear vaguely similar garments marked with a cross. There is a proper infirmary, with a proper infirmarian attached to it. The latrines are so impressive as to be almost of a monastic standard, spotlessly clean and with running water to carry away the ordure. Of the few younger brethren, the majority are crippled or slightly mad; one has obviously been stricken down by a wasting disease, and another is a blind youth whom I saw—rather to my astonishment—emptying the piss-pots of those incapable of visiting the latrines themselves.

It was in the infirmary that I espied the object of my quest. He was peeling bandages off somebody's bedsores, and I saw at once why he was needed. Only a strong arm could have pinned down the writhing, squealing sufferer, whose lesions had adhered painfully to the bloody cloth, and whose enfeebled intellect was not amenable to persuasion.

I marked the determined set of my quarry's jaw—so at odds with the drooping slant of his smoky eyes—and turned away before he could see me. 'There is a stout heart,' I observed to Brother Bongratia, when we had lingered for just a moment on the threshold. 'I would find it hard to undertake such duties, day after day.'

'Ah, Loup earns his keep,' my companion replied cheerfully. 'He had one foot in the grave when we found him, but now, as you see, he could lift twice his own weight. Very quick on his feet, too. And *this* is the cellar . . .'

So the name of my mysterious pursuer is Loup. That is the sum total of what I bought today, for an outlay exceeding thirteen *sols*. At least, however, I was not forced to visit every hospital in Narbonne. And I am particularly grateful that I was able to avoid the leprosaria.

I returned home in time for my second meal, which I collected from the kitchen. Here I found most of the Moresi clan, excepting, of course, my tenant's elderly mother. Though still fairly infirm after her bout of illness, she had clearly managed to struggle off to St-Sebastien—where, as a rule, she practically takes up residence during Holy Week. Hugues was good enough to rise in greeting. He urged me to join him at the table, cuffing his eldest daughter to clear a space on the bench beside him. But I declined, with thanks. It is not my habit to eat with the Moresi. To share a meal with someone is to invite familiarity, and I prefer to maintain a distance between myself and those with whom I reside.

It does not trouble me in the least that Hugues thinks me very proud and unfriendly. I know this because his voice is far more penetrating than he realises. Since my own opinion of Hugues is even less flattering than his opinion of me, I have not taken offence.

'Thank you, no,' I said, in response to his hearty invitation. I was far too tired to think of an excuse, so my tenant—who was in an uncharacteristically genial mood—produced one for me.

'The boy tells me that you have been making charitable visits to hospitals,' he remarked. 'That would be enough to turn *my* stomach. I expect you would rather have a spoonful of broth, or milk.'

'Bread and lentils will be sufficient,' I replied, accepting a little of each from Hugues's wife. Martin immediately sprang up, offering to carry the lentils for me. His father, meanwhile, declaimed on the subject of hospitals.

'I would rather give alms to the hospitals than to the Church,' he said. 'Give alms to a monk or priest and the money will be spent on filling his belly. Give alms to a hospital, and you are truly helping the poor, now that the consuls of the city control our hospitals.'

A grunt was my only refuge, since I was not of a mind to indulge Hugues's evident desire for a debate on the merits of ecclesiastical administration. His views, in any case, were not of a kind that merited encouragement; once again, they filled me with unease. While Hugues does not bear himself like a typical Beguin, the sentiments that he expresses are sometimes enough to make my blood run cold.

With a nod, I therefore took my leave. Martin followed me upstairs to my workroom. Here I had already poured wine for myself, and uncorked my pot of honeyed almonds. (Honeyed almonds are my greatest weakness, even during Lent.)

'There,' I said, bestowing a handful upon my apprentice. 'Take some.'

'Oh.' His response was a sudden intake of breath. '*Thank* you, Master!'

'Did anyone come knocking today? Any priests from the Archbishop's palace?'

'No, Master.' He peered at me, his demeanour anxious. 'Is that bad or good?'

'What do *you* think?' It was an idle remark, and probably a foolish one. For the boy took me seriously.

'Good?' he hazarded, and looked gratified when I said: 'Of course.'

'Most priests are bad,' he remarked, nodding sagely, 'because they dress in rich clothes, and drink the wine of fornication.'

I nearly choked on my almonds. As I coughed and spluttered, Martin patted me timidly on the back.

'Are you all right, Master?' he said, after the paroxysm had eased.

In fact, I was not all right. I was aghast. I am still aghast.

My heart sank as I surveyed my apprentice, who gazed back expectantly, eagerness warring with apprehension on his face. My own face was a blank. I have trained myself to assume such a mask at moments of dismay. Yet that stare of mine, which I am unable to suppress . . . that stare must have made him nervous.

He fidgeted, and looked away.

'So you agree with your father?' I said at last, moving my head so as to catch his wandering eye. When I did, he flushed.

'My father?' he echoed, then nodded shyly. 'Oh, yes.'

'But still you will go to Mass on Sunday?' This I was determined to find out. Eschewing Mass at Easter is the surest way of identifying oneself as a heretic to all the world.

'Yes, Master,' Martin replied. 'Do—do you think I should not go?'

'Of course you should go! Did I say otherwise?'

'No . . .'

'There are good priests as well as bad priests. It makes no difference. Each will be judged by God, according to his sin.'

'You mean—when the Carnal Church is destroyed?'

I sat down abruptly. My knees have a tendency to fail me sometimes. They fail me even when my face does not.

'Go now,' I said. 'Go back and finish your meal.'

'Master—'

'Go.'

'You are not angry with me?'

'No.'

'If I have said something wrong—'

'Later. Not now.' I took a deep breath. 'Go on. Your food will be getting cold.'

He went at last, with many a stealthy backward glance. But I showed him nothing, in either my expression or my posture. Not until I heard the door to the kitchen bang shut did I allow myself the luxury of closing my eyes, and slumping in my seat.

I have been thinking ever since. Thinking and thinking. Is my tenant a Beguin after all? While his past observations about greedy priests can be explained away (though not, of course, excused), his son's reference to the Carnal Church brands them both like a yellow cross.

Can I really be such a fool? Have I been sharing my house with a heretic for the last few years, all unknowing? Is heresy the true cause of Hugues's splenetic nature?

Of course I was not that well acquainted with the Beguin heresy before I spoke to Bernard Gui. Upon noticing how plainly Hugues dressed, I had put it down to his humble trade, and the fact that he spends so much on wine. How can a genuine Beguin be an habitual drunkard? Unless the drunkenness is only a ploy, and the time that he claims to spend at the Inn of the Star is in fact spent with other Beguins? With Na Berengaria, for instance? *She* lives near the Inn of the Star.

But I would be prepared to swear an oath that Hugues is genuinely drunk when he staggers home to beat his wife. Nor, despite his penetrating voice, have I ever heard him refer to Pierre Jean Olivi, or St Francis, or Berengaria, or anyone else connected with the Beguins.

I hardly know what to think.

If Hugues is a Beguin, recognised by other Beguins, then his children are doomed. They have imbibed poison straight from their father's mouth—much as I did, so long ago. I had thought to curry favour, by parroting the lies that I had heard from my relatives, and by running errands for the liars. God help me, I was misled by my own desperate need for commendation.

And Martin is the same. He would do anything to win his father's grudging approval. He would sell his soul, just as I did. If Hugues is ever charged with heresy, Martin will be questioned also, and it will be the end of him. He will waste his youth away in the Capitol Tower, or some such place. He will have to endure the rats at night. Or the brutal attentions of the gaolers. Or worse.

But this fretting is pointless. I have to think *logically*. All will be well if Hugues is ignorant of Na Berengaria and her circle. And he must be, for I have seen no evidence of association. Berengaria and Guillelma were strangers to Martin when they came here. Never once, during the last four years, have Blaise, Guillaume, Perrin or Berengar Blanchi visited this house, on any pretext whatsoever. Imbert paid a visit, but his business was with me.

If Hugues is a lax Beguin (as a habitual drunkard would have to be), then he might not mix with earnest Beguins such as the ones I know. He might nurse his beliefs in isolation. He might air them occasionally at the Inn of the Star; perhaps he has a likeminded friend there. And this being the case, he is no concern of mine. The trail that I follow links Berengar Blanchi to Imbert Rubei to Berengaria Donas. Hugues stands far outside the net. I have no *positive* proof that he was ever in it—and God grant that I shall never find any. After all, what do I know? Only that his son used the words 'Carnal Church'. Perhaps Hugues once employed the term while railing against tithes. There is every possibility that it might have caught his attention years ago, when the grave of Pierre Olivi was still an object of veneration, and the anniversary of his death was still celebrated with feasting, votive offerings, and inflammatory sermons from rabid Spiritualist friars.

I must not indulge my imagination. I must not permit my fears to cloud my judgement. Martin is still safe as things stand. Before I begin to worry about him, I should determine whether his father is known to Na Berengaria's circle. I should follow Hugues the next time he sets out for the Inn of the Star.

That will help to determine matters.

There are so many tasks to be accomplished. I must discover why Loup has been pursuing me. I must find out if the connection between Sejan Alegre and Berengar Blanchi is of any importance, or whether it is a coincidence merely. I must establish the whereabouts of Jacques Bonet, alive or dead. And I must decide whether my apprentice is truly at risk.

Firstly, however, I must calm myself.

Nothing useful can be done when one's emotions are governing one's mind.

XV.
Day before Maundy Thursday

From now on I shall tread very, very carefully—or my next step might prove to be my last.

I put Martin to work all day, scraping skins. He raised no objection, and I wanted him out of his father's way. When he first entered my workshop, I asked him where his grandmother was, and he looked at me in astonishment.

'She is sitting by the fire. In the kitchen,' he said.

'Will she be going to church, today?'

'Perhaps.' He shrugged. 'She will go on Friday. She told me.'

'The next time she goes, Martin, you should accompany her.'

He blinked, and his mouth formed a perfect 'O'.

'Your grandmother sets a far better example than your father does,' I continued, trying not to sound pompous. 'Your father is in error when he fulminates against priests and bishops. We are none of us well placed to judge them—that is God's task. Instead we must concentrate on our own sins, for which we have full responsibility.'

My apprentice heard me out with the most peculiar look on his face. At first I thought him bewildered. Then his mouth twisted, and his cheeks coloured, and his gaze dropped to the floor.

'Do you hear?' I said, wondering greatly at this response. 'It grieves me that your father should speak without due consideration, in front of his own family. No good will come of such defiance. I myself have no quarrel with the Church, and I cannot believe that it has ever caused *you* any offence. Has it?'

I waited, but Martin did not reply. Bending my head, I saw that he was blinking away tears.

Much to my astonishment.

'What is it?' I said. 'What ails you?'

He shook his head, still avoiding my regard.

'Does it hurt you to hear me speak of your father in this way?' I pressed him. Again, he shook his head. 'Have you some quarrel with a particular priest?'

'No, Master.'

'Then what is it? Come, tell me.'

I believe that he might have obeyed, had his restless eye not suddenly alighted on the view of the street from my window. Seeing him wince, I glanced around.

Hugues Moresi was heading down Stump Way, towards the Rue de Sabatayre.

'Ah,' I said, and fixed my attention once more on the boy. 'Where is your father going? To the Inn of the Star?'

He nodded, miserably. No doubt he envisaged another round of beatings later in the day. And although he himself was no longer at risk, he must have feared for his mother.

'I am very sorry, Martin,' was all that I could offer him. 'You may stay here, if you wish. For as long as you like. Other than that . . .'

Other than that, I had nothing to suggest. Though I am lawfully entitled to expel Hugues from my house, I have no power to interfere between husband and wife.

Martin understood this. He nodded again, even more miserably than before, and cleared his throat. I anticipated some enlightening remark, perhaps on the subject of his father's beliefs, or his father's violence, or even his father's condemnation of me. But I was disappointed.

'Which skin shall I scrape, Master?' was all that he said. And I respected his reticence. How not? I myself can hardly be described as forthcoming.

Besides which, if he has been entrusted with his father's secrets, I would not expect him to divulge them. Not without good cause.

So I wordlessly helped him bind a skin to his frame, before leaving him with some vague excuse about repaying a debt. In fact, I was heading straight for the Inn of the Star. I wanted to see whether Hugues Moresi spends as much time there as he claims. For I learned long ago not to believe everything I hear without confirmation.

The Inn of the Star stands so close to the church of St-Sebastien one can sometimes listen to the canons chanting while one swills down generous amounts of good local wine.

The Old Market and the hospital of St-Jacques are also within spitting distance; as a result, the inn is never wanting for patrons, even during Holy Week. When I arrived there this morning, I was surprised to see how busy it was. Several horses waited patiently outside, the subject of endless negotiations. A *joglar* sat tuning his instrument. Beggars prowled. Dogs scavenged. Pilgrims argued over the rate of exchange for their foreign coins.

Hugues Moresi had joined a crowded table, where a game of dice was underway—though I am not sure that gambling is permitted during Holy Week. No doubt he and his friends are indulged in this matter owing to their repeated and regular visits to the inn. Certainly they had possession of the very best table in the house, and were being generously supplied with food as well as drink. One look at Hugues told me that he would not be stirring from his seat in the immediate future. He had the appearance of a man perfectly satisfied with his lot.

He also had the appearance of a man who was quite at home. I heard him address one of the maidservants by name; I saw him pat the innkeeper's unshaven cheek, and fondly abuse him. Such familiarity, in an establishment of that kind, is only earned by faithful and persistent patronage.

Watching him from behind a knot of jabbering tanners, I decided that Hugues was no ordinary Beguin. And I began to doubt very much that he was planning to visit Berengaria Donas. I saw no indication of anything save a firm intention to get drunk, play dice and argue with his friends about the merits of imported wine.

It did not seem to me that Na Berengaria's circle would have tolerated such conduct.

Therefore I withdrew from the immediate vicinity of the inn, and started towards the Rue de Sabatayre. On my way, I was naturally obliged to pass the Donas house, and for the second time that morning attempted to do so without attracting the notice of anyone living there. The shop seemed to be open, though in a half-hearted manner; the downstairs shutters were partly folded back, and the door stood ajar. There was movement within. I could see nothing but an indistinct flurry of dark shapes, enfolded in shadow, as I kept to the other side of the street. Nevertheless, I sensed that somebody was about to leave the shop. My suspicions were confirmed when a faint farewell reached my ears, and I glanced over my shoulder to see who was sallying forth—making sure, at the same time, to screen myself from observation behind a pair of large women who had stopped to lean on their brooms and trade insults.

Imagine my surprise when I spotted Berengar Blanchi.

If he saw my face at all, it would have meant nothing to him. At our last meeting I had been well disguised as a blind beggar, and today I was dressed with propriety in dull, unexceptional clothes. In any event, he is not the sort of man to remember faces. His gaze is turned ever-inward, as I observed when I began to pursue him, keen to find out where he would go next. Only a blind man or a visionary would have walked straight into that tethered pig.

Needless to say, I did not turn on my heel and bound after him like a faithful hunting hound. To have done so would have required that I pass the Donas shop for the third time this morning, in full view of any occupants who might have been watching Berengar Blanchi walk away. Instead, I risked losing my quarry by darting into a backstreet that runs parallel to the Rue Droite, hoping that he was on his way to the Bourg, and would not be making any unexpected detours before he reached Caularia Square.

Happily, I was correct in my assumption. When I followed the next cross-street back to the Rue Droite, I found myself just a few paces behind Berengar, and lingered on the corner briefly (pretending to have grit in my eye) so that the distance between us might widen a little. Not that he would have seen me. He was oblivious to his surroundings, and nearly caught me out as a consequence. For as we approached the bridge to the Bourg, something about it seemed to penetrate the fog of abstraction that blinded him. He started, and whirled around—having walked straight past his destination.

His sudden reverse took me by surprise. I was given no opportunity to conceal my face, which was exposed to his direct regard. Fortunately, nothing about my appearance snagged his attention; his dark yet luminous gaze swept over me as he identified his exact whereabouts, ignoring people in favour of buildings. Then he loped gracelessly back through the Alquiere Gate, nearly brushing my shoulder as he passed.

It was a frustrating moment. There was no doubt in my mind that, by turning so sharply on his heel, Berengar must have caught the eye of any idle observer. To have imitated his actions would have looked absurdly suspicious. As a result,

I had to keep moving forward. I had no choice but to cross the bridge, cursing inwardly all the while.

Not until I had reached the gate to the Bourg did I feel safe enough to retrace my steps. By slapping my brow, I demonstrated to the world at large that I had forgotten something important. And I returned to the Cité at a brisk pace, hoping against hope that Berengar Blanchi would still be in Caularia Square.

It had crossed my mind that the whole manoeuvre might have been a deliberate tactic, to shake me off. Certainly it was the sort of thing *I* would have done, had my position and Berengar's been reversed. Yet I was not convinced. Nothing else in his manner had indicated to me that he was alert to my presence. If he had been, he would have looked back. Just once, to mark my position. I had thought that he might, when he tripped on a pothole outside the chapel of Bethleem. I had been anticipating a single, stealthy glance. But he had exhibited not the slightest interest in anything behind, beside or ahead of him, pressing on as if barely conscious of his stubbed toe.

Scanning the busy square upon my return from the bridge, I saw no trace of him. And I knew that I could not afford to stand and stare without a plausible excuse. So I approached the entrance of the Viscount's palace, where many petitioners, beggars, mercenaries and lazy old men are wont to sit in the shade at all hours, awaiting a summons or simply watching the world go by. People will often arrange to meet at this same spot. You will frequently see loafers gossiping with the guards, or lingering beneath the awning of a nearby shop, examining fruit and leather goods. Therefore, when I took up a position under the Mauresque Tower, and peered at the milling crowds as if in search of someone, I was subjected to no unwelcome scrutiny. Why should I have been? At least half a dozen other men were similarly engaged.

At first I did not see Berengar. He was not in the square. And I was about to admit defeat when my gaze wandered towards the Archbishop's palace—which stands directly opposite the Viscount's abode, just as the Archbishop himself stands in direct opposition to the Viscount. Looking straight down the cavernous entrance to the palace courtyard, I noticed two men talking. One was a guard, who had about him a certain archiepiscopal gloss. The other was Berengar Blanchi. After a short discussion, during which Berengar's companion pointed towards the cathedral, the two men parted. Berengar headed for St-Just. I watched him disappear through its southern door before I ventured to move so much as an eyelid. And even then I did not follow him.

In all truth, I was unmanned. It seemed to me very ominous that Berengar Blanchi, of all people, should be making inquiries at the Archbishop's palace. For what possible reason would a devout Beguin do any such thing? Unless, of course, he wished to communicate with his cousin, Sejan. About something that might concern his visit to Berengaria Donas.

I can still feel the chill that invaded my gut at this point. I had the same instinctive reaction nine years ago, on Mount Vezian, when that so-called woodcutter took up his axe. After the first tide of panic has surged through my veins, it recedes before a sudden, icy calm, which compels me to act with the most detached yet implacable deliberation. I know exactly what must be done, and I do it. Yet it is my will alone that propels me. I cannot summon up any kind of emotion. All my fear, desire, anger, self-pity—all of it is briefly discarded, until such a time as I have leisure to indulge my feelings.

It was therefore in a state of intense yet impassive resolution that I approached the archiepiscopal attendant, who had taken up what must have been his customary gate-keeping position. In a dry voice, I told him that I was looking for my friend Berengar Blanchi. Berengar, I said, had instructed me to meet him at the Archbishop's palace. He was a tall man, thin, with big brown eyes, wild hands and an eager way of talking. He was dressed from head to toe in dark grey.

'Oh. Him,' said the guard, sounding bored. 'He was just here. But he left.'

'Why?'

'Because Father Sejan isn't working here today.' A careless gesture. 'I told your friend to ask at St-Just.'

With a nod, I signified my thanks. Then I moved towards the half-completed cathedral, though not with any intention of chasing down Berengar Blanchi. I wanted merely to convince the Archbishop's guard that I genuinely wished to find my friend. Had I headed off in some other direction, he might have been suspicious. He might have wondered what I was doing.

In fact, I was trying to avoid Berengar. Though desperate to overhear his conversation with Sejan Alegre, I knew quite well that any attempt to eavesdrop would fail. Even in the dusty, noisy nave of the cathedral, I would almost certainly be seen—and recognised—by the priest. As for the cloister, it would afford me even less concealment. Had I been dressed in a habit, I might have had a chance. But no layman, however insignificant he might be, can ever escape notice in the canonical quarter.

That is why I skirted St-Just and hurried home. All my thoughts were bent on reaching the refuge of my workroom. Though outwardly calm, I was becoming increasingly agitated. For it seemed to me that there was one obvious reason why Berengar Blanchi might have visited his cousin directly after paying a call on the Donas house.

God help me, what if they *know*?

When I reached my house, I had to collect myself before confronting Martin. I did not want him to notice anything unusual about my appearance. So I paused at the bottom of the stairs, taking a few deep breaths as I untied my cloak. I remember feeling suddenly exhausted, and almost unequal to the climb.

But I accomplished it, at last, only to be greeted at its conclusion by a worried-looking apprentice. Evidently my tread on the stairs is not usually so slow.

That, at least, is what he told me.

'Are you ill?' he demanded, and I shook my head.

'Of course not.' Something about my tone discouraged further inquiry. He returned to his work, and I went through the motions of attending to my own. But I was unable to concentrate properly; having nearly ruined a good pigskin,

I finally went downstairs and shut myself in the cellar, far away from Martin's inquisitive presence.

I had to think.

Supposing that Father Sejan is a friend of the Beguins? Supposing that he and his cousin are on good terms? If that is the case, then he might have become acquainted with Jacques Bonet through Imbert Rubei, Berengar Blanchi's friend. And anyone even remotely familiar with Jacques Bonet would have recognised his description in the Archbishop's report.

Father Sejan might have asked himself: Why is the Archbishop searching for a corpse that looks like Jacques Bonet? And why should he be sending information about this search to a humble parchment-maker?

Even if Jacques is still alive, I am in grave peril. Even if there is not a single Beguin in Narbonne who knows that Jacques was an inquisitorial agent, it must be obvious to Father Sejan, at least, that *I* am not who I claim to be. Why else would Germain d'Alanh, the archiepiscopal inquisitor, be sending me details about a missing Beguin at the behest of the Archbishop?

Perhaps Father Sejan asked his cousin to warn Berengaria Donas, and to make inquiries. Perhaps his cousin did so this morning, stopping to tell Sejan about it on his way back home. Perhaps the entire Beguin population of Narbonne is now busily discussing how I might be disposed of.

No, no. This is foolish. I am becoming overwrought. I am *not thinking clearly*. I must set down what I know, fact by fact, and consider the logical sequence.

All the following people are acquainted with each other: Berengaria Donas, Imbert Rubei, Berengar Blanchi. Berengar Blanchi's cousin is Sejan Alegre, who knows that I have an interest in the corpse of Jacques Bonet. It is *possible* that Sejan met Jacques Bonet. It is therefore *possible*—though not certain—that he has informed Berengar Blanchi about my interest.

On the other hand, I may be wrong. Sejan might never have met Jacques Bonet. He might be unsympathetic to his cousin's beliefs. His cousin's visit to the Donas house might have been a coincidence. With Easter Sunday fast approaching, he and Na Berengaria very possibly met to discuss a suitably Beguin way of celebrating the feast.

And then, since he happened to be in the Cité, Berengar might have visited Sejan on a whim.

Which explanation is more probable? I hardly know. It hardly matters. What matters is that I find out whether I am under suspicion.

Otherwise I will be taking my life into my hands, if I walk unprotected into Na Berengaria's house on Sunday.

XVI.
Maundy Thursday (morning)

I slept badly last night, plagued by ugly dreams. It seems that I shall never escape my years in the Toulousain, and in the mountains. They lie in wait for me always, much as I lay in wait for the man I killed.

Once, long ago in the spring, I was journeying towards Catalonia using a shepherds' high road. It was still very cold, but the sun held a promise of warmth. There were flowers in the valleys, and green buds higher up. I was young, then, and more easily able to forget my cares. My legs were stronger, and my spirits more responsive to external influence. I remember whistling as I walked along, alone up there among the snow-capped peaks. My new sheepskin cloak had made me very happy.

And then an evil smell reached me, soiling the fresh breeze. The further I walked, the worse this stench became. As I drew closer to its source, the green haze of new growth became somehow sickly in my eyes, and the twittering birds no longer charmed me. Some subtle poison was affecting

God's glory, turning it to ashes and rot. Finally, upon mounting a large boulder, I saw the source of the corruption, and turned away and vomited.

A corpse had been nailed to a cross, up on that high, lonely track. It was an old corpse, dead before winter. Black with age and frost, it hung by only one arm, since the weathered sinews of the other had parted around the nail or wedge used to secure it. I did not examine it closely. I know not whether it was the corpse of a man or woman. I saw only grinning teeth, and empty eye sockets, and hair or rags aflutter in the breeze. Then I ran, still retching. I retched and prayed with equal fervour. I traced a hundred crosses over my breast.

Ever since that time, I have been unable to enjoy even the simplest of God's gifts without a vague and nagging sense of trepidation. It seems to me that every good meal holds within it the threat of famine—that every day of peace is only a prelude to war. As for life itself, what is life but a gateway to death? I live with that sure knowledge always. We must every one of us live with it. Over and over again, I have heard the priests warn me that death is the only certainty in this life. (And therefore we must prepare ourselves for eternity.)

Yet I am unable to confront the possibility of death with resignation. I lose sleep, and concentration, and all appetite. My brain works itself into a fever. I find myself pacing at night like a trapped beast. Though to others I present an inscrutable façade, my thoughts rage about my skull, and my heart batters against my ribs as if trying to escape.

These are all symptoms of indecision, however—indecision and inactivity. As soon as I have a plan, and may carry it out, my symptoms ease. That is what occurred this morning. After a troubled night, I faced a more tranquil day. For I had decided what to do.

Once again, I allowed Martin to work. This I did purely out of concern for him, since it gave him refuge. It gave *me* no refuge, however. I was unable to indulge myself wholly in strategic speculation, owing to the fact that Martin watches me as a sailor watches the sky. Every movement, every sigh, every shift in the aspect of my features is always carefully noted. Months ago, when I first realised this, I thought that he was moved by fear, and that he watched me as he watched his father, alert to the threat of approaching squalls. Then I thought that he wanted to please me by anticipating my wants and moods. Now I am unsure even of this. Perhaps he only watches me for the sake of watching—because I have *trained* him in the art of watching.

He no longer opens his face to me like a daisy in the sun. Those brown eyes are no longer clear to their very depths. Something is there: a shadow. A dark fleck. A hesitation, if you will, such as an honest soul must feel when forced to dissemble.

He is holding something back. Of that I am sure. Yet it is not something of which he is entirely ashamed: I sense a hidden excitement. Could it be his father's heresy? (God forbid.)

Whatever it is, it presents no threat to me. Not in his view, at any rate. He would not betray me—not willingly.

This morning, when I told him that I would join his family at Mass on Sunday, his smile seemed to illuminate the entire workroom. I could not detect a trace of falsity in that smile. And I was glad, though at the same time felt a tiny prickle of discomfort.

My main purpose in accompanying Hugues's family is not that I may share with my apprentice the joy of Christian worship. My intention is to decide whether Hugues himself is more accustomed to praying while seated, and with his head turned to the nearest wall. I have never observed him with any great attention in church. To do so, I think, might be enlightening.

But I must not allow Martin to shame me with his innocence. There can be no shame attached to the pursuit of obdurate heresy. I know this. My master assured me of it many times. He took my chin in his hand once, and searched my very soul with his eyes, willing me to cast out those few remaining traces of resistance. 'What can you or I know of God's plan?' he said. 'What can we know of the judgement that awaits any one of us before His throne? Would you rather betray God, or betray your own heart? They are not one and the same, Helié. Do not be led into *that* error.'

And I never have. God grant that I never shall. If I remain strong, I shall even endure the pain wrought when God's will and the heart's inclination diverge.

It leaves me so tired, though. When I came to Narbonne, I had thought to avoid all intercourse, and live like a hermit monk, free of any occasion for shame or despair. Now once again my life is a well of secret conflict, and I am tormented by the responsibility for another's wellbeing.

But I should have known that there would be no refuge. Every safe place is merely an antechamber to endless peril. Even the firmest ground is nothing more than a thin layer of ice, liable to give way at any moment.

I allowed Martin to work, as I have mentioned. And I left him to watch over my house after the bells rang for tierce in the cloisters. I laid down my chalk and said: 'Martin, I must go out for a short time. And while I am gone, you must not unbar the door to *anyone*, no matter who it might be. Whether lay or cleric, male or female. Do you understand?'

'Yes, Master.'

I had been too emphatic; it showed in his startled expression. I smiled, but the smile came too late. So I did something stupid.

I patted his cheek.

Never having touched him before, I could have done nothing more likely to cause alarm. Terror leapt into his eyes; I saw it there clearly. Only God knows why I had been moved by such a foolish impulse. Had I thought to offer him comfort? Had my fear of what the day would bring caused me to bestow on him just a small acknowledgement of my fond regard, in case no other opportunity should present itself? (Though this, I knew, was an unlikely outcome.)

My intentions were unclear even to me. All I know is that the gesture was meant to reassure, and that it had exactly the opposite effect.

'Master,' he cried, 'where are you going?'

'Only to visit a friend,' I replied.

'No! Don't! Not if . . .' He bit something back.

'Not if what?'

'You—you should be careful.'

'*I* should be careful?' The impact of my sudden stare made him flinch. 'Why do you say that?'

'Because you seem worried?' He put it to me as a question, though it was not a question at all. It was an observation.

I was taken aback.

'What makes you think so?' I said.

He opened his mouth, but no sound emerged.

'Come,' I insisted, wanting to know. 'What tells you that I might be worried?'

'Your face,' he mumbled.

'My face?'

'There's nothing on it.'

He was right, of course. My expression was as blank as one of my own parchment folios.

Yet he had read it so easily that it might as well have been covered in script.

'My worries are not your burden,' I said at last, almost winded by his acuity. 'You have your own troubles, Martin. You should not concern yourself with mine.'

He dropped his gaze, his lips pressed together, his jaw locked down on what he may have wished to say in response. The most important thing he has learned from me is that one never regrets silence as often as one regrets speech.

'Keep watch,' I requested. 'Tell me if anyone calls here while I am gone.'

'Yes, Master.'

'I shall return very soon, child. Have no fear.'

Needless to say, I spoke with more confidence than I felt. Had Martin seen me in the cellar shortly afterwards, he would have realised it. For as well as wedging a knife into my boot, I threaded a long, sharp needle into my tunic. Then I donned the hooded cloak that I had sewn many years ago, when I was still a shoemaker and skilled at stitching. This cloak can be pulled inside out, very rapidly, through one small hole. Within the time it takes to say the *Gloria excelsis*, I can transform my pale green cloak into a dark brown one—and thereby, perhaps, escape detection.

The cloak was green when I wore it to Na Berengaria's house. I had to knock on the closed door, and upon being admitted, I plunged straight past her stepson—who had the bleary look of someone freshly roused from his bed. Before he could stop me, I entered the kitchen.

Here I found the master of the house, seated at the table, hunched over his account books. His chin bristled with grey hair. His blunt-fingered hands were spattered with fresh ink. His wife sat nearby, as beautifully groomed as her ageing husband was rumpled and untended. Her brow was puckered; her generous lips were pursed. I knew at once that there must be a discrepancy in the figures.

Her face lit up when she saw me. There can be no doubt about it: genuine pleasure was inscribed upon her features, along with a very natural surprise. Later it occurred to me that I must have represented a welcome relief from the task of addition and subtraction. Even so, a great weight was lifted from my heart.

Had Berengar Blanchi told her the truth about me, I would not have been received with such cordiality.

'Master Helié!' she exclaimed, rising. 'You are most welcome!'

'A fleeting visit, I promise,' was my hurried reply. For I had seen her husband's frown, and knew that I was interrupting his calculations. 'I wish to ask you something, merely.'

'Yes?' said Na Berengaria, with an encouraging look. Her husband, in contrast, folded his mouth into a lipless line.

'I have met a man who seems—um—sympathetic to the teachings of our blessed master.' Watching her like a hawk, I saw no suppressed start or wince. 'I wonder if you would allow him to accompany me here, on Sunday?'

'But of course!'

'With his three grown sons?'

'They will be welcome also!'

In which case, I thought (as I studied the woman's face), my own status cannot be a matter of debate in this house. For if Na Berengaria has been informed that I am secretly looking for Jacques Bonet, why would she encourage me to bring friends along to the next gathering? Why would she embrace four unknown men? Especially if there are plans afoot to ambush me here on Sunday.

I glanced at her husband, and saw that he was not well pleased. His expression became gloomy as his gaze ran doggedly down a column of figures. Yet I am not persuaded that he knows the truth, either. If he did, surely he would have raised some objection, instead of assuming the demeanour of a man whose wife's mad schemes were no concern of his, thank the Lord.

I cannot understand that marriage. Perhaps Berengaria brought a substantial dowry to it. There can be no other explanation for the way her husband silently endures what he so obviously deplores. Any other man would have beaten his wife to a pulp long ago.

'We are meeting here tomorrow as well,' Berengaria told me. 'Would your friends like to mourn Our Lord's crucifixion with us?'

'Tomorrow?' I wondered if this was a stratagem to lure me in without my guards. 'After Mass, you mean?'

'Why, yes. As it happens.' For the first time, Berengaria's smile receded. It was replaced by a slightly pensive look. 'Do you attend Mass at St-Sebastien, Master Helié?'

'I would be foolish not to, Na Berengaria. Since the priests there would certainly want to know why.'

She nodded, in a resigned fashion. 'That is very true,' she said. 'How I wish that we could still receive the Holy Sacrament in the Franciscan priory, as we used to! But most of the friars there now condemn the martyrs of Marseilles as heretics, and are therefore heretics themselves.'

When she sighed, I sighed with her. It seemed to be expected. I did not, however, lose sight of my purpose. If the invitation was a pretext, I wanted to see how she would respond when I called her bluff.

'I will come with my friends, tomorrow,' I declared. 'They will have no objection, I feel sure.'

'Good,' said Berengaria—and I would swear an oath that

her approval was genuine. 'Who *is* your friend, Master Helié?' she wanted to know. 'What is his rank?'

'He is a blacksmith,' I replied. 'As are his sons.'

A blacksmith, as everyone knows, has a well-developed musculature, and an easy familiarity with steel implements of all kinds. He is also very much the inferior of a rich draper. So I cannot be sure whether the slight shift in Na Berengaria's smile signified her dismay at how well defended I would be, or whether she was simply adjusting to the fact that she must soon find herself on intimate terms with a hulking great blacksmith and his enormous, sooty sons.

The latter, I think. Otherwise she would have asked more questions. Had I been in her place, I would have expressed concern about the wisdom of admitting four unknown blacksmiths into her confidence. At the very least, I would have wanted to know more about them.

But she seemed willing to put herself at enormous risk, simply because I had vouched for these men. Would she have done anything so reckless, if she thought me an agent of the archiepiscopal inquisitor?

'A blacksmith,' she mused. 'He will be the first among our number. Does he live in the Cité?'

'In the Bourg,' I replied, edging towards the door.

'Indeed! I wonder if Imbert Rubei knows him?'

'Perhaps,' I said. 'Good day to you, Na Berengaria. I must go now. Blessed be the name of Jesus Christ.'

I left before she could press me for a name. I shall have to think of one. And I shall have to think of a plausible excuse when the sturdy blacksmith and his sons fail to attend the next meeting. What if Berengaria wants to pursue them herself? God knows, she has an ardent nature. If I admit that I have been unable to convert my 'friends', she might very well undertake to do the job for me.

I have dug myself a pit, and fallen into it. Climbing out will be difficult. But it was unavoidable—and now, at least, I am reassured. Unless I have learned nothing of human nature in the last ten years, Berengar Blanchi did not mention the Archbishop's report to Berengaria Donas.

So why did he visit her?

I was pondering this mystery when I turned into Stump Way, and saw something that made my heart miss a beat. A man was standing with his ear pressed against my front door. It was Loup, from the hospital of St-Just. After watching him for a moment, I realised that he was in fact talking to someone inside. To Martin, perhaps?

Then he caught sight of me. Slowly, hesitantly, he moved away from the door, and advanced in my direction with increasing confidence as I, in turn, strode forward to meet him. There was no attempt at concealment. Nor did he demonstrate the guilty air of a man caught out in the performance of an underhanded act.

On the contrary, he hailed me in a cheerful voice distinguished by faintly French intonations.

'Are you Master Helié Seguier?' he inquired.

'I am.'

'Then I have a message for you.' He placed in my hand a crumpled parchment folio, folded three times but unsealed. 'Your boy would not take it.'

'I told him to keep the door shut. My stock is very valuable. Who wrote the letter?'

'I don't know,' Loup replied, and strode off without a backward glance—though not as if he was in any particular hurry.

By this time, I was aware of my neighbours' scrutiny from various upstairs windows. So instead of lingering to examine the document, I walked quickly towards my shop. Upon reaching it, I employed the three double-raps with which I customarily alert Martin to my presence; he unbarred the door almost at once, and started gabbling before I had even crossed the threshold.

'Master, did you see him? The man? He had a letter for you—'

'I spoke to him. I have the letter.'

'You told me not to admit anyone.'

'I know. You did well.'

'It was lucky that you came back!'

'It was,' I agreed, and sent him to fetch my meal from the kitchen. I then hurried up to my workroom, where I discovered that the elaborately folded parchment was merely a covering used to protect and conceal the letter inside. This letter was written on the very highest quality vellum, folded twice, and properly sealed.

The seal bore an imprint of a dog with a torch in its mouth. My master once explained to me the meaning of this picture, which is based on a kind of Latin pun.

Domini canis. Hound of God.

It is the sign of the Dominicans.

XVII.
Maundy Thursday (evening)

I must now conclude this morning's entry, which was cut short for reasons that will soon be explained.

The letter, as I said, was stamped with a Dominican seal. I examined this seal thoroughly before I broke it, and was quite convinced that it was genuine. For I am no stranger to the Dominican seal. Every curve and hollow of its design is familiar to me.

So is the script of Bernard Gui, my master. Sometimes, when afflicted by a sense of my own profound isolation, I have taken his letter of recommendation from under the cellar flagstone and studied it, as one might study a beloved face. Therefore I recognised at once that I had been sent a forgery. The new letter was signed with Bernard Gui's name, but it was not signed by Bernard Gui. I knew this even before I compared it to the old letter.

There are many, many ways in which I can prove my theory. To begin with, in imitating my Master's hand, the forger laboured for too long over the shape of each character.

As a consequence, although he copied the elongated Ts and Qs quite well, his ink was laid down too heavily. Bernard Gui is a prolific writer; as well as the many letters and reports that he produces year after year, he has also written numerous works of theology, liturgy, history, hagiography and geography. A man so liberal with the written word does not use his pen like a chisel, carving the text into his parchment. Instead his quill tends to skip and fly, so that the ink dries thin and pale, and sometimes disappears altogether.

Bernard Gui also employs contractions, *but only when he is writing in Latin*. When writing in the vernacular, he never contracts anything. He told me why on one occasion, after he had accidentally dropped a stray Latin document onto the floor and I had picked it up. Upon glancing at the document, I had been amazed at the number of little letters written high—and in very small characters—beside the big ones. Bernard Gui explained that these little, high characters give a shortened form of common Latin words, and that they are often used by educated men, who can recognise what they stand for. Uneducated men like myself, however, are not accustomed to reading, and are unfamiliar with most words, even in the vernacular. Consequently, no one wanting to be clearly understood by the semi-literate would substitute V for 'vos' when writing in the vernacular, even though he might employ the same contraction when writing Latin. (The two words have an identical meaning in each language, as I discovered many years ago.)

Looking at the forgery, I realised that the man responsible for it had used as his model a Latin document written in Bernard Gui's hand. And he had copied the Latin contractions wherever the vernacular gave identical or similar words, not being fully acquainted with my master's habits.

Had he been better informed, he would not have used contractions in my letter. Indeed, he would not have used the alphabet at all. The most suspicious aspect of the entire text was the fact that it had not been encoded. Not once, during my long association with Bernard Gui, has he ever sent me an unencoded, written message.

Instead, he resorts to numbers.

Down in the cellar, under the loose flagstone, there lies a long scroll of parchment on which are recorded column upon column of numeric codes and ciphers. Bernard Gui possesses an identical scroll. By consulting it, my master is able to communicate with me entirely in numbers, each of which corresponds to a different word, letter, or group of letters. It has therefore been his custom in the past to send me messages that look rather like this: *XXIV-VII-CCX, LXIV-XIX* . . .

Not that he often writes to me. In my whole life, I doubt that I have received more than five encoded messages from Bernard Gui. He knows how anxious I am to protect my false name and identity; he understands that even an encoded letter can imperil my very life. So he refrains from intruding on my daily rounds unless driven by the direst necessity. And he would never, *ever* put me at risk by sending an unencoded letter.

That is why I did not for one moment believe that the summons was from him, though it purported to be. In full, the letter reads:

To Helié Seguier, Parchment-maker of Narbonne.

From Bernard Gui, Inquisitor of Heretical Depravity, deputed by the Apostolic See to the Kingdom of France.

You are summoned to the Priory of St Dominic, in La Moyale, on the day following Easter Sunday, directly after compline. Report to the gate facing the Pont de Las Naus and await further instructions.

In the name of our Lord Jesus Christ, amen.

After recovering from the first shock of this peremptory order, I began to study it with close attention. And I drew certain conclusions from it, some of which I have already listed.

Firstly, the forger must have consulted a Latin document written in Bernard Gui's hand.

Secondly, he must have custody of a Dominican seal.

Thirdly, he is ignorant of my real name.

Most insulting of all, he has used a piece of my own split-skin vellum. And unless I am grossly in error, this folio lay among the quires that made up my last delivery to the Dominican priory at La Moyale.

It therefore seems evident that someone from the priory wrote my forged letter. It cannot have been Jean de Beaune, for Jean de Beaune knows my real name, and left Narbonne some time before I made that delivery of parchment. Nor can it have been Sejan Alegre. A regular canon like Sejan would not be given free access to a Dominican seal and, in any case, I would have recognised his script.

I think it unlikely that the forger is either a city priest or a highly educated monk. Someone of that description would know better than to use Latin contractions when writing in the vernacular; such ignorance suggests that the forger cannot read Latin at all. And this again rules out Sejan Alegre, just as the seal, the parchment and the use of Bernard Gui's real script as a model rule out every single one of the Beguins whose acquaintance I have made since Christmas.

So who wrote this letter?

A nameless Dominican, evidently. A Dominican who employed Loup to deliver his correspondence and follow me around. But why would a Dominican want to lure me to the priory at La Moyale by pretending to be Bernard Gui? Why not simply order more parchment? Why this elaborate trick?

I was pacing up and down, wringing my hands, when Martin returned from the kitchen. And I was short with him, I must confess. I told him to go home—that I would summon him back when he was required. His glance strayed immediately to the letter, which he had identified as the source of my change of mood. (He is no fool, that boy.) He said: 'Master, how can I help?' Whereupon I replied: 'By going away. Now.'

Reluctantly, he went. And I gave myself entirely to the task of thinking through my dilemma.

I first saw Loup when he was waiting outside Na Berengaria's house, on Palm Sunday. He did not follow me there; I would have noticed him if he had. I therefore asked myself: what brought him to that particular place, at that particular time? Could he have known that I was expected? Or had he been told to watch the house, and see who was welcomed into it?

He had followed me home from the meeting. Why? Why choose me? Why not Guillaume or Perrin or Blaise? Because I was a new face, perhaps.

It is quite possible that someone else has been keeping an eye on Na Berengaria's friends. Someone who employs Loup as a spy. Someone who also, very probably, uses him to deliver forged letters.

Not Jean de Beaune, I decided. Not Bernard Gui, either.

But who?

Clearly, I had to find out. I also had to find out whether Sejan Alegre had mentioned me to his cousin Berengar Blanchi. Perhaps not. If he had, why would Berengar keep the news from Na Berengaria? Yet still I was uneasy. I dislike coincidences. I disliked the fact that Berengar Blanchi had gone to consult with Sejan straight after visiting the Donas shop. To my mind, it smacked of conspiracy.

Round and round I paced, cursing my own ignorance. I could see no way of interrogating my suspects without revealing too much about myself. Bribery is always a terrible risk. If I were to approach Loup, and pay for his information, what was to stop him from reporting back to his master? Nothing—unless I used blackmail as well. And as far as I knew, he was as virtuous as St Catherine.

Then it hit me. The jovial porter! Immediately I rushed to this journal, and flicked back through several past entries, until I reached my description of the fat and cheery porter who had admitted me into the hospital of St-Just.

In a moment of carelessness, he had used the term 'crooked stick'. His exact words, as recorded here previously, were: 'Come in, come in. Sit yourself down and be at ease. You will find no crooked stick among our brethren, for we are happy to welcome all who seek admittance.'

Now it happens that, in this context, a 'crooked stick' means a threatening person. It is not a common turn of phrase—not hereabouts. Yet I have heard it uttered before, among the Cathars of my country. When a believer enters a Cathar house, his first remark will often be, 'Is there a crooked stick here?' (By which he means to ask: Is it safe to speak freely?) Whereupon, if it *is* safe, the response will be, 'Do as you wish.' Or, if it is not safe, 'Be seated.'

It was therefore evident that the porter at the hospital of St-Just had either been a Cathar or had mixed with Cathars at some time in his life. I realised that he might have borrowed the term 'crooked stick' unknowingly. Yet I thought it sensible to challenge him. For if he was ignorant, then I would risk nothing. And if I could bend him to my will, then he would be the perfect source of information about Loup's visitors.

To protect myself, I retrieved Bernard Gui's letter of recommendation from the cellar. But I did not head off immediately towards Caularia Square. My previous visit had occurred somewhat later in the day; I did not want to reach St-Just only to find that my porter was not at his post for some liturgical reason. So I occupied myself by writing up this journal, until the bells of St-Sebastien told me that

I could approach the hospital with every expectation of finding my quarry guarding its door.

On my way to the hospital I kept alert for anyone who might be in pursuit, doubling back several times and circling the entire canonical quarter before returning to the site of the hospital. I even ducked into St Bethleem, and surreptitiously turned my cloak inside out. Though I saw no one of a suspect demeanour, I was very, very careful. For I had decided to conduct myself as if I were in the heart of the mountains, with heretics and assassins lurking behind every rock.

When I knocked at the door of the hospital, it was opened by the man whose cooperation I was seeking. He recognised me, and grinned widely. 'Ah!' he exclaimed. 'Our benefactor!'

To which I replied: 'Can we do something for our betterment?'

It was a test, and he failed it. I have mentioned that this greeting is a kind of code, by which Cathar believers and *perfecti* recognise each other. The porter certainly knew it. Taken by surprise, he was unable to conceal his horror. His expression changed. His dimples were expunged. Instinctively, he tried to slam the door.

But I prevented him, throwing myself against its oaken panels.

'Let me in,' I murmured, wedging myself into the gap that he was endeavouring to close, 'and you will come to no harm.'

One should always attack without warning, especially if one is small of stature; it confounds one's opponent, and gives him very little time to collect his wits. Confused and frightened, the porter had no choice but to admit me. He stepped back, and I entered.

Then I closed the door.

'What is this foolishness?' he spluttered, in a feeble attempt to regain lost ground. His round, red face was already damp with sweat. 'What harm could I possibly come to, little man?'

'*You* know,' I said quietly.

'I do not!'

'You do,' I insisted. 'Where are you from?' (Because I could detect the trace of an accent.) 'Albi? You are far from home. As am I. Are you in hiding?'

'Get out of here—'

'I shall. If you answer one question.'

'You—you are making no sense.' He glanced around, fearful that we might be overheard. By this action he exposed himself as a timorous man, easily overborne (despite his weight). 'Begone, or I'll throw you out!'

'If you throw me out, I shall wait for someone else to emerge. Bongratia, perhaps. And I shall tell him everything that I know.'

'You know *nothing*!' the porter squeaked.

'I know enough to interest Germain d'Alanh. Anyone who talks of crooked sticks must naturally interest *him*.'

The porter flapped his jaw, but no sound emerged. He looked stricken. Aware that we might be interrupted at any moment, I allowed him no more room to manoeuvre.

'If I had wished to harm you, I would have harmed you already. You must realise that. And be assured that I *could* destroy you. For I paid my dues long ago. I can show you the scars, if you wish.'

The porter groaned. He put his plump hands over his face as I continued, remorselessly.

'I was punished, and I repented. Just as you have repented. You *have* repented, have you not?'

'Yes! Oh yes!' he croaked.

'I thought as much. No practising Cathar would go undetected for long on the very doorstep of the Archbishop's palace.'

'Please!' He uncovered his face to reveal wet and frantic eyes. 'I have repented! I am a good son of the Church now! It was so many years ago—it happened when I was a boy—'

'Inquisitors have long memories.'

'What do you *want*?' His voice rose uncontrollably; he grimaced before continuing, in a hoarse whisper. 'I have nothing of my own! You must see that!'

'All I want is an answer to my question.' I spoke calmly, yet with all the force that I could muster. 'If you give it to me, I will go away and leave you alone.'

'What question? About what?'

'About Loup.'

'Loup?'

'You know him. He lives here.'

The porter stared at me in complete bewilderment.

'He has grey eyes,' I went on, 'and burns on his hands, and hair about this long—'

'Yes, yes! I know Loup! What of him?'

I steadied myself with a deep breath. For in revealing what I wanted, I was entrusting the porter with a precious fact about myself.

Had he only known it (and known what to do with it), he might have used this to his advantage.

'Tell me who comes here and asks for Loup,' I said. 'Tell me about his visitors.'

'*Loup's* visitors?'

'Yes.'

The porter seemed taken aback. Worse than that: he hesitated. For one awful moment, I expected to hear that Loup never did receive visitors.

Happily, the moment passed.

'His friend Leonet comes,' he said, his jowls wobbling. 'Leonet is a mercenary. A bad lot, that one.'

'Anybody else?'

'Loup has no family. You realise that, don't you?'

'Who else?'

'The priests use him sometimes. When they need something carried or moved, they come here.'

'Which priests?' I swallowed my excitement. 'Describe them.'

'*Describe* them?' It was as if he had been asked to kill them; despair mingled with disbelief on his face. 'All priests look alike to me,' he protested. 'They live across the road, in the cloister.'

'Have you any names?'

'Father Sejan Alegre. Father Etiennet Cuissard. Father Etiennet died, though,' the porter added. 'That was a great loss to St-Just.'

'When? When did he die?'

'Oh . . . last year. A long time ago. Ascension Day.'

'Any other priests? And monks? Friars?'

'No.'

'When did Father Sejan last come here?'

The porter blinked.

'This morning,' he said. 'Why?'

'And Leonet the mercenary?'

'I don't know . . . Last week?'

'Thank you.' I had my answer. 'Be assured, your secret will be safe with me,' I advised him, and turned to go. His astonishment was manifest.

'Is that all?' he asked.

'Yes.'

'And you swear that you will tell no one?'

I paused on the threshold, my hand hovering over the latch. 'In the name of the Holy Virgin, I swear that nothing *I* say will ever convict you of heresy,' was my promise.

It was safely made, since no heretic can be convicted on the sworn statement of one witness alone. But in any event, my task is to hunt down active Beguins. Bernard Gui expressed no great interest in repentant Cathars.

If he should ask, I will not lie. Until then, however, I intend to forget about the porter's past sins. Sejan Alegre's present transgressions are far more important.

That priest is ubiquitous. He has been talking to Berengar Blanchi. He knows about my interest in Jacques Bonet. He gave Loup the forged letter, though he did not—I am quite certain—forge it himself.

He may even have instructed Loup to follow me home on Palm Sunday. And now that I think of it, Palm Sunday fell just two days after Sejan Alegre first came to my shop, with an order for parchment. If the parchment was ordered then, it must have been because the Archbishop's report was ready to dispatch to me.

So by that time Sejan would have had grounds for suspicion.

Without doubt, Sejan Alegre knows someone from the Dominican priory. Because only someone from the Dominican priory could have forged that letter. And only someone from the Dominican priory would be aware of my meeting with Bernard Gui. Sejan Alegre, therefore, must realise that I am my master's familiar.

Does this explain the mysterious summons? Perhaps Father Sejan is a secret Beguin. Perhaps he intends to lure me away from the crowded streets of Narbonne so that I may be killed (with the help of a friendly Dominican). But if he *does* fear me, then why not inform the other Beguins? For he has not, I am sure. Had he done so, Na Berengaria would have been horrified at my suggestion that I bring four hefty blacksmiths to her house on Good Friday.

Conceivably, there is another explanation. It may be that Germain d'Alanh has uncovered information vital to my quest, and has asked his scribe, Sejan Alegre, to convey this to me in a surreptitious manner. Very possibly, Father Sejan has been commanded to watch over me by the archiepiscopal inquisitor. Or even by Jean de Beaune.

I have until Monday to decide. Three days. By then, I must have a strategy in place.

XVIII.
Good Friday

God help me. What shall I do?

I had everything so carefully planned. Yet now—now I am at a complete loss. Events have moved too quickly. My heart has betrayed me. I am such a *fool*!

This morning I was in control. I had made certain decisions. It had occurred to me that the forged letter might be a test—that Sejan Alegre might be in league with all the other Beguins, and might be seeking to discover the extent of my loyalty. What if he was uneasy, but still unsure? I thought: If I go secretly to the rendezvous on Monday, then I will prove beyond doubt that I am Bernard Gui's agent.

So I determined that I would call Father Sejan's bluff. By a fortunate chance, the letter was ambiguously worded. While it *could* have been a command issued by a master to his servant, it could with equal justification have been read as an official summons. And it gave me the perfect means of proving my innocence.

I concluded that the most natural response of any true Beguin who had received such a letter of citation would be fear, dismay and a fervent desire to flee. In the circumstances, he would almost certainly consult his Beguin friends. And what better time to do it than at the Good Friday gathering? My plan was as follows: I would take the letter to Na Berengaria's house, I would show it to her—with every manifestation of acute panic—and, at the same time, I would use it as an excuse for coming alone. 'My blacksmith friends,' I would say, 'might not be inclined to join us upon learning of this summons.'

Naturally, I understood the risks inherent in my plan. If Germain d'Alanh was behind this fraudulent communication, he would be left wondering whether I was still faithfully Catholic. If Na Berengaria knew nothing of it, she might herself become frightened, and flee Narbonne. In pursuing my chosen course, I would be releasing the proverbial wild beast into the proverbial market square: there was no way of foretelling the outcome, save that it would probably involve a great deal of upheaval.

But really, I had no choice. And I told myself that, the moment I felt in any way threatened, I would leave. I would collect my bundle of secret things and slip away. God knows, I have done it before. And always I have found temporary refuge in Toulouse, under my master's protection.

I was reluctant, however, to bring him only half the story. I still wanted to know what had happened to Jacques Bonet. That is one reason why I did not pack up and go this very morning. My intention was to see if I could wring any further information out of Berengaria Donas, since she is *obviously* better acquainted with Berengar Blanchi—and therefore, perhaps, with Imbert Rubei—than I had at first anticipated.

It was a sensible strategy, I think. It would have worked. But now, God help me, I am completely undone. Everything is ruined.

I went to the Donas house directly after Mass. I took the forged letter with me. Before leaving, I saw Martin returning from church with his grandmother, and was pleased that he had taken my advice to heart. So I admitted him into my workroom, hoping (as ever) to shield him from his father's dubious influence. I told him that he could remain in my quarters while I was out. Though I did not think it altogether proper that he should engage in anything resembling his usual work on such a holy day, I did give him a job to do. A very beautiful and ancient codex had been left in my custody, because one of its pages had been damaged beyond repair. The chapter of Notre-Dame La Major had asked me to match the old vellum as best I could, in order that a new page might be copied and inserted into a rebound volume.

I therefore instructed Martin to sift through my stock in search of a possible replacement folio. This, of course, meant that I was entrusting to my thirteen-year-old apprentice an object that is almost certainly worth more than this entire house *and* its contents put together. Be assured that I did not do it lightly. I impressed on him the value of the codex. I reminded him that if he should damage or harm it in any way, I might very well end up on the street.

Martin solemnly promised that he would refrain from touching the book unless absolutely necessary. He swore that he would go nowhere near it with any candles, lamps, drinks or foodstuffs. He would blow his nose and close his mouth, he said, before leaning over its pages.

Then he asked me where I was going.

'To visit some friends,' I replied, studying him closely. He turned his face away, but not before I saw his mouth twist.

To my astonishment, he actually muttered something under his breath.

'What was that?' I queried.

'Nothing, Master.'

'You spoke.' If there is one characteristic that I absolutely detest in an apprentice, it is a tendency towards muttered asides and half-concealed reprobation. This must have been evident in my voice, for its sharpness unnerved him. He tensed, and looked at me with the most unconvincing show of bravado that I have ever witnessed.

'If they are your friends, then why are you so afraid to visit them?' he croaked, unsuccessfully attempting a tone of careless flippancy.

I could have hit him, at that moment. For it was true: I *was* afraid. Though I had spent a good portion of the night weighing risks and judging possible outcomes—though in my head, I was certain that I would be safe at Berengaria's house—my heart still betrayed me. My pulse was jumping. I was undoubtedly paler than usual. And I was hiding my apprehension behind an expressionless face, as always.

It became suddenly clear that Martin knew me too well. Much too well for my peace of mind. Much too well for *my own protection.*

Why in God's name did I fail to realise this before?

'Forgive me, Master,' he whispered. Staring into his eyes, I saw tears there, and knew that I must have frightened him with my silent, stony regard. 'I—I am so very grateful . . .' he stammered.

'Yes.' I knew that. In fact, he was far too grateful. 'Gratitude is no excuse for insolence, my friend.'

'Master—'

'Take care of that codex. Tell me if anyone comes. I shall return shortly.'

I need hardly add that I was fully armed with knife and needle. I had the forged letter concealed in my clothes, and the burned finger in my purse. I remember thinking, as I walked towards the Rue Droite, that I would be sorry to leave Narbonne. Though I was born in a village, I find city life more to my taste—and Narbonne is a city that suits me very well. The people here are less passionate than the people of Toulouse. While they have a well-developed understanding of what is due to them, the Narbonnaise are at the same time practical; they would far rather negotiate than fight, and were never attacked nor besieged by the French, since they realised very quickly that no good would come of resistance.

I have learned that lesson myself, over the years, and can sympathise with their point of view. For a small man, open defiance is never a sensible option. There must always be a certain measure of cooperation if one is to survive.

At the Donas house I was admitted by Blaise Bouer. When he glanced from left to right, it became obvious that he was expecting four blacksmiths as well.

'Blessed be the name of Jesus Christ,' I observed, adding: 'There has been a complication.'

I have no doubt whatsoever that he was genuinely disappointed. His thick black brows snapped together; he screwed up his mouth and stuck out his jaw. But he said only, 'Blessed be the name of Jesus Christ,' and walked ahead of me through the dim shop into the kitchen.

Here I found the lady of the house, together with Guillaume Ademar, Perrin and Guillelma. Their eyes, too, skipped from my face to the empty space behind me, as if expecting it to be filled. The same question was written upon every countenance.

'My friends are not coming,' I explained, responding to this silent interrogation. 'I thought it best not to invite them after all.'

Na Berengaria blinked. She was sitting on a stool with Olivi's *postilla* cradled in her lap. I was struck anew by her noble mien and luminous, fine-grained skin.

'Why is that?' she asked. 'Has something happened, Master Helié?'

'Yes.' I advanced towards her, conscious of Blaise's looming form behind me, and Guillaume hovering at my flank. I remember being aware that, if suddenly leapt upon, I was well positioned to duck under the table and use it as a shield while I plucked my knife from its place of concealment.

Producing the summons, I laid it gently on top of Berengaria's book.

'This arrived yesterday, while I was away from home.' With my right index finger, I drew attention to the seal—and then to the name at the bottom. 'You see who sent it.'

Berengaria's breath caught in her throat. Her hand went to her mouth, before tracing a cross over her breast. I stood aside as her friends gathered about her, jostling each other for a look at the document that most of them could not even read.

Only Blaise was literate enough to extract meaning from the text. He hissed through his teeth, and swore an oath that attracted many accusing looks. Berengaria simply raised her eyes to mine.

'Bernard Gui!' she exclaimed—and a gasp was wrung from every person present. I saw nothing but the most convincing exhibitions of shock and horror, wherever I turned. I thought: They are ignorant of this. They *must* be ignorant. Only look at their faces!

'Is this a summons?' Blaise demanded, as if truly uninformed. Meanwhile, Guillelma was tugging at my sleeve; she wanted to know what Bernard Gui had said in his letter. So did Guillaume. The sudden babble of questions briefly masked the sound of knocking, and only when Blaise called for silence did a steady *tap-tap-tap* become audible from the front door.

There was a squeak of alarm—uttered by Perrin, I think. He had been goggling like a fish, confusion writ large upon his face; now he covered his open mouth with one hand.

Every head swivelled.

'Surely not . . .' Berengaria murmured, and clutched at my arm. 'No one followed you? From your house?'

'No.' I was confident of *that*, if nothing else. 'I would have seen.'

'It is Berengar Blanchi,' said Blaise, in an authoritative tone. 'I know his knock.'

Berengar Blanchi? I absorbed this unexpected news in silence, as around me the Beguins expressed doubt and consternation in low-pitched voices. Blaise left the kitchen. My hostess stood up, apparently at a loss. In one hand she held her book; in the other, my forged document.

'Perhaps you should hide them,' Guillelma suggested. But I did not want to lose sight of my letter.

'No.' I retrieved it from Berengaria's slack grip. 'This was sent to me. I may need it.'

Guillelma shook her head, however.

'Not if you leave the city,' she said, and turned to Berengaria. 'He should go. He should leave Narbonne.'

'It *is* Berengar Blanchi,' announced Guillaume, who had stationed himself at the door to the shop. 'Only he won't come in, for some reason.'

'Wait. Hush. Let me think.'

Na Berengaria laid her book down on the table, frowning. She stood for a moment in an attitude of deep concentration, her brow furrowed and her mouth shielded. For my part, I had missed nothing of importance. I had made a mental note of Perrin's bewildered expression, and the way Guillelma was wringing her delicate hands. I had marked the sick look on Guillaume's face, as he swallowed repeatedly.

Not a trace of calculation was visible in the eyes or actions of anyone in that room.

Guillelma said to me: 'What does the letter say? Read it.'

So I did, though I would have preferred not to. With my gaze on the text, I was vulnerable to attack. But nobody moved during my brief recital. And when I finished, the silence—the stillness—caused me to hold my own breath.

At last Berengaria roused herself from her reverie.

'Could your friend be responsible for this? The blacksmith?' she inquired. Whereupon I knew, without a shadow of a doubt, that she was innocent of all duplicity. Even *I* could not have formulated such a disarming response, delivered with such perfectly expressed indecision.

It was an immense relief, of course. Yet also strangely saddening.

'You mean—he might be an informer?' I asked. Berengaria winced, as did her three companions. Perhaps they were not accustomed to naming their fears so bluntly.

I was beginning to wonder what had happened to Blaise.

'What do *you* think?' said Berengaria, addressing me. 'Can *you* understand this?'

'No.' And I was speaking the truth. 'I cannot tell you why this has happened.'

'Could you have been recognised? By someone from Carcassonne?'

'Perhaps.'

'You should leave,' Guillelma reiterated. 'Do not wait to be caught. He should leave Narbonne!'

'Shh.' Berengaria captured her young friend's restless, twisting hands, quieting them with a gentle pressure. 'These decisions cannot be made in haste. They must be carefully considered.'

'Something's wrong!' said Guillaume.

I had already sensed this; Blaise had been away for too long. The sound of a cry, muffled and cut off short, confirmed my misgivings. There followed a flurry of movement. Guillaume disappeared into the shop. Berengaria released Guillelma and moved after him, passing through the doorway. Then I heard a sharp *bang* and I tensed, ready to face whatever might ensue. I can honestly say that I had not the slightest inkling of what my response should be. Would a man under threat of internment seek to satisfy his curiosity? Would he pursue his friends, or remain skulking inside?

Watching the two women hurry away, I realised one thing. No one doubting my intentions would have left me alone with the unworldly Perrin, who seemed finally to have grasped that all was not well. 'W-what is it?' he stammered, looking to me for enlightenment. 'Is it Bernard Gui? Has he come here?'

'I think not,' was my dry retort. I considered moving the concealed knife from my boot to my belt. And then I heard something terrible.

It was Martin's voice.

My body recognised that high-pitched babble before my brain did. I distinctly recall the way the blood rushed up to my head, even as I was still engaged in analysing—and identifying—the sound. For a moment I convinced myself that I must be mistaken. An angry growl had replaced the shrill yammer; scuffles and grunts from somewhere nearby propelled young Perrin across the room, towards the back door.

Then, as he unbarred it, Martin's muffled voice became audible, from outside in the courtyard.

'He knows me! He does! *I'm* a believer, too!'

My knees betrayed me at that point; I staggered, as if from a blow. Fortunately, no one observed it. Perrin's gaze was fixed on the back door, which burst open to admit a tangle of bodies. Three people lurched over the threshold: Blaise Bouer, Berengar Blanchi, and—between them—my unfortunate apprentice.

Blaise held him by one arm, twisting it. Berengar's fingers were entwined in his thick black hair. Tugging and jerking, the two men hauled Martin into the room. He was grimacing with pain, his eyes screwed up, his head bent back, his legs buckling.

A door slammed. I took note of that, though otherwise I stood frozen and speechless.

'What are you doing?' Na Berengaria's sharp inquiry preceded her. She must have closed the front door and returned through the shop, because all at once she appeared beside me, flapping her hands. 'Who is this?'

'A spy!' snapped Blaise. Or perhaps it was Berengar Blanchi who spoke; I cannot be certain. I was distracted at that instant by the force with which Martin was abruptly thrown to the floor. Yet I remained where I was. Motionless. Mute.

'A spy?' Guillelma echoed, from somewhere behind me. And our hostess said: 'He is only a boy.'

'He was watching the door. Hiding and watching,' Berengar offered, in an agitated voice. Martin, meanwhile, had looked up. I found myself staring straight into his eyes, which widened and dilated.

'Master!' he yelped. 'I—I meant no harm, I was afraid for you—'

'Master?' said Guillaume, who had also reappeared.

'I am no spy!' Martin continued. 'I believe what *you* believe! I do, I swear!'

'Quiet!' snarled Blaise and, seizing Martin's collar, he yanked the boy to his feet in one swift, powerful movement. 'Do you know him?' Blaise demanded, practically shaking his captive under my nose, like a dead chicken. 'Do you?'

That was a terrible moment. One of the worst I have ever experienced. Above all else, I wanted to preserve Martin's anonymity. It was crucial that no one discover his name because, once identified, he could (and would) be betrayed. I understood this. I could foresee the entire disaster unfolding in front of me: the arrests, the interrogations, the desperate denouncing of remote acquaintances. *A young boy—he said he was a believer . . .*

Inquisitors have long memories.

'*Master!*' The poor child's voice cracked. Finding me dumb—paralysed, if you will—he turned to Na Berengaria, his hands clasped together in supplication. 'I am Martin Moresi! His apprentice! I believe everything—I have read it! Pierre Jean Olivi! He spoke the truth!'

It is hard to convey what I felt, on hearing this. Yet all I did was bow my head, and blink once. I did not groan. I did not clutch at my hair, nor pound my own temples with clenched fists. Neither my wits nor my training deserted me.

I took a deep breath, and spoke as calmly as possible.

'He is my apprentice,' I confirmed. 'He must have followed me here.' And I fixed upon Martin the most forbidding, coercive glare that I have ever employed. 'Hold your tongue, now,' I said flatly. 'Or I shall deprive you of it.'

But the warning came far too late.

XIX.
Good Friday (continued)

I had to stop. Pure weakness. My hand started shaking; I was unable to write. Broke the nib and blotted the page.

God grant me strength.

I used up all mine today, standing in that dingy kitchen. Curious how the mind works at moments of intense strain, when all one's overwrought faculties are engaged in presenting a tranquil façade. Never in my life have I been so acutely observant—and I am not a man who normally misses much. I noticed the wine-stain on Guillelma's sleeve, and the spot on Perrin's forehead. I noticed the fibres adhering to Na Berengaria's hems. I committed to memory odd things like the gleam of sweat on Guillaume's double chin, and the pattern of red veins on Blaise's eyeball. It was as if I hoped to prepare myself for any possible threat from every possible direction, without, at the same time, appearing to be on guard.

Not that this was a decision consciously made. My instincts guided me, as they often do. My instincts and my training.

'So this *is* your apprentice?' Na Berengaria queried, after I had silenced Martin. 'He's telling the truth?'

'Yes.'

'I remember him!' Guillelma suddenly exclaimed. 'He was watching us from an upstairs window—when we left your shop, Master Helié. I looked up and saw his face!'

'No doubt.'

'Then why was he spying?' asked Blaise, and went on to describe the circumstances of Martin's apprehension. Apparently, when Blaise had emerged from the front door to admit Berengar Blanchi, he had spotted my apprentice peering around the side of the house. On catching the tailor's eye, Martin had ducked back into the side alley where he had been lurking—and this suspicious behaviour had caused the two Beguins to give chase. They had caught him near the gate that opens onto the Donas courtyard.

'If he is truly a follower of the Poor Brethren, why not simply join us?' Blaise growled, still clutching Martin's collar. 'Why listen under windows?'

'Oh, Master Helié,' said Na Berengaria, in worried tones, 'surely this boy cannot be the reason behind your summons? He—he cannot be an agent of Bernard Gui, do you think?'

'No!' My immediate response was much too loud. It made everyone jump. 'No, no,' I continued, speaking more quietly. 'That is impossible.'

'Why?' Blaise was not about to back down. 'What other reason would he have to follow you here secretly?'

I was about to say something about boys and their games when Martin answered for me, defying my wish that he hold his tongue. 'Master Helié is always very careful!' the little fool yapped. 'He is afraid to tell anyone that he comes here, even me. I thought that he might be angry at me for prying.' When he turned his face towards mine, I saw on it a look of such anxious devotion that I briefly lost the power of speech, and was unable to reprove him. 'But I believe the same thing, Master,' the boy continued. 'I believe that—that the poor Franciscans are the true apostles of Christ, and that the priests who persecute them are heretics. I *believe* that. I would not betray you.'

All the while, as I listened to my apprentice condemn himself out of his own mouth, I observed his many little characteristics as if I had never noticed them before: the dusting of chalk on his clothes; the thickening, downy growth on his upper lip; the dark circles under his eyes. Martin occasionally lisps his Ts, and has a crooked canine tooth. He will be quite tall and strong one day. I can see it already in the emerging width of his shoulders, and the comparatively large size of his hands and feet.

Just now, however, he is still small and slight. Still vulnerable. A child, merely.

What am I going to do?

'So you know of the blessed Pierre Olivi?' Na Berengaria gently inquired of him. 'Your master has told you about his teachings?'

'No. I mean yes, but . . .' Martin's glance skipped from her face to mine, and back again. 'I read his books. Forgive me, Master, I—I found them. In their hiding place. I found them and I read them.'

'And thereby came to believe?' said the matron.

'Yes. I believe as my master believes.' Another pleading look. 'My master is a good, pious, clever man. He is always right. He knows what the true faith should be.'

This, I think, was the greatest blow of all. Listening to Martin's paean of praise, I realised that Hugues had not infected his son with heretical opinions—the fault lay entirely with me. *I* had led my apprentice into error. First I had won his loyalty. Then I had trained him in the art of vigilance. Then I had aroused his curiosity with my secretive conduct.

Had I intended to corrupt him from the very start, I could not have done it more efficiently.

I nearly groaned aloud at the horrible irony of it all. Swallowing my emotion left me with a sore throat; my neck muscles are still aching now. At the time, I was unable to speak, though everyone was awaiting my comment.

At last, after a long pause, Na Berengaria said to Blaise, 'Let him go. How can he talk if you choke him like that?' The tailor promptly released Martin (though with some reluctance, I decided), and our hostess led the bewildered child to a bench. Here she proceeded to question him, in the most benevolent way, about his beliefs.

I would have intervened more quickly, had not Berengar Blanchi required an explanation. He grabbed my arm almost as if he expected me to fly away. At close quarters, I was more than ever struck by his odd demeanour. Though he and Blaise are both tall and dark, the resemblance between them is very slight. For Blaise rejoices in a solid, heavy presence, while Berengar—with his dishevelled locks, jittery movements and wild, distracted gaze—gives the impression of a man only partly tethered to the earth. It therefore surprised me very much when he said, abruptly, 'So *you* are the parchment-maker?'

'Yes,' I replied, pretending not to know him. 'And you are?'

'This is Berengar Blanchi. A faithful believer,' Blaise supplied. Beyond him, I caught a glimpse of my apprentice earnestly responding to Na Berengaria's motherly interrogation. But I was unable to help.

Not while I was being detained by Berengar Blanchi.

'The lady spoke of a summons,' he said, his face so close to mine that I felt his moist breath. 'What summons? Why did she mention Bernard Gui?'

'Show him,' said Blaise. Whereat I held up my forged letter for Berengar's perusal, slipping from his grasp as his attention strayed to the parchment. He took it, and read it.

Martin, meanwhile, was being subjected to Guillelma's questions also.

'The Archbishop is a heretic, and so is the Inquisitor of Marseilles,' she was saying. 'You realise that, do you not?'

'I—I know nothing of inquisitors . . .'

'All inquisitors are heretics. Because they persecute the Evangelical Church.'

'Oh.'

'They are in error who seek to deny the rule of St Francis,' Na Berengaria explained, in a far more genial, less hectoring tone than that employed by her young friend. 'A man who takes a vow of absolute poverty cannot be forced to break it. Not even by the Pope.'

'Who is the Spiritual Antichrist,' Guillelma interjected. 'Do not forget *that*.'

Seeing Martin nod, I thought it advisable to act. So I came up behind him, and placed a firm hand on his shoulder.

'Come,' I said. 'You must leave now. You were not invited.'

Martin peered at me, opening his mouth to reply. Before he could speak, however, our hostess answered for him.

'He may not have been invited, Master Helié,' she said, 'but he is welcome. Everyone is welcome here, who will bear witness to God's truth.'

'No one is too young for salvation,' Guillelma added, to my intense annoyance. Then Blaise interrupted us.

'We were talking about this letter,' he said loudly, from across the room. 'What does it mean? What advice can we offer? Something has to be done, Mistress, you know that.'

Na Berengaria conceded that she did, as Berengar Blanchi glanced up from my summons.

'Bernard Gui!' he exclaimed, stabbing the forged name with one long, bony finger. 'Why would Bernard Gui want to see this man? Bernard Gui is the Inquisitor of Toulouse! He has no authority here! Does he?'

No one seemed to know. *I* could have told them that a papal inquisitor has almost limitless jurisdiction—but of course I did not. Guillelma was the one who spoke.

'Master Helié comes from Carcassonne,' she pointed out, with far too much self-confidence. (She is only a girl, after all, and one of lowly rank.) 'Maybe Jean de Beaune has asked Bernard Gui to help him.'

Several reproving looks were thrown in her direction, while Martin wriggled like a puppy. Glancing down, I saw the fear in his eyes. All this coupling together of my name and Bernard Gui's had unnerved him.

I squeezed his shoulder hard, willing him to be quiet.

'Perhaps someone has seen me.' I spoke with carefully judged diffidence. 'Someone from Toulouse or Carcassonne, passing through Narbonne. In Carcassonne I was known as a supporter of the Spiritual Franciscans. Someone might have given my name to Bernard Gui, under duress.'

'Then you must leave.' Na Berengaria's tone was decisive. 'You cannot stay. You must go into hiding, before they arrest you.'

Here, at last, we came to the crux of the matter. Though not wholly unexpected, Berengaria's decision elicited a mixed response. Martin gasped. Guillaume hissed through his teeth. Guillelma nodded enthusiastically, as Perrin gazed about him in a puzzled yet trusting way.

'Leave Narbonne, you mean?' I asked cautiously, conscious of Martin's stiffening muscles beneath my fingers. Na Berengaria inclined her head. Blaise growled, 'Not through the gates, though.'

'No,' our hostess agreed. 'Not through the gates.'

She went on to explain that the gates might be watched. It had happened on other occasions; she had once been forced to conceal several 'beloved brethren' in her vineyard, which abutted the wall of the city. From here, at night, they had climbed the wall and made their escape into the open fields beyond.

'But where should I go?' It behoved me to respond with dismay, as any peaceful citizen might; I did so to the best of my abilities. 'What will happen to my house, my—my business . . . ?'

Instead of answering, our hostess appealed to Berengar Blanchi.

'Imbert will help, surely?' she said. 'As he did before?'

Berengar's thoughts must have been elsewhere; he was staring into space, reciting something under his breath. Blaise had to nudge him.

Even then, it took the distracted visionary a moment to recollect where he was.

'Yes?' he said, blinking.

'Imbert will help, will he not?' Na Berengaria reiterated. 'I know he did before. He arranged a passage on that barge to La Franqui, remember?'

'Oh. Yes,' came the vague reply. At which point I took the kind of risk that I normally avoid, and asked a very precise question.

'You smuggled someone down the river? Hidden on a barge?'

'Imbert Rubei did,' said Berengaria. 'He has many friends among the bargemen and merchants.'

'Was this one of the people who climbed the wall?' I wanted to know, and she shook her head.

'*They* went to Béziers,' she sighed. 'But it is no longer safe at Béziers, for those under suspicion. It is no longer safe anywhere close to Carcassonne, or Toulouse. That is why Imbert sent Jacques Bonet on the barge.'

I need hardly describe my feelings at *that* moment. At last! Something of my tension must have conveyed itself to Martin through my hand. For he looked up, startled.

'And where did your friend Jacques actually go?' I asked, quickly adding, to explain my interest, 'Will I be going there too?'

Na Berengaria seemed unable to reply. She hesitated, and appealed once again to Berengar Blanchi. 'I was never told where he went,' she admitted. 'Imbert was in charge of all that—we none of us were involved, in the Cité. Do *you* know, Master Berengar?'

'No.' Berengar suddenly thrust the forged letter at me, with such unexpected vigour that I almost jumped. Politely, I took it from him. 'Imbert thinks it best that we know nothing,' he intoned, as if preaching a sermon. 'If we know nothing, we can reveal nothing.' He seized my shoulder, and fixed me with his bright, disturbing gaze. 'A friend of our faith, who works for the Archbishop, discovered that the archiepiscopal inquisitor was about to have Jacques Bonet arrested—and warned us just in time,' he explained. 'Jacques was smuggled out. Thanks to the efforts of Imbert Rubei, he was saved from the clutches of our persecutors.'

Now this, of course, was a lie. And even in my troubled state, I thought to myself: who is lying here? Berengar Blanchi? Imbert Rubei? Or Father Sejan Alegre himself? For I realised at once that Berengar's 'friend of the faith' must be Sejan.

Alas, I was unable to give the matter as much attention as it deserved. Not at that time, when so many other problems were occupying me.

'I shall speak to Imbert,' Na Berengaria promised, before I could request further information. 'I shall speak to him as soon as I can, and advise you what you should do, Master Helié.'

'I tell you what he should *not* do,' Blaise broke in—and everyone turned to regard him. 'He should not come back here.'

There was a murmur of agreement. Guillaume glanced uneasily at the door. Guillelma said energetically, 'He should not have come today. What if he was followed?'

'He *was* followed,' Blaise reminded her, fixing a stern eye on Martin. Whereupon my apprentice once again became an object of scrutiny.

I placed my free hand on his other shoulder.

'Martin is a loyal friend,' I insisted.

I may have allowed a hint of steel to enter my expression. Certainly every gaze fell before mine. Only Blaise dared even challenge me, for all that I am hardly taller than Guillelma, and carry less weight even than Perrin.

'In that case, we should make the boy swear,' said the tailor. 'If he swears an oath on the body of Our Lord Jesus Christ that he wishes us no harm, then I shall be satisfied.'

Inwardly, I was much relieved to hear this suggestion. For Martin, I knew, would be eager to comply. And I gave thanks to God that I was not dealing with Cathars, or Waldensians, or Pseudo-Apostles, since none of these heresies permits the swearing of oaths, no matter how desperate the circumstances.

Among my Beguin companions, in contrast, there was general agreement that an oath would suffice as proof of Martin's goodwill. So he fervently swore his oath, hand upraised, while I struggled to devise a new plan.

I found it hard to think, however. Perhaps I was still recovering from the shock of Martin's appearance. God knows, I was eager to depart from that noisy house, and find a peaceful place where I might consider recent developments. In addition, I wanted Martin separated from the Beguins as soon as possible. But escape was not so easily accomplished. I had to stay there while we prayed together—for Martin's soul as much as for my own safety. Then there was a reading, followed by the usual veneration of Na Berengaria's charred relics. The sight of my apprentice kissing one of these articles made me feel sick.

Fortunately, no one seemed troubled by my sudden pallor, or the dampness of my brow. Perhaps such symptoms were unsurprising in a man confronted with the imminent threat of imprisonment.

'Have no fear, Master Helié,' Na Berengaria kindly remarked. 'I shall speak to Imbert Rubei, and decide upon a course of action. You will not be arrested. We none of us want that.'

'Our *own* safety depends upon your freedom,' Blaise observed. He is, without doubt, the most pragmatic of the matron's circle, and proved this with his next comment. 'You should not come here again. In case your house is being watched.'

'Then how are we to communicate?' was my very natural question. It preceded a long silence, as those around me searched for an answer. When Na Berengaria advised, in a tentative voice, that I could perhaps seek refuge in Imbert's house—where we could easily converse without fear of arousing anyone's curiosity—Berengar Blanchi's perturbation was immediate and unexpected.

'*No!*' he cried. 'Not there!'

We all gaped. Even Blaise looked surprised. Though Berengar is of an excitable temperament, this response seemed excessive even for him.

Only Na Berengaria showed any signs of understanding. She coloured, and made haste to withdraw her proposal.

'No, of course,' she amended. 'Of course not there.'

'Why not?' I asked. Our hostess frowned. Berengar Blanchi fixed her with a fierce, warning look. I wonder even now what he was warning her against. What does Imbert's house conceal, that it must be protected from every incursion?

'If he goes to the Bourg, he must pass through the gates,' the irrepressible Guillelma suddenly remarked. 'He might be arrested if he does.'

'Yes.' Na Berengaria all but pounced on this timely excuse. 'Yes, Master Helié must not go near the gates. The Bourg is closed to him.'

'Then how *should* we converse?' Guillaume demanded, and there ensued a long, somewhat fractious discussion concerning the method by which I might receive directives in the future.

Blaise supported the notion of a written message, hidden in a basket of fruit and delivered to my door by a 'neighbourhood child' of spotless reputation. Na Berengaria objected that this plan did not allow for the exchange of news. Berengar Blanchi was utterly opposed to the setting down of even the smallest detail in writing. (I must say, I concurred with his opinion.) Guillaume wondered aloud if it might be possible to meet in a church outside the parish, where we would be unknown, but he was instantly overruled. His friends pointed out that every church in Narbonne was currently stuffed to the roof with Easter worshippers. 'You want a *priest* to hear them?' Guillelma scoffed, before suggesting the Donas vineyard. Blaise, however, refused to countenance this.

'If Helié is to stay there and hide until his escape, then well and good,' the tailor said. 'But if there is too much coming and going, someone will suspect. Na Berengaria must not be implicated.'

And the argument continued. I myself contributed nothing at first. Martin was tugging at my sleeve, his expression one of such urgent inquiry that I could not ignore it; only after I had hushed him with a gesture did I return my attention to the debate.

It was becoming quite heated. After concluding that it would never resolve itself if allowed to proceed, I decided to put an end to the matter.

'Leave it to me,' I said.

Silence fell. Every eye sought my face.

'The meeting is my problem. The escape is yours,' I said. 'Be satisfied that I shall seek you out tomorrow, surreptitiously. No risks will be taken with your safety or mine.'

'But—'

'Please allow me this, Na Berengaria.' All at once I felt utterly drained—tired to the bone—and unable to endure another moment within those four walls. 'You may trust my discretion. This is not the first time I have fled an inquisitor. I do have some notion of what it involves.'

If I had unsheathed a sword, I could not have been more persuasive. Perhaps the weariness in my voice had some effect. Whatever the cause, Na Berengaria yielded. They all did. Even Blaise had nothing more to say on the subject. I saw Perrin close his eyes in prayer, and Guillaume nod slowly.

'Oh, Master Helié,' said Berengaria, with real compassion, 'do not let your courage fail. You will find a resting place at last. When the seventh era of the Church arrives, the Holy Spirit will be poured out in abundance on Christ's true disciples, and God will hide His elect from all harm, and after the death of the Antichrist there will be no more malice or sin, and everything will be for use in common, and love will govern the whole of mankind for a hundred years. When that happens, your suffering will be rewarded, and your long exile will be at an end.'

'God grant us His succour,' I replied. In other circumstances, I would have been deeply touched by this impulse to comfort me. But knowing what I knew, it only made me feel worse. I wondered: Why has God sacrificed this woman? Is her pride so offensive that it eclipses even her generous heart?

I took my leave hurriedly, incapable of further pretence. On our way back home Martin wisely refrained from all speech; he was perhaps watching my face, and knew enough to anticipate my wishes. Only when we reached my front door did he finally remark, in a very small voice, 'I am so sorry, Master.'

'In,' I replied, waving him over the threshold. One last scan of the street convinced me that we had not been pursued. Nevertheless, I was careful to close the door firmly behind us before asking any questions.

'How did you find me?' I wanted to know. 'You were not following—I would have seen.'

'Master, I . . .' He hesitated. With all the windows shuttered, my shop was so dim that I could barely see his face. But I sensed that he was trying to suppress a mounting panic. 'Master, I guessed,' he revealed.

'You *guessed*?'

'My father saw you leaving that shop, once. When he was returning from the inn. He made a joke . . . about the lady, you see.' Martin became flustered. 'Not that *I* ever thought—that is, my father is very—'

'I know what you mean.'

'It was a draper's shop, Master. And then yesterday, when you seemed frightened to go out—you came back covered in so many loose threads. Threads of a hundred different colours and lengths and thicknesses. They were everywhere.' Martin's tone was all at once imbued with an unmistakable authority. 'I thought that you must have gone to the draper's again, and that the draper's must be a perilous place. That is why I went there too, after you left. I was . . .' He faltered, swallowing. 'I was afraid that you might not come back,' he finished, almost in a whisper. 'I was afraid that you might be arrested.'

'Because you knew my secret?'

'Yes, Master.'

'How?'

'Because of the cask,' he explained, mumbling with embarrassment. 'Once, when you moved it, some of the water must have spilled. I saw the drag marks later, before they dried. And so I moved it myself, to see why you had.'

I looked at him for a long time, speechless. What could I possibly have said? That the pupil had outstripped the teacher? I should have been proud, I suppose, but I was heartsick. I could have wept.

This is what comes of ignoring the lessons of the past. *This* is what comes of a life too closely observed.

I should never have hired him.

'So you did move my books.'

'Yes, Master. I'm sorry. I'm sorry for lying.'

'Go,' I said. 'Go to your family.'

'But—'

'We can talk later. I must think.'

'Master, let me help!' His voice broke on a sob as he clutched my sleeve. 'Please, you can't—you can't go away! Not by yourself! You can't leave me!'

'Shh!'

'Master, I am in danger too! I am a Beguin! You must let me come with you!'

'*Will* you be quiet?' I clapped my hand over his mouth, and spoke to him so fiercely that he cringed. 'Do you think me a fool? God help me, I understand our position far better than you do—you cannot *comprehend* what is happening here! Now leave me in peace! Give me some time!' Pausing to catch my breath, I suddenly realised how distressed he was. His taut posture and ragged breathing caused me to regret my outburst.

I released him, and spoke more quietly.

'I have to think, Martin. Are you listening? I must consider our choices. Unless I make the right decision, we are lost. Do you understand?'

He nodded.

'Then go. Please. I will not forget you, I swear.'

It astonishes me that he obeyed. For all he knew, I was about to effect my escape then and there, leaving him to weather the consequences. But he trusts me, for some reason. Though all I have done is lie, and dissemble, and lead him into error, still he trusts me.

Is this God's punishment, for all my sins?

XX.
Easter Saturday (early morning)

Once I knew a girl named Allemande. She was illegitimate, the daughter of a poor shepherd, and worked as a servant in the house of one Raymond Boret. She looked after the bread, and washed the clothes. Sometimes she brought in the harvest. Had she not been slightly simple, she might have resented her position—for she was treated badly. Raymond Boret often beat her, and made her sleep in the barn. He was equally violent with his wife and his mother. All in all, he was an unfeeling, rough-tongued, autocratic man, who thoroughly deserved the fate that overtook him.

It so happened that I was the agent of his downfall. Though not a particularly fervent believer himself, his house was a safe haven for various Cathars related to him by blood and marriage. And I know this because I myself lodged there. Six years ago, when I was still a cobbler, Raymond Boret took me in and gave me a bed. I paid for it, naturally; he was not a generous soul. I also chopped wood, and ran the occasional errand for him. Most of all, I earned my keep by listening to his stories. He loved a full house, because it gave him an audience—but when no other guests were in residence, and when the womenfolk were busy with their chores, he could always come in search of my willing ear. In this way I learned everything there was to know about the population of his village, and a good deal as well about connected families living higher up in the mountains.

After seven months, I had collected enough information to keep my master busy for twice that length of time. And I felt no compunction at all about informing on Raymond, who in his cups had admitted to the rape of his own niece, and to having defrauded a friend by selling half his sheep without passing on the sum that had been paid for them.

I felt that the world would be a better place without Raymond Boret.

But in cases such as this, there are always other people implicated. Thanks to Raymond's pervasive influence, his entire household was infected with Cathar opinions. His wife had been in no position to protest against feeding and housing *perfecti*. His daughter had been expelled by her own husband for her heretical leanings. His mother was more devout a Cathar than any of them.

As for Allemande, she had allowed herself to be converted. The *perfecti* had impressed her with their fasting and preaching. At the same time, however, she had not altogether rejected the saints or the Holy Virgin. Her thinking was rather muddled on this subject.

In all truth, she was a biddable, sweet-tempered, ignorant young girl, who came to regard me as someone blessed with unlimited knowledge and a saintly disposition, if only because I could read simple texts, and made no effort to force her when we were alone. (Cobblers, I fear, are notorious for their lustful natures.) I know that she admired me very much, for she would follow me around like a dog, and was forever scenting my clothes with herbs, or bringing me sweetbreads. In the end, I succumbed to temptation—for she was perfectly willing, and as pretty as a lamb. But my weakness left me in an awkward position. Naturally, I wished her no harm. For while she might have been a heretic, she had sinned only because she was obedient and simple-minded. Her error was not founded in pride.

I must confess that I tried to warn her. Though I was running the gravest risk, I took her aside one day and told her to leave. I said that Raymond Boret's household was doomed, and that she should seek work elsewhere as soon as possible. I told her that I myself was not staying. I even gave her money, and one of my winter cloaks. Yet all this meant nothing in her eyes, because I would not take her with me.

It was for my own safety that I left her. A veiled warning would not have earned my master's condemnation, but active assistance was another matter. So I cast her adrift, knowing all the while that my attempt to shield her was half-hearted, at best. Had I *truly* sought to protect the girl, I would never have informed on Raymond Boret—since it was inevitable that he would be arrested, and would then seek to win favour by naming names. Unless, of course, he escaped. Perhaps I was half hoping that she might pass on my advice, thereby enabling the Boret clan to flee over the mountains before I had a chance to make my report. Perhaps I had too much confidence in the refuge offered by the Pyrenees at that time; it is, after all, a very long way from Toulouse to Catalonia, and six years ago the Bishop of Pamiers was not zealous in his persecution of heretics. Not like the current bishop, who exceeds even my master in his fervent dedication to the task of rooting out error among his flock.

In all honesty, I am still unsure as to the reasoning behind my decision. Reason, I daresay, had very little to do with it. I acted without fully comprehending my own motives, and was thereafter affected by a kind of numbness as I sought out Bernard Gui, acquainting him with most (though not all) of the facts. He knew that something was wrong. No man so gifted in the art of exposing secrets could have been unaware that I had suffered a mysterious blow, whose effects not even I understood, back then. I told him that I was finished. That I was too widely suspected to be of any further use. And this was the truth, though not the whole truth.

The fact is, I needed time to recover.

It was not without due consideration that I chose Narbonne as my bolt-hole. Narbonne lies far from Toulouse, but not so far as to require a different language. In Narbonne, I knew that I would be very unlucky to encounter anyone with whom I might have been associated in the past. My greatest fear (and, paradoxically, my greatest desire) was that I might accidentally discover what had befallen Allemande. It was my hope that she had found a haven in Catalonia. During moments of weakness, I would try to imagine her there. But while I was anxious to know her whereabouts, I could not face the far more likely possibility that she had been arrested, and imprisoned in the *mur* at Toulouse. I could not countenance such a disturbing thought. That is why I tried to banish the whole subject from my mind. Whenever it surfaced, I would repress it with severe force. And by this means I have been able to live from day to day, quietly, as a soldier might live while recovering from his wounds.

Then Bernard Gui reappeared. Had it not been for Bernard Gui, I might never again have confronted the kind of choice that faces me now. But his reappearance has ripped open old scars, and shone a blinding light in my eyes. I seem to have advanced *not one step* in six years. Here I am, back where I started. Torn between heart and head.

There are two possibilities, neither of which appeals. Yesterday I sat pondering them for a very long time. I knew that, for a wise man, the correct path would be the path of self-preservation. This would involve making a full report immediately, either to Germain d'Alanh, Jean de Beaune or Bernard Gui. It would *not* involve approaching either my parish priest or the Dominican priory, as Bernard Gui advised, since I am convinced that someone from that priory is a friend of the Beguins. And parish priests are notoriously unreliable.

The old Helié would have gone already. He would have slipped away this morning, bound for the Dominican priory at Carcassonne. But I left that Helié in the mountains, years ago. I left him there when I left Allemande.

Once upon a time, there would have been only one possible course of action open to me. No alternative would have crossed my mind. Yesterday, however, I realised that I had a choice. I could either make a report, or I could withhold my information.

I remember gazing at the familiar furnishings of my workroom, as I slowly realised that whatever I decided to do, these comforting objects would soon be lost to me. Narbonne, in fact, would be lost to me. If I made my report to Jean de Beaune, and the Beguins were arrested as a consequence, I would be ill advised to show my face in the city again. Oh, I might very well live unmolested. The truth might not emerge—and even if it did, it might not trouble the majority of Narbonne's citizens. But one cannot live comfortably as an unmasked agent of the inquisitors. There is always the fear that somebody, somewhere, will exact revenge for all that he has lost.

If, on the other hand, I failed to make a report, then what would follow? Retribution, inevitably. The inquisitors would seek me out. Not at first, perhaps; not for a while. Perhaps not until Pentecost, or later. In the end, though, Bernard Gui would grow uneasy. He would demand an explanation. And what explanation could I possibly give that would satisfy my master?

Suppose I went to him now. Suppose I said to him: 'I was afraid to approach you, because I have accidentally led my apprentice astray. He has imbibed grievous error, and testified to the fact in front of many witnesses. Yet I believe that, with my guidance, he will renounce his heresy and embrace the true faith once more.' Would Bernard Gui grant me the custody of Martin's soul? Would he say to me: 'I entrust you with the boy's eternal salvation'?

Perhaps he would, but I very much doubt it. I myself was once a heretic, after all. And when I vanished from my master's sight, he was disconcerted. He was *displeased*. His faith in me—if it ever existed—must have been undermined.

Besides which, I am no priest. What right have I to claim pastoral authority? No monk on earth would feel justified in abandoning an errant sheep to *my* care—especially not a monk who has spent fifteen years as an inquisitor of heretical depravity. While Bernard Gui might very well be sympathetic to my plight, he would not allow his sympathy to interfere with his God-given work. I can almost hear him point out that, although I possess great discernment, I have not the skill to penetrate the depths of a human heart.

For all my efforts, I would not be able to shield Martin. That is the truth with which I grappled yesterday afternoon. Were I to attempt some form of trade—were I to offer up information in exchange for the boy's freedom—I would no doubt find myself incarcerated. Why pay for something, after all, which can be extracted at no cost to oneself?

It became apparent to me that Martin would receive a summons if I were to betray the Beguins, and that I could only prevent his arrest by disappearing. By becoming a fugitive. I turned the prospect over and over in my mind, studying it from every angle. There were various considerations, none of them serious. My property could be disposed of long before anyone thought to confiscate it; by the time a search was instituted, any agent entrusted with the sale of my possessions would already have surrendered the sum that was realised—and could not be blamed for having done so. In other words, as long as I planned carefully, I would not be left destitute.

I would, however, lose my trade. Never again would I be able to work as a parchment-maker, or even as a cobbler, since Bernard Gui has known me in both guises. But this does not much concern me. I have skills enough to train as a tanner, or a bookbinder. I could probably earn my keep mending clothes, if necessary. I have no fear of starving.

My fear concerns Martin. As I pondered his predicament, I realised that my disappearance would only postpone his inevitable fate. Were I to vanish, on the very heels of Jacques Bonet, Jean de Beaune would do one of two things. He would either send in another familiar, or he would lose all patience, arresting the Hularts, and everyone associated with them—Berengar Blanchi included. At which point names would be divulged. And Martin's, almost certainly, would be among them.

It occurred to me that Martin had been right. Only by taking him with me would I protect him from the inquisitors.

I confronted this unpalatable fact with the utmost dismay. Avoiding detection is hard enough when one is alone; it is doubly hard when one is accompanied. And though Martin has some talent for dissimulation, he is not by any means skilled enough to become somebody else. Not for any great length of time.

Yet I knew, with a kind of awful certainty, that I could not leave him. Once the possibility of taking him had entered my head, it remained lodged there. No matter how much I paced, no matter how often I turned my thoughts to other matters (such as Berengar Blanchi's curious lie about Jacques Bonet's imminent arrest, for instance), I was unable to ignore my own burgeoning compulsion. Having abandoned Allemande, I do not possess the strength of mind to abandon my apprentice.

Were I to walk off without him, I would never recover. It would break me. Allemande damaged me somehow, but Martin would break me. I would lose part of what it is that keeps me alert and whole and able to survive in isolation. When I tried to imagine myself on the long road ahead, all alone, I could see nothing at my journey's end but an empty void—a complete absence of far, far more than just one small child. Exactly what I would relinquish, I am unable to define exactly. Myself, perhaps.

In any event, I made my decision. After pacing the room for a good while, I sat down again, and stared at my hands as the light faded. Though utterly familiar to me, they also seemed strangely removed, as if they were attached to someone else. Had they really bludgeoned a man to death? It was inconceivable. Such an act seemed beyond the capabilities of anything so small and weak and worn.

Then I got up and went to find Martin. It happened that he was waiting in the courtyard, beside the door to my shop; very possibly he had been waiting there since our last exchange. I did not ask him if that were so. I simply invited him back upstairs, where I placed him on my own stool. In the dimness, his eyes looked enormous. He stared mutely, afraid to speak.

I seated myself opposite him, on top of my linen chest. And I said, 'I am no Beguin, Martin. I am no heretic. And nor should you be.'

His mouth opened in astonishment.

'The Beguins are wrong,' I continued. 'You have to understand that. If you adopt their beliefs, then I cannot help you.'

'But—'

'Listen to me.' I lowered my voice, and leaned forward so that our foreheads were almost touching. Though I had no real expectation of being overheard, I could not prevent myself from adopting this attitude. 'The books that you found are full of lies. It grieves me that you should have read them. Martin, there is only one true church, and it is the Church of Rome. I am a faithful son of that church. I would that you were, also.'

His expression was pitiful to behold. I have never seen such confusion on any face.

'It seems as if you have strayed into error out of loyalty to me,' I added. 'But you were misled. That is why I am confident that you will turn away from sin, now that you know the truth. I wish that you had known it before.'

By this time Martin's bewilderment had given way to a more complicated emotion. He narrowed his eyes, gazing at me intently. I pressed on regardless.

'Would you recant your heretical beliefs? For my sake and for your own? Would you do that?' I inquired. 'Please. It hurts me that I should have done you such harm.'

'But the books—'

'They are wrong.'

'Then why do you have them?'

I had been expecting him to ask this; he is no fool, after all. Yet I found myself almost incapable of forcing out a reply. The secret had been a secret for so long—I felt that giving utterance to it might bring down some dreadful calamity upon us.

Eventually, after a long hesitation, I told him the truth. And in so doing I took a risk that I would not have taken if I had been in any doubt as to the depth of his regard for me.

Because I was entrusting him with my life. Make no mistake about that. I would have done nothing so foolhardy, had his soul not been in danger.

'Martin,' I said, 'those books were given to me by the Inquisitor of Toulouse. I am his agent. I have served him since I was not much older than you.'

He caught his breath, and I waited. It is no easy task to accept that a friend is really a stranger. I saw Martin swallow my unpalatable revelation like a sharp bone; he grimaced, and frowned, and for an instant I thought that he might recoil. If he had, I would not have blamed him. Even among the highest prelates in Christendom, a papal inquisitor has very few friends. And among the lower orders he has none at all—except a handful of people like me.

It must be confessed that I watched Martin with great vigilance, poised to take action lest he bolt for the door. Though I doubted that he would, one must always be prepared for the worst. And let me add that he would have suffered no hurt, had he decided to betray my secret.

I would merely have confined him somewhere while I made my escape.

'Then you have been spying on them?' he said at last, in a very small voice. 'On the Beguins?'

'Yes.'

'For the Inquisitor of Toulouse?'

'Yes.'

'Why?'

I could have told him what my master had told me. I could have lectured him on the fatal arrogance of heretical creeds, and why there are certain tasks—like the slaughtering of vermin—which, though unpleasant, must be undertaken for the purpose of ensuring a healthy existence.

But I did not. Instead my reply was merely, 'Because I believed that I had no choice.'

He was silent. All at once I could not endure his solemn regard, and turned my face towards the window.

'The Beguins are misguided—you must not think otherwise,' I continued. 'Nevertheless, I cannot betray them. Not now. If I do, they will give your name to Jean de Beaune, and you will be arrested.'

'They—they might not tell . . .' Martin stammered, at which point I realised that he understood fully the consequences of what he had done.

'They will tell,' I stated flatly. 'Believe me.'

'Then—'

'If I run, you will be safe for a while—but only until the Beguins are found out. And they *will* be found out. They are too rash to escape detection forever.' I noticed that it was growing dark very quickly, and wondered if I should light a lamp before we were both engulfed in impenetrable darkness. 'If you come with me,' I added, turning back to him, 'you will never be discovered. I can promise that. I have one skill in which I excel above all other men, and that is the skill of disappearing. It is what has kept me alive all these years.'

There was another pause. As Martin leaned over to scratch his leg, his shadowed face was completely hidden from view.

After a while he said, in muffled accents, 'Will I be able to return?'

'No.'

'Not ever? Not even when I am old?'

'Martin, understand this.' I spoke a little coldly, perhaps, but the point had to be made clear. 'If you leave here with me, you will be dead to your family. It must be so. For if you ever approach them again, they will only be able to ensure their own safety by betraying you to the inquisitors. Would you force them to make such a choice?'

'I—'

'You must do as you think fit. I cannot decide for you. I merely offer you my protection because I am the one who has destroyed your life.'

His drooping spine jerked upright. 'Oh *no*, Master!'

'Yes.'

'No, no, you—I—there was never *anyone* as good to me as you!'

I stood up then. Truth be told, I could not bear to hear him expand on this subject. His words were like coals of fire heaped upon my head.

'Your mother cares for you,' I insisted. 'You must think carefully before leaving her, because once you have made your choice, it cannot be unmade.'

'Master—'

'Think. Think while I light a lamp.'

I took a lamp, and went downstairs and ignited it. Having done so, I discovered that I was sweating—and for a short while remained in the shop, trying to recover my appearance of equanimity. I did not want Martin to see me with ragged breath and trembling lips. It would have caused him to doubt my strength of mind.

The fact is, I had run a very grave risk. And no one, after endangering himself in such a way, is likely to remain unaffected. No matter how brave and resolute he might be.

I myself can lay claim to only a modest amount of courage. Therefore I suffered the inevitable reaction.

Finally (by various means which I have perfected, over the years) my agitation was conquered. I was calm again. So I picked up my lamp and climbed the stairs, telling myself all the while that I was a hundred kinds of fool. No man in my position should be encumbering himself with a boy. Though shackled by his conscience, a sensible familiar—having made his offer of protection—would have prayed that this offer was not accepted.

Yet despite all my fears and doubts, I nursed deep within me a kind of reluctant hope. For I had realised that, against a lifetime's expectations, I might not have to die a lonely death.

'Master,' he said, before I had reached the top stair. 'Master, I have decided.'

'Already?'

'Master, I want to go with you.'

XXI.
Easter Saturday (noon)

I have been very busy since I made my last entry in this journal. Events are outrunning my ability to record them.

Last night, after Martin had made his choice, I sent him back to his family. I told him that our escape would have to be carefully planned, and that I would need time in which to make preparations. Then, my fate having been sealed, I sat down to contemplate the future with a much cooler head than I had boasted hitherto. As I mentioned before, once uncertainty is banished, and I have a definite purpose or destination in mind, then I am apt to become more tranquil.

I made various decisions concerning my property. There is a public notary whose services I engaged when I purchased this house; he is an able, distinguished and immensely discreet old man, incapable of defrauding or misleading his clients. I believe that I might safely employ him to sell my house and pass on the proceeds without endangering his reputation in any way. Of course, he could not with decency be approached until Monday at the earliest. No sane man would try to transact any kind of business on Easter Sunday.

As for my destination, after much thought I decided that I would take a barge from La Barque to the coast, and there find a passage east—from Leucate, perhaps. The trick would be to avoid setting sail from any port at which I had landed, for in that case my movements could easily be tracked from records such as the pilgrim lists in the communal cartularies. (Marseilles, I know, keeps excellent lading and passenger records.) Once landed, I could perhaps make my way on foot to another port—the busier the better—and from there board a galley headed for Genoa, or Sicily. Italy would be safer than Provence, I think, now that the Pope is living at Avignon. And I know from talking with Bernard Gui, and Pierre Autier, and even some of the tanners down by the river, that many exiles from my country can be found in the northern marches and southern tip of the Italian peninsula. I would not, in either Messina or Lombardy, be as visible as I might elsewhere prove to be, as a lone foreigner. And I would also have the comfort of a shared tongue.

Naturally, the expense of such a journey will be very great. So although I can afford to wait for the price of my house—as long as it reaches me before Pentecost—I must sell all my tools and furniture as soon as possible. This will cause no little stir. I was wondering how the sale might be effected in a stealthy manner when my eyelids began to feel heavy, and I realised that it was growing late.

Once in bed, I drifted off without much delay. Before unconsciousness claimed me, however, my drowsy thoughts did snag on two features of my latest visit to the Donas shop. First of all, I pondered Berengar Blanchi's remarkable lie. At the time of its utterance, I had been preoccupied with other matters. But the more I considered it, the more it suggested to me that something was not right. Jacques Bonet, as I knew well, had not been in imminent danger of arrest. On the contrary. So where had this lie come from? Surely not from Jacques himself? Though he might have been desperate to escape Jean de Beaune's clutches, only a fool would have claimed to be the subject of an inquisitorial investigation. Because such a lie would easily have frightened his heretical friends into killing him.

Of course, he might indeed have been a fool. I have heard nothing to suggest the opposite. But even so, I was puzzled—and aware of a growing disquiet. If the source of the lie was Berengar Blanchi, or Imbert Rubei, then their motives demand some sort of inquiry. In my opinion.

The other mystery concerned Imbert's house. The proposal that I be concealed there had met with an extraordinarily sharp response. Berengar had been adamant that Imbert's privacy not be invaded. And Berengaria Donas, upon being reminded of this, had been abjectly apologetic.

It seemed to me that Imbert must be hiding something—or someone—in his house. Not Jacques, though; of that I was convinced. Jacques had not been seen in the vicinity of Imbert's house in six months, according to the innkeeper who lived opposite. How could Jacques have been confined indoors for *six months*? Unless he was dead. But if that were the case, his corpse would have been removed. Or at least hidden. It would not be so openly displayed that visitors would have to be discouraged, surely?

I was speculating on this matter when I fell asleep. Some time later, I awoke to see that it was still dark outside, and my heart sank—for I knew that I would not be able to sleep again. (The symptoms of extended wakefulness are familiar to me, after many years of restless nights.) I therefore rose and went to write in this journal, completing my last entry just as dawn's light began to arouse Narbonne. Then I dressed myself. Make no mistake, it was still very early. I had no expectation of seeing even Martin at this point, let alone any of my neighbours.

I was consequently very much taken aback when someone knocked on my front door. I had just begun to take inventory of my stock, in preparation for its sale; when I threw open the shutters, and peered out my workshop window, I saw that a shrouded figure stood below me, barely visible in the filmy light.

The creak of hinges alerted my visitor. Before I could issue any sort of challenge a pale face was lifted, and I recognised Berengaria Donas. She placed a finger to her lips.

Then, with more urgent gestures, she indicated that she wished to talk with me in private.

My amazement can easily be imagined. On my way down to admit her, I armed myself with a knife from my workshop—since it is always best to be prepared. The thought crossed my mind that, should Adhemar or any of my other neighbours chance to observe Berengaria's entry, word would soon spread that I had a lover. What other cause but dalliance would drive a woman to seek my company at such an hour?

'You should not have come,' I whispered, as she brushed past me on the threshold. 'You could have been seen.'

'There is no one about,' she rejoined. 'Besides, I wore my hood up.'

'Even so.' I barred the door, and surveyed her with a kind of wary interest. Her cheeks were flushed, and her eyes bright. She looked excited. 'Why are you here?' I asked.

'To bring news.' With her customary self-assurance she flung off her cloak, and seated herself on the nearest stool. Her sweeping glance seemed to take cognisance of, and at the same time summarily dismiss, every humble item in our immediate vicinity. 'Berengar Blanchi came again yesterday,' she went on. 'He had spoken to Imbert Rubei. They have devised a plan for your rescue.'

'Then you had better relate it to me upstairs.' I did not want my tenants to overhear this. 'If you have no objection.'

She admitted to none—and indeed, she had always presented the appearance of a woman sublimely unconcerned about her own reputation for marital virtue. Perhaps she regards this as a petty preoccupation, compared to the much more worthy principle of evangelical poverty. Perhaps her wealth gives her a confidence not easily felt by those who must rely on the goodwill of family or friends, and who are therefore obliged to regulate their conduct.

Or perhaps she is one of those rare souls who are oblivious to questions of gender and purity. I can understand this. While some clerics of my acquaintance never cease to fret over every aspect of the subject, I myself regard it as being of limited interest.

There are far more dangerous and perplexing things to worry about, in my view.

'That is a fine linen chest,' said Berengaria, upon reaching my workroom. 'Sturdy but simple. Is it oak?'

'Yes.'

'Very handsome. There is no sin in preserving one's cloth from harm, as long as the cloth is plain.'

'What did you want to tell me, Na Berengaria?'

'Only this.' She turned from the chest. 'If you will pack up a few possessions, and come to my house as soon as possible, I will hide you in my vineyard. Then tonight you can climb over the city wall. Imbert will meet you on the other side, and take you to a boat moored downstream. In this way you will not have to pass through the gates, and no one will detain you.'

Now it so happens that last night, along with all my other musings, I had asked myself what I should do with regard to the Beguins. And it had crossed my mind that leaving them ignorant might not be the best choice. On the one hand, I was reluctant to share my secret with such a painfully injudicious group of people. On the other hand, my first object was to delay for as long as possible the Beguins' arrest—since this would inevitably result in Martin's name becoming known to Jean de Beaune, and the Moresi becoming subject to interrogation.

It had occurred to me that if the Beguins could be persuaded to leave Narbonne (or, at the very least, to avoid welcoming into their midst yet another inquisitorial agent), then I myself would be better protected. So when Na Berengaria revealed her plan, I did not put her off with vague protestations. Nor did I make promises that I had no intention of keeping.

Instead I studied her face, noting its fine-grained skin and noble measurements, its indestructibly artless yet somewhat imperious expression. It must be said that I can find in my heart no trace of contempt for this woman. Exasperation, perhaps. Impatience, certainly. But her generosity has been of a very rare order, and her disposition is one of the most upright and amiable that I have ever encountered among the heretics of this world. Being myself steeped in duplicity, I recognise no trace of it in her. Were she not so proud, she would be altogether admirable.

I understood that she would not knowingly betray me, once the truth had been revealed. That is why, without preamble, I suddenly remarked: 'Your concern for me is misplaced. I am in no danger from Bernard Gui, at present. Nor from any other inquisitor of heretical depravity.'

She blinked. But she said nothing.

'That summons was neither written nor sent by Bernard Gui,' I continued. 'It was forged by someone known to Father Sejan Alegre—for what purpose I am still unsure. Perhaps to test my true allegiance.'

'But—'

'Wait.' I held up my hand. 'Hear me out, then judge for yourself. I know Bernard Gui's writing very well. Because I myself am an agent of Bernard Gui, just as Jacques Bonet was an agent of Jean de Beaune.'

Still she seemed not to understand. Her evident perplexity gave way to no look of dawning horror.

'Jacques Bonet was instructed to seek out any unidentified Beguins of Narbonne,' I explained. 'But he vanished. So I was told to discover his whereabouts. I am no Beguin, Mistress. And never was.'

'No.' She shook her head, a stunned half-smile flickering across her stricken features. 'No, you're—you're lying.'

'I *have* lied to you. But no longer. You must believe me when I say that I have had a change of heart.'

Her breathing quickened. All at once, her face lost its colour; it became ashen, and she stumbled backwards. The truth had suddenly hit her—as truth often will—with the force of a crossbow-bolt.

I caught her arm to steady her.

'Listen to me,' I said. 'You will come to no harm through *my* actions. I intend to leave here as soon as possible. I intend to disappear. But if you remain, Mistress, you will suffer the same fate as the men and women whose relics you venerate.' As she lowered herself weakly onto my linen chest, gaping like a fish, I tried to impress upon her the extremely vulnerable nature of her position. 'Do you understand?' I went on. 'Your group is in grave danger. You have been far too trusting. You have freely embraced two impostors; if you embrace one more, you will surely come to grief.'

'Jacques Bonet.' She was staring at me, wide-eyed. Her hand flew to her mouth. 'Not Jacques. No. Not Jacques!'

'He secured his freedom by pledging his service—'

'But he was at Imbert's house! He was *living* there!' Her voice cracked on a shrill note, as she moved both hands to her temples in an attitude of the most profound anguish. 'God help us, what if he *saw*? What if he *knows*?' She caught her breath, and sprang to her feet. 'What if he told them?' she whispered, clutching my wrist.

'Told whom?' I demanded. 'About what?'

Already, however, she had let me go. She glanced towards the stairs, and was about to bolt when I detained her. Though she is a tall woman, and sturdy, she is not my equal in strength. She could not shake me off.

'Wait,' I said.

'He must be warned!'

'Who?'

'Imbert!' There were tears in her eyes. Every vestige of benign self-confidence had left her. 'I have to tell him! They're not safe any more—they have to be moved! Let *go*, you fool!'

'Wait,' I repeated, and turned her frantic face towards mine. Her flesh beneath my fingers was as soft as silk. '*What* has to be moved? Tell me.'

She hesitated, open-mouthed. Slowly she seemed to realise the full import of what she had just revealed; with enormous effort she recovered a small portion of her customary composure.

'I—I cannot say,' she replied. 'It would be a sin to tell you.'

'A sin?'

'Yes.'

'A sin.' I released her chin, but not her arm. 'That would suggest Imbert is concealing something very precious. Even holy.' I studied her with interest. 'More remains, perhaps?' Her sudden quiver confirmed it. 'Whose remains?'

'Please—'

'Remains that demand far more protection than the relics in your own house, which have been exposed to the gaze of a virtual stranger.' I was thinking aloud, and reviewing a certain conversation in my head. 'Remains that have been hidden even from your friend Blaise . . .' Suddenly, by some divine intervention, the answer came to me. It was so obvious, yet so incredible.

I gasped, and my grip on her arm tightened.

'The bones,' I said. 'The bones of Pierre Jean Olivi.'

I felt absolutely confident, and my confidence was well founded. Berengaria did not attempt to deny that I was right.

Rather, she burst into tears.

'Oh, *please*!' she sobbed. 'Please . . .'

'Shh!'

'Do not betray me! Do not—please—I have broken my vow . . .'

The rush of calculation that followed close upon my discovery prevented me from offering her any comfort. I stood quite still, as half a dozen different notions fought for supremacy inside my skull.

Then gradually her distress penetrated the cloud of abstraction in which I had lost myself. She had collapsed back onto my linen chest, a mere shadow of the stately woman who had entered my workroom. It saddened me somewhat, to see her brought so low.

Nevertheless, I would not be distracted from the subject at hand.

'I thought that Olivi's bones were destroyed.' Such had been the gossip, in any event. 'I thought that the Dominicans took them.'

'They did,' Berengaria whimpered. 'But Father Sejan gained custody of them, and gave them to Imbert Rubei.'

'How?'

'He paid money. Our money. Mine and Imbert's.'

'To whom?'

'I know not.'

'A Dominican?'

'I know not.'

'It must have been paid to a Dominican. A Dominican who was charged with their disposal.' I have to confess, I was growing excited. 'The same Dominican who forged that summons, I guarantee it!'

'What?'

'Listen to me. This is important.' Dragging over my stool, I sat down opposite Berengaria, and placed a hand on her knee. 'Father Sejan has known for some time that I am an agent of Bernard Gui. He has *known* that I was told to look for Jacques Bonet.'

'How—how could he—?'

'Never mind that. He discovered that I was making inquiries about Jacques Bonet's corpse.'

'His *corpse?*'

'Shh! Listen.'

'You mean he is *dead*?'

'That I cannot tell you. But make no mistake, Mistress—Sejan can. And Imbert too, perhaps.'

Berengaria then fixed me with a look so pitifully baffled, so defeated and dismayed, that it smote my conscience. I forgot to consider my own advantage, and sought only to clarify matters for her.

'Sejan discovered that I was making inquiries about Jacques Bonet. But did he tell you that? No,' I pointed out. 'Instead, he alerted his friend the Dominican. And the Dominican, because he lives at the priory, was able to tell him that one Helié Seguier, a parchment-maker, had met with Bernard Gui. Sejan and his friend must then have concluded that I was an agent of the inquisitor. Whereupon they forged a summons—still without telling the rest of you.'

'I—I don't understand . . .'

'Neither do I. But I can hazard a guess as to what they were about.' Noting her blank expression, I leaned forward, impelling her to meet my gaze. 'Only consider,' I said firmly. 'The day before I received that forged letter, Berengar Blanchi came to you. I saw him leave your house. He went straight afterwards to his cousin Sejan, at St-Just. Why did Berengar visit you that day? Was it to ask about me?' Her eyes were stunned, empty of all comprehension. 'Think!' I snapped. 'Please! It was last Wednesday!'

But she was latching onto inessentials. 'How do you know that Berengar Blanchi and Father Sejan are cousins?' she asked, in childish astonishment.

'Just answer my question! *Is that when you first told him about me?*'

'No. At least—no.' At last, with a visible effort, she turned her attention to Berengar Blanchi. 'He already knew about you,' she admitted. 'I had mentioned your name to Imbert when I went to buy silk—'

'When was that?'

'Oh—'

'Was it before Palm Sunday?'

'Yes.' She nodded, unable to detach her gaze from mine. 'The day before. And a few days later Berengar Blanchi came, and wanted to know if I had told you about . . .' The words caught in her throat. She had to swallow them, and try again. 'About the bones,' she sighed at last.

'Ah.'

'I was not to tell you about the bones. On any account.'

'Did Berengar say why?'

'Because they are a great secret.' All at once the tears welled up in her eyes; I could see them gleaming. 'And now you know!' she whispered, clearly appalled at her own weakness.

'Your secret is safe with me. I am a graveyard of secrets.' With a strong sense of satisfaction, I began to piece together all those disparate elements that for so long had seemed unrelated. On the Thursday before Holy Week, Na Berengaria had invited me to Sunday prayers. On the Saturday following, she had mentioned this to Imbert. On the day after, Sejan had sent his creature Loup to track my movements as I left the Donas shop.

Meanwhile, Sejan had delivered to me the Archbishop's report. And by Wednesday of Holy Week, Berengar Blanchi was insisting that I not be told about Olivi's bones.

Unless I am mistaken, Sejan must have consulted his friend, the unknown Dominican, on Monday or Tuesday of Holy Week and learned of my visit with Bernard Gui. Whereupon, having pooled the information gathered from three sources, they had seen what it implied, and started to panic.

I stood up, and began to pace the floor.

'For a week now, Sejan and his friend the Dominican have been aware of my secret. There can be no doubt of that,' I mused aloud. 'They forged the summons because they were convinced of my treachery.'

'But how can you possibly know?'

'I *know*. I know Bernard Gui. I know his writing. I know his habits. He would not have sent me that letter. *Sejan* sent me that letter, and the Dominican wrote it. My question to you is: Why?' I stopped, and swung around to confront Berengaria. 'Was it to see how I responded? Clearly, if I had obeyed without protest, I would have proven myself a spy. But in that case, why were you yourself not informed? *Why?*'

She waited. And indeed, I was not expecting an answer. For while the woman might be damned, she is in many ways honest and ingenuous. Although busily condemning herself to certain death with every word that she utters and every stranger that she trusts, she would never condemn another to the same fate.

'It is my belief that the priest and the monk are planning to kill me,' I said. 'For what other purpose would they want to lure me into the grounds of the priory at such a late hour?'

'Oh no.' Sure enough, she refused to countenance such a suggestion. Instead she shook her head, with mounting energy. 'No, no. Impossible.'

'Then why was I the one to tell you my secret? Why did *they* not inform you?'

'Because—because—'

'Because they must have known that you would object to their plan!' It seemed so clear to me that I became impatient with her obtuseness. 'You might be a heretic, Mistress, but you are no murderer. You would not wear *that* sin on your conscience.'

This compliment failed to appease her. She covered her face with her hands, as if to escape from an intolerable sight.

'You must be wrong,' she faltered. 'I cannot—your mind is—these are wicked thoughts . . .'

'The world is full of wicked thoughts. You must understand that, or you will perish.' Believe me when I say that it required some strength to continue. I was all at once mortally tired; forcing Na Berengaria to accept the truth was far more difficult than I had anticipated. 'Berengar Blanchi told you a lie when he said that Jacques Bonet was about to be arrested.' This was another fact worthy of remark. 'I should like to know where that lie came from. Perhaps from Jacques Bonet, though I have my doubts. While he may have hoped to fashion a quick escape by telling such a lie, he must have known that it might easily have the opposite effect, and frighten his friends into killing him. On the other hand, if the lie came from Sejan, or Imbert, or Berengar himself, then what is the reason for it? Why dream up such an excuse for Jacques's sudden disappearance? The only reason I can think of is guilt, and fear. Because Jacques is dead.'

'No!' Na Berengaria clamped her hands over her ears. 'I refuse to listen any more! Jacques escaped!'

'How do you know?'

'He did! He did!'

'*How do you know?*' But I had spoken too loudly, and made haste to lower my voice. 'Did you see him?' I hissed. 'Did you speak to him?' Exasperated by her attitude of rejection, I went over and prised her hands off her ears. 'Do you really comprehend what this means?' I demanded. 'A monk of St Dominic was paid money to disobey his superior. He committed a heretical act by surrendering those bones to Berengar Blanchi's cousin. *You* might be happy to martyr yourself in the name of Pierre Jean Olivi, but no venal Dominican will want to follow your example! He will do everything in his power to prevent it. Any man facing ruin, and perhaps even death, might contemplate murder to protect himself—especially a man who has already risked his life for *money*.' As Berengaria's hands twisted in mine like a pair of small, captive creatures, I clasped them with iron resolve, and would not allow her to look away. I bent down, so that my head was level with her own. And I held her gaze pinioned.

'If Jacques Bonet was living with Imbert, there is every chance that he uncovered the secret of Olivi's bones,' I said. 'In which case, he might have identified the source of those bones. And if our Dominican friend knew it, he might have felt sorely threatened. He might have behaved rashly. Rashness is not out of character, I think. It was rash to sell you those bones in the first place. God knows what he needed the money for. A whore? A poor relative? A blackmailer?'

'What shall I do?' It was a mere breath of sound, accompanied by a glance of abject entreaty. 'What am I going to do?'

'You need to find out what is happening—and so do I. This Dominican cannot be trusted. If he has killed Jacques, then clearly he will stop at nothing to protect himself. Nothing. Do you understand?'

Of course she did not. She searched my face for enlightenment, and I stamped my foot in frustration.

'Berengaria, *think*,' I groaned. 'You are not stupid. Suppose that I disappear. What will he believe? He will believe that I have gone to Bernard Gui—and he will be very frightened. Though unaware that I have learned of Olivi's relics, he must realise by now that I have furnished myself with a lot of Beguin names. Your own. Imbert's. Even Berengar Blanchi's. The trail will lead any good inquisitor to Sejan Alegre, and from Sejan to his friend the friar.'

'What are you saying?'

'I am *saying* that the Dominican will kill again. If he feels that he is in danger.'

'Oh no!' She recoiled.

'Why not? If he has killed once, why not again? Sejan is the biggest threat to him. And Imbert, too. Imbert has the bones. If the bones are ever discovered, it will be obvious that whoever was given the job of burning or discarding them must be culpable.' Conscious that her hands were now motionless, I dropped them. I straightened. And I remarked, with some relief, that she was knitting her brow in thought. 'As for you, Mistress, you know about those relics,' I added. 'You are in as much peril as Imbert. Oh, yes.' (For her head had jerked up in alarm.) 'You should think very, very carefully about your future dealings with these men. At present, they are a much graver threat to you than Jean de Beaune.'

'Advise me, then.'

'What?'

'Advise me.' A trace of the old Berengaria was evident in her tone: the composed, imposing, authoritative Berengaria. She lifted her chin and squared her shoulders. 'You, Master Helié—you are clever. Cunning. Far more so than the men against whom you have warned me. What would you advise me to do?' Suddenly, her voice cracked. 'How am I to protect my friends from such wickedness?'

Once again, she was placing her trust in the wrong person. There was I, a traitor. A liar. A spy whose own interests would best be served if Berengaria *was* dead—and all her friends along with her. After all, without their testimony, how could Martin ever be condemned? If they were every one of them dead, I could make my report freely, in the certain knowledge that I would not be implicating Martin by doing so. Since even Bernard Gui cannot extract names from a corpse.

Yet despite my demonstrated perfidy, Na Berengaria persisted in believing that I would help her—perhaps because I had helped her already. Standing at the window, surveying the bleak, raw, morning sky over the rooftops, I marvelled at my own imprudence. A wise man would have abandoned her to her inevitable fate. A wise man would have told her some lie, to prevent her from alerting Sejan and his friends too soon, before preparing for a hurried and secret withdrawal.

But what is true wisdom? *God hath chosen the foolish things of the world to confound the wise*; I remembered this lesson as I marked the small signs by which my neighbours attested to their wakefulness. I noted Adhemar's daughter, trudging towards the well. I traced the passage of a piss-pot's contents as they were hurled out of an open door. I smelled smoke, and heard Martin's mother calling to her fowl. In every small action, I detected many things—including the hand of God.

And I thought: Why should I run like a skulking, frightened rat from this unholy monk? From this pitiful priest?

'We can lay a trap,' I said, turning back to Berengaria. 'Tonight, if you want. We can lay a trap for the Dominican.'

XXII.
Easter Saturday (afternoon)

Blaise Bouer just arrived bearing fresh news. The trap has been set: Na Berengaria has made her final arrangements with Imbert Rubei.

She left here this morning not long before Martin brought me my food. Her stated intention was to seek out Imbert immediately, but she must have explained matters to Blaise first. That is why I had to wait so long. I completed my second journal entry during the long hours between tierce and sext, while Martin emptied the vats downstairs, bucket by bucket.

I had explained to him that the job must be done quietly, for I did not want excessive amounts of hustle and bustle to draw the attention of my neighbours. Ideally, I should like to be far from Narbonne before anyone realises that I am gone—though Martin will not, of course, be prevented from alerting his family. I can hardly expect him to leave without saying goodbye. Nevertheless, I made it clear to him that when the time does come, there will be no loud lamentations or lavish farewell feasts. A sudden announcement will precede one hurried exchange of paternal advice and heartfelt good wishes. Then, without fanfare, we shall quit Narbonne.

'Not tonight, however,' I assured him. 'Tonight we are only *pretending* to quit Narbonne.'

And I described to him my plan, which only made sense after I had also described our entire predicament. Believe me when I say that it was not an easy task. Nor was it speedily accomplished. Poor Martin sat with a creased brow and a slack jaw as I summarised all my convoluted speculations about Sejan, Berengar, Loup, Imbert, Jacques and the unknown Dominican. In some cases, of course, I had reached no final conclusions. While Sejan and the Dominican are quite evidently implicated in Jacques Bonet's disappearance, I am uncertain about Berengar Blanchi. Like Na Berengaria, he may have been duped into believing that Jacques Bonet *did* escape. He may not have formulated the lie that he told; perhaps he has been used, as a tool and a messenger, by his cousin Sejan—or by Imbert Rubei. Imbert's role is also unclear, though I am inclined to be more suspicious of him. If Jacques Bonet was supposed to have been smuggled out of Narbonne by one of Imbert's friends—and then was not—Imbert Rubei must surely have known his true fate.

I expressed some of my doubts to Martin, who had to keep asking for clarification with regard to dates and times. He was also largely uninformed about the disappearance of Pierre Olivi's bones. ('I knew they were buried at the Franciscan priory,' he remarked, 'but I never knew that the

Dominicans moved them.') Nevertheless, being a clever boy, he came to grasp the fundamental points of my narrative. And when he learned that he would be taking part in the unmasking of a corrupt Dominican, he became very excited. *Too* excited. Watching his eyes gleam, and his wide, disarming grin engulf almost half his face, I realised suddenly that, for all his intelligence, Martin is still thinking like a child. He has a child's view of the world; to him it is still a vivid and exciting habitation of good and bad men in heroic conflict—of epic journeys, angelic intervention, and pots of gold waiting in hidden places.

To some degree, I was already aware of this. I had known of his fondness for scriptural narrative and colourful gossip. I had sometimes fed his desperate hunger for stories culled from my past (heavily edited). But it had not occurred to me, until then, that his attachment to me was based on more than the contrast between his father's rough handling and my own more gentle deportment.

All at once, it became apparent that Martin sees me as a figure of mystery and adventure. My secret life, once uncovered, must have seemed to him immeasurably thrilling when compared to his own plodding, disregarded, under-nourished existence. First I had introduced him to the delights of the written word. Then I had opened his eyes to the hidden meanings of dress, speech, gesture and the positioning of telltale scars. Finally, I had revealed myself to be a man absorbed in all manner of intrigue and subversion.

Is it any wonder that he threw in his lot with me? That he has decided to forsake his family to follow my star?

But it is done for the wrong reasons. For childish reasons. *When I was a child, I spake as a child, I understood as a child, I thought as a child: but when I became a man, I put away childish things.*

What will happen when Martin becomes a man? For he will not remain a child long—not if he comes with me.

God grant that, in taking him from here, I will inflict on him less harm than he would suffer if he stayed.

'Martin,' I warned him, 'this is no game, such as you play with your brothers and sisters.'

'No, Master.' His tone was reproachful. 'Of course not.'

'You must be vigilant. Cautious. You must do *exactly* as I tell you.'

'Yes, Master.'

'I would prefer that you were not involved. It worries me. But I have no choice—I must ensure that the Dominican is distracted. And he would be suspicious if anyone else appeared in your stead.'

Martin nodded eagerly. His solemn manner, though well meant, did not convince me that he truly understood the dangers that confronted us. So I got up and went to my frame, which stands near the workroom window. From beside it I retrieved the sharp metal stylus with which I customarily mark up my finished skins.

'Here,' I said. 'Take this with you tonight. Conceal it under your clothes. If anyone should attack you, shove it directly into his eye, if possible.'

It would be wrong to say that Martin flinched. But he certainly blinked, and looked startled enough to reassure me.

Perhaps I have finally managed to impress him with the seriousness of our situation.

Blaise needed no convincing. He came, as I said, not long ago—surprising me a little. (For I was expecting Na Berengaria.) Martin was downstairs when the tailor knocked, and called me away from this journal; having been instructed not to open the door to *anyone*, my apprentice very properly sought permission before even replying to Blaise's request for admittance.

I immediately sent the boy back upstairs. And I was very careful when I unbarred the door. Though I see no particular reason to distrust Blaise, I did not quickly relinquish the heavy slab of wood with which I secure my shop, even after he had crossed the threshold. One must always be prepared, as I have said.

'Na Berengaria sent me,' he announced, slamming the door behind him. He thereupon fixed me with a look so openly contemptuous that I immediately understood two things: first, that Berengaria had revealed to him my entire secret, and second, that he was not inclined to be as forgiving as she was.

I had anticipated no freely bestowed absolution from Blaise Bouer. He is an altogether different type from the lady he serves, being driven by an obscure, festering resentment. This anger, while it gives him courage, must inevitably saddle him also with the most ferocious and abiding grudges.

Nevertheless, it has worked to my advantage. Granted that there is nothing a rancorous man appreciates less than being fooled. Granted that I myself had fooled him. A violent and uncooperative response would not be unexpected, in such circumstances.

But it must not be forgotten than I am practically a stranger to Blaise. Berengar Blanchi and Imbert Rubei, in contrast, call themselves his friends and brothers in Christ. Yet they betrayed him by neglecting to warn him about my identity. They kept secrets and told lies. They did not treat him as a true friend.

The treachery of friends is always more difficult to endure than the treachery of strangers.

I had anticipated that Blaise would be outraged by the mere thought of his fellow Beguins conspiring together without his knowledge. And I was not disappointed. Though he surveyed me much as a knight might survey a dung heap, I sensed that the full force of his anger was being directed away from me.

'She has revealed all,' he growled. 'And I have come with her final instructions.'

'Not here,' I said quietly. 'Upstairs. No one will overhear us in my workroom.'

Though plainly disinclined to take advice from a stinking papal lackey, he must have seen the sense in this proposal. For he pursued me up the stairs, only to find Martin waiting at the top.

'Is this the same boy?' Blaise asked suspiciously, eyeing the stylus in Martin's hand. 'The one we surprised outside the house?'

'Yes.'

'Is he a creature of the inquisitors, also?'

'No.' I spoke calmly. 'He is innocent of guile, and God will therefore punish anyone who seeks to harm him.' Placing a hand on Martin's shoulder, I added, 'Once I myself have dispatched his assailant to an early grave.'

The tailor snorted. 'With poison, no doubt. Or some other underhanded method,' he snapped. '*I* am not a skulking, lying sneak, Master Helié. If I intend to harm someone, I speak of it openly. I do not come to him in the guise of a friend, and knife him when his back is turned.'

'I am pleased to hear that, Master Blaise.'

Having established that he was an honest man, the tailor went on to recount the events of the day. Apparently, Imbert had been visibly disconcerted by Na Berengaria's request that Martin accompany me over the city wall. He had raised various objections: that the bargemen were expecting only one fugitive; that two would cost more than one; that a boy could not be trusted to keep his mouth shut or obey orders. When Na Berengaria had insisted that I would not leave without Martin, he had put her off with a promise to 'think about it'—and had ejected her from his house. He would, he said, have an answer for her before the end of the day.

'He had to consult his fellow conspirators,' I remarked, upon hearing this. 'It is my belief that Imbert is well acquainted with the activities of the Dominican. Berengar Blanchi may be ignorant, but not Imbert, I feel sure. Therefore he would have wanted to speak to Sejan, at the very least.'

'Perhaps,' said Blaise. 'In any event, Imbert came to the shop not long ago with his agreement. Your apprentice, here, will be included.'

'First over the wall?'

'First over the wall.'

I must explain the reasoning behind such a strategy. The original plan, as presented by Imbert Rubei, was that I should be hidden in the Donas vineyard until it was safe to climb over the city wall. At the base of this portion of the wall—which rises hard out of a field of olives—I would be met by Imbert Rubei, who would conduct me to a barge moored at La Barque, on the river.

But I have a strong suspicion that the barge will not appear. Rather than being conducted to a place of refuge, I will probably be killed. Who exactly has undertaken to accomplish this act, I have no way of knowing; any number of people might be capable of it. Imbert. Sejan. Even Berengar Blanchi.

It is my belief, however, that the Dominican, at least, will meet me at the bottom of that wall. He has already tried to summon me to his priory with a forged letter. And if that was his first attempt to have me killed, then he was almost certainly planning to do it himself.

Naturally, I cannot be certain of this. But the possibility is strong enough to merit extreme caution henceforth. That is why Blaise and I will conceal ourselves in the vicinity of the chosen olive grove far ahead of time. That is why Martin must be sent over the wall, as a distraction—for while my apprentice is climbing down his allotted length of rope, the attention of those awaiting him will be wholly directed towards his descending figure.

At which point, Blaise and I will surprise the attackers into surrendering their weapons. And, perhaps, into telling the truth.

But Blaise had misgivings.

'Do we really need the boy?' he objected. 'If you came over yourself, I could lie in wait with Guillaume, or Perrin.'

'*Perrin?*' I blinked, assailed by a mental picture of that fragile, passive, unworldly creature. 'Are you joking?'

'Well—perhaps not Perrin,' Blaise conceded. 'But Guillaume—'

'Is the size of a house,' I finished. 'It will be hard enough to find cover for ourselves, let alone a man of Guillaume's considerable girth. So unless Na Berengaria's sturdy husband is willing to lend us his assistance . . . ?'

'No,' said Blaise.

'No. I thought not. And Guillelma, though doubtless willing, would not have the required strength. Therefore we *shall* need Martin.'

Blaise had to agree. We made arrangements to meet each other at the Royal Gate, after the bells have rung to signal the end of nones. This will give us a couple of hours before the gates close at sunset; we shall have ample time in which to conceal ourselves somewhere advantageous.

'Though it worries me that we must hide ourselves in the fields of St Felix,' Blaise fretted. 'The olive trees there are neither very high nor very thick. They are well spaced, and there are no stooks or barns or fences—certainly none close to the walls.'

It is a problem, I had to agree. Neither of us are well acquainted with the area adjacent to Na Berengaria's vineyard, on the other side of the city wall. We cannot be certain that we shall find there an overgrown hollow, or a bushy copse of wild oak. So I hit upon a solution.

'Have Na Berengaria gather up all the wood she can,' I suggested. 'Olive wood, if possible. Vine branches, logs, faggots—scrappy fuel, in part. Just as long as it hasn't been shaped or worked in any way. Then have her bind it together in several large bundles, and throw them over the wall at the end of nones.'

Blaise began to nod.

'So that we may collect them!' he exclaimed.

'And heap the wood up over us.' I wanted to be sure that he understood. 'As if the monks of St Felix have been clearing and stacking, but have yet to haul in the timber.'

'A very good notion.' For the first time, Blaise regarded me with something like approval. 'But what of the noise when we emerge?'

'We must construct a kind of tunnel, or exit. In any case, my intention is that we attack so quickly that they have no time to respond to any noise.' I cocked my head. 'Have you considered your weapon, Master Blaise?'

His manner immediately became furtive. Glancing about the room, he lowered both his head and his voice.

'A sword,' he murmured.

'A *sword*?' This was wholly unexpected. 'You have a *sword*? *You*?'

'Shh.' He seemed offended at my astonishment—for all that he is a tailor, and no knight or mercenary. 'I *have* served on the city militia, you know.'

'Is that how you came by it? Through some comrade in arms?'

'That is my secret,' was his rather pompous reply. 'Be assured, however, that I know how to use it.'

'Then I am confident in our victory.' What else could I say? 'My own weapon will be a dagger. But I will undertake to do my part, since I am no stranger to combat.'

Martin's eyes brightened to hear this; I am convinced that he was about to request details of my campaigning experience. Since it has involved crushing a man's skull with a rock and an axe, however, I quickly forestalled him.

'Go back to the Donas house now, and tell Na Berengaria about the wood,' I said to Blaise. 'You must take Martin with you, so that you can leave him with her. It will be her task to conduct him to the vineyard, and help him over the wall.'

Blaise nodded.

'For myself, I have one more job to complete while you are so engaged,' I continued. 'It is my belief that we will certainly flush our Dominican friend out of hiding if he has incontrovertible proof that I am a spy—and *that I do not suspect him*. Therefore I shall send a letter to the priory, addressed to Bernard Gui. The letter will be dispatched by hand of messenger—I shall pay a beggar, perhaps, or a pedlar—and it will alert our Dominican friend to the fact that I have agreed to escape Narbonne with Imbert's help. My stated reason for doing this will be the desire to uncover yet more Beguin sympathisers, such as the bargemen entrusted with my safety. When the Dominican sees this letter, it should make him believe that I will simply walk into his trap, all unsuspecting—'

Suddenly, I stopped. A thought had struck me with all the impact of an arrow. I stared at Blaise.

'What?' he said, frowning.

'I know who it is.'

'Eh?'

'The Dominican. I know who it must be.' Thinking aloud, I counted the reasons off on my fingers. 'He would be the logical choice for the job of discarding Olivi's bones. He would know who has arrived and who has left the priory. He would know how to read langue d'oc but not Latin, because he is a lay brother. And he could be sure that if I sent a reply to his forged letter, it would not reach the hands of any other Dominican.'

Blaise waited. Martin waited. I looked from one to the other.

'It has to be the priory porter,' I said. 'Brother Henri.'

This meant nothing to them. Why should it? They would have had no reason to visit the Dominican priory, or knock on that little door leading into the cloister. Nor would they have been subjected to Brother Henri's brusque and discourteous welcomes. And they were clearly disconcerted when I laughed, because the matter did not seem to them in the least humorous.

But it is. I find it very funny that I shall be able to revenge myself, at long last, on a man who has slammed the door in my face at least half a dozen times.

There remained little else to say, or to prepare. I did warn Blaise that he should dress in very dull colours before joining me at the Royal Gate; greys, blacks, browns or muddy greens will be suitable. I also advised him to don a hooded cloak. And I requested that he bring some rope or cord, with which to bind our captives if necessary.

'You must understand,' I said, as he opened his mouth, 'that these men may very well be dangerous. The Dominican, especially, has demonstrated a good deal of cunning, and a venal attitude that does not bode well; his anger and his discontent are manifest on his face. He may have no compunction about killing every Beguin in Narbonne if it ensured his safety. Which it *would*, Master Blaise. Have no doubt of that. With every one of you dead, he would no longer have to fear exposure.'

This point was well worth making—and the tailor absorbed it in silence. As he did so, I turned to Martin.

'You must go with Master Blaise now,' I said. 'Have no fear of what your parents might say; I will provide them with some excuse for your absence. With luck, we shall find ourselves back in this room before cock-crow, since I have every intention of returning over the wall after this affair is concluded.' Squeezing the boy's shoulder, I stooped until our eyes were level. 'Meanwhile, I would have you place yourself in Na Berengaria's care. She is a good woman, and will let you come to no harm.'

Martin's brow puckered. He glanced at Blaise, before leaning close to my ear.

'But she is a heretic,' he whispered. 'You said that the Beguins are wrong, and sinful. How could she then be good?'

There is something that Bernard Gui used to say to me, many years ago, when I was very young. *I thank thee, O Father, Lord of Heaven and Earth, that thou hast hid these things from the wise and the prudent, and hast revealed them unto babes*, he would say, with a crooked smile. It happened rarely, but always in response to some simple question of mine, which had left him oddly confounded. He explained to me that this expression of gratitude was derived from the Holy Scriptures, and that it contained an abiding truth: that sometimes even the wisest of men must receive a lesson from the simplest, and that God hath chosen the foolish things of the world to confound the wise. Because, in the words of our Lord, whosoever therefore shall humble himself as a little child, the same is greatest in the kingdom of Heaven.

'Helié,' my master told me once, 'to be great in the kingdom of Heaven is to be truly enlightened. And sometimes, only a child has the humility to see plainly what lies in front of his nose.'

I remember this remark so clearly owing to the wonder—and the rueful affection—that were evident in his voice. I felt peculiarly blessed at that moment. It was perhaps the moment at which I delivered my soul into my master's care.

As for Bernard Gui's own feelings, they are now revealed to me. For my reasoning has been suddenly overset. When Martin asked me his question, all my calm assumptions were yanked awry, upended, and exposed to an unwelcome amount of penetrating light.

I saw, in a flash, that Na Berengaria's excessive pride and Martin's excessive humility had lured them into the same error. I saw that her sins and his must therefore merit equal forgiveness; that the goodness so manifest in Martin might likewise be manifest in her. And I saw that, just as all the heretics are wrong to seek perfection in any man, so too is the Church in condemning all heretics for being misguided or mistaken. Because there is none wholly good but one, and that is God.

I thought: who am I to pass judgement on this woman, when I would extend to my apprentice infinite mercy? How is it possible that all her many virtues should be wholly undermined by her deluded beliefs, when Martin's are not?

Sitting here now, awaiting the moment when I might leave my house and make for the Royal Gate, I am a different man from the one who last wrote in this journal. My mistake was an excess of humility. Like Martin, I followed my master into falsehood. For just as the Beguins err, so too does Bernard Gui. Both believe themselves wholly right, and their opponents wholly corrupted.

I differ from them in this, and have for some time. I realise that now. Pride is at the root of error, it is true, but for one reason: it drives away all charity. How can we truly know who is doomed to eternal damnation? We cannot. We cannot *presume* to know—or to act. *Vengeance is mine; I will repay, saith the Lord.*

Martin may yet endure God's vengeance. So too may Berengaria Donas. But since they have committed no great crimes here on earth, I would hesitate to condemn them to a secular punishment. They have not killed anyone. They are not thieves. Nor are they given to lying, or cheating, or any form of violence. Their sin is rooted in a gentleness of spirit. Wherefore, because the heart is God's domain, I will judge them only by their acts. As should Bernard Gui.

When Martin looked at me, and asked his simple question, I was for a moment quite nonplussed. I could not think how to explain why Na Berengaria should be good, when she was at the same time sinful. So I said only, 'All things work together for good to them that love God,' repeating a phrase that I had once heard preached by a Dominican in the priory of Toulouse. Then I kissed Martin on both cheeks, to acknowledge my indebtedness. And I sent him away with Blaise Bouer.

Now that I have reflected on the matter, I know what I should have said. I should have said that there is no perfect goodness here on earth—but that where the spirit has no guile, and the heart no hardness, iniquity must surely yield a small place to virtue. Furthermore, I should have said one more thing, which is this: that where love is, must also reside the Holy Spirit. For the fruit of the Spirit is love. And what harm can justly be inflicted on the dwelling place of the Holy Spirit?

Perhaps, at the Last Trump, Berengaria Donas will be judged as one of the goats. But if by chance she is a lamb, how then can I lead her to the slaughter? God has chosen to gather the lambs with his strong arm, and carry them to His bosom. How can his lowly servant do any less? Is it not my *duty* to protect those in need of protection?

This is what I will say to Martin, when next I see him. And God grant that events will not conspire to withhold from him a better understanding of why I have sacrificed so much for his sake.

Extracts from the confession of Blaise Bouer, tailor of Narbonne

C. 1325

I first met the man calling himself Helié Seguier four years ago, on the feast of St Benedict. It was in Caularia Square, where I had gone to watch seventeen Beguins burned at the stake. Here I saw Helié collecting remains from the ashes. He was wearing a scarlet cloak and handsome Spanish boots. I noticed little else about him at the time, except that he was small.

Suspecting that he was a fellow believer, I approached and asked if he had known the woman whose remains he had just collected. He replied that he had not, but that he would have wished to. His voice was so soft that I could not place his accent. Because I was afraid that agents of Jean de Beaune might be watching, I went away, wondering how I might arrange a more private discussion.

Some days later, my friend Guillaume Ademar saw Helié Seguier on the streets, and followed him home. Berengaria Donas then went to visit him. She told me afterwards that he was undoubtedly a follower of Pierre Olivi, and that she had asked him to deliver some parchment to her shop. So I next saw him at Na Berengaria's shop.

I was with Na Berengaria and Guillelma Roger when he made his delivery.

I remember how, on that occasion, he seemed very suspicious of us all. This made me feel confident of his honesty. Moreover, he did not look dangerous. His demeanour was meek; his pallor suggested such a lack of blood and heat that I assumed he must be quite timorous, and was reassured. I cannot recall his individual features. I believe that they were small, like his stature. He kept his eyes cast down for the most part.

At the meeting, he told us that he was from Carcassonne, and had been a supporter of the Spiritual Franciscans. He appeared to be greatly afraid of the inquisitor Jean de Beaune. Because of this, I did not admire him. I considered him weak. Though he piously venerated our relics, and donated parchment to Na Berengaria, I decided that he was not a man with the strength to undergo martyrdom. Also, I resented his wealth. He must have been quite rich, though not as rich as the Donas family.

Helié then came to our next Sunday gathering at Na Berengaria's shop. He brought money, and his own relic. Na Berengaria, Guillelma Roger, Guillaume Ademar and Pierre (Perrin) Espere-en-Dius were present as well. They welcomed Helié warmly. Berengar Blanchi was not there. Nor was Imbert Rubei.

After that, I did not see Helié again until Good Friday. On this occasion he brought with him a letter of summons from the inquisitor Bernard Gui. (At least, that is what it appeared to be.) He also brought his apprentice—though I still do not know if Helié had ordered his apprentice to follow him. I understand now that the man calling himself Helié Seguier was enormously cunning, like a fox. But I was unaware of this four years ago.

Helié's apprentice was caught hiding outside Na Berengaria's shop. The boy's name was Martin; I do not know his father's name. He professed to be a believer. Again, I cannot tell if he truly was. When Martin was brought into the shop, Helié Seguier remained calm. That is why I am uncertain as to whether the boy was following his master's instructions or not.

The rest of us were more concerned about Helié's letter of summons. It was decided that he must be smuggled out of Narbonne as soon as possible. I was afraid that, if arrested, he would reveal all. I did not believe that he could withstand an inquisition. So I agreed with Na Berengaria that she should consult Imbert Rubei quickly, concerning the method of Helié's escape. Looking back, I am sure that Helié contributed little to the discussion. He was usually quiet. It was easy to forget that he was present sometimes.

The next day, Na Berengaria came to my house. I had never seen her so anxious. She told me that Helié Seguier was an inquisitorial spy—and that Jacques Bonet had been an agent of Jean de Beaune. She also told me that Father

Sejan Alegre had been aware of this for some time, and that Imbert Rubei might also know it.

At first I did not believe her. She had to persuade me that Father Sejan had conspired with a Dominican to forge the letter of summons. She was afraid that, together, they might have killed Jacques Bonet. I scoffed at this notion; I thought it preposterous. But then she explained to me about the blessed Pierre's bones. I had never been told about his bones. It *offended* me that I had never been told about them, or about the suspicions that were held about Helié Seguier. But when I heard that the bones had been bought from a Dominican, I understood why this monk would stop at nothing to conceal his part in the exchange. For Dominicans are violent men, servants of the Whore of Babylon, and drunk with the blood of martyrs.

I do not know why Helié Seguier had suddenly decided to reveal everything to Na Berengaria. *She* thought that he had been touched by the Holy Spirit, but I am not so sure. It is my opinion that he was moved by unchaste feelings for Na Berengaria, who is very beautiful, though not submissive. Whatever the reason, he had devised a plot for the capture of Father Sejan's Dominican friend. And it was this plot that Na Berengaria related to me.

She had already arranged with Imbert Rubei that Helié should hide in her vineyard, and escape over the city wall that night. (It was simply a matter of bribing one of the guards, whom I had befriended during my spell in the militia.) This seemed like a good enough arrangement. But according to Helié, he would not then be concealed on a barge, as

Imbert Rubei had promised. Instead he would very probably be slaughtered by the Dominican, who would wait on the other side of the wall. Helié therefore suggested that we lay a trap. He wanted to ambush the Dominican, and make him tell the truth about Jacques Bonet, among other things. Helié suggested that if Martin was sent over the wall first, it would provide enough distraction to allow us to surprise the Dominican, and overwhelm him.

I must admit that I had my doubts about this plan, and its purpose. To begin with, I was not completely convinced, in my heart of hearts, that Jacques Bonet was dead—or that Father Sejan had conspired with a mysterious friar to kill him. I worried that Imbert Rubei *would* appear at the base of the city wall, to help Helié Seguier, and put us all to shame.

Furthermore, I despised Helié. I thought him not only dishonest, but weak and cowardly. I could not imagine that he would be of any use whatsoever if by chance he was correct, and we were forced into a struggle. These were my feelings when Na Berengaria acquainted me with recent events, on the morning of Easter Saturday. I asked her why we could not approach Imbert frankly, and demand that he reveal all. Na Berengaria told me that, just before she had left him, Helié had advised against being honest with our brothers. He said that we would thereby lose our advantage, and perhaps suffer as a result.

I disliked such duplicity. I thought it unworthy of us. Though I wanted to help Na Berengaria, I was a reluctant confederate.

At my next meeting with Helié, however, all my doubts were swept away. This meeting occurred at his house, and Martin was also present. It is difficult to describe the change that I witnessed in Helié Seguier when I spoke to him. His meekness was entirely gone. He spoke fluently and firmly; his manner conveyed complete assurance, for all that he was as small and pale as ever. When he told me that the Dominican would have no mercy, I believed him. I could hardly do otherwise, when he remained so calm, and fixed me with such a hard, level gaze.

His eyes were green. I remember that now. They were green like seawater.

It soon became clear to me that he was quick-witted. I heard him thinking aloud, and was impressed by his cleverness. Where once I would have scoffed at his advice concerning weapons and concealment, I realised almost at once that any counsel he chose to give me would be well worth following. So I agreed with everything he said. And I promised to meet him at the Royal Gate, after the bells had rung at the end of nones.

Then I left the house, taking Martin with me. I led him straight to Na Berengaria, who conducted both of us to her vineyard. Here Martin was concealed in a kind of hut. After that, I went about collecting wood, as Helié had requested. Na Berengaria gave me permission to gather up vine stakes, vine branches and faggots. She helped me to make up two large bundles, which she undertook to throw over the wall at the end of nones. Guillelma Roger agreed to carry one of these bundles. We had no choice but to inform her of our plan, since she was at the Donas house when I arrived there with Martin. But we told nobody else.

At the end of nones, I met with Helié Seguier at the Royal Gate. He had recommended that I wear dull colours, and I did. He himself was dressed in grubby greys and browns, with a hood thrown over his head. His face (what you could see of it) was heavily begrimed, as if to prevent it from shining white in the dusk. I could not see his knife, though he assured me that it was concealed on his person.

My own sword had been secreted in a bundle of firewood. Instead of trying to smuggle it through the city gates, I retrieved the weapon once we had reached the right olive grove, and had discovered the two bundles. Though one bundle had broken apart upon hitting the ground, the other was still tied tightly around my sword. Helié Seguier seemed to admire this ploy. He even commended me for it.

Much to our relief, there was a kind of depression or trench in the earth not far from the proposed site of Martin's descent. By piling up wood over this gully, we were able to create for ourselves a good hiding place. We had to work quickly, not wishing to be accosted by any passing traveller, labourer or militia guard. But we were fortunate. Not a soul came anywhere near us before night fell, by which time we were safely lodged in our little den, with its carefully constructed rear exit.

I do not know how long we waited there. The sun set and the moon rose, during which time Helié Seguier uttered not a single word. He barely moved, as far as I can remember. When darkness engulfed us, I almost began to wonder if he was there beside me. Even his breathing was inaudible. When at last we heard the sound of footsteps, however, Helié put his mouth to my ear.

'There,' he whispered. 'Look.'

Through the spy hole that we had fashioned, I could see a moving light. This was not a lamp or candle but a lantern, and it was soon set upon the ground. In its glow, I could discern a cloaked and hooded figure. The base of the city wall was visible as well. So was one end of an unfurled rope, which had been dropped from the high ramparts.

No one else could be seen, though, and for that I was thankful. I had begun to doubt Helié Seguier's ability to bring down any man by himself. Already he had demonstrated a want of muscular strength during the construction of our hiding place. Despite his dogged tirelessness, he had not much force. Or so it seemed to me at that time.

When the hooded figure suddenly drew close to the base of the wall, and the rope started to twitch about, Helié gave my sleeve a sharp tug. That was our agreed signal. I let him go first. It was Helié's belief that, should a misplaced step announce his approach, our quarry would perhaps hesitate to flee before such a puny opponent. He might even attack Helié, if unaware that I was nearby. Above all, it was important that this wicked man should not be allowed to escape.

Therefore Helié went first. He did not stumble. I myself took a slightly different path, skirting the pool of light shed by the lantern. We closed in on our quarry's flanks, surprising him completely. He was alerted to my proximity before Helié's because I had more weight, and my tread was heavier.

But when he spun around, brandishing his knife, my sword was already aimed at his heart.

With Helié's dagger suddenly pricking his back, he was given no choice. He had to surrender. And he did, relinquishing his knife to my care. As Helié had predicted, he was a Dominican lay brother, recognisable by his garb. He was also as ugly as a breeding sow, all bristles and dewlaps. Nevertheless, because he was so big, I watched him closely.

Helié could not give the man his undivided attention at first, for Martin soon reached us, and had to be helped down from his rope. Helié did that, while I watched the Dominican. Even in the poor light, I could see the man's face turning red.

'Would you rob a servant of St Dominic?' he demanded of me. 'Do you think I have money to steal? Look! I have nothing!'

'That is not what *I* have heard, Brother Henri,' said Helié, pushing his apprentice behind him.

At this, the Dominican swung around. Although he had not recognised me, he did recognise Helié. I was afraid that he might attack, and placed the tip of my sword between his shoulder blades as Helié fell back a step. But the Dominican was too astonished to act decisively.

'You!' he said.

'Are you surprised?' said Helié. 'Were you expecting someone else?'

The Dominican then recovered his wits. He said that he *had* been expecting Helié, and that he had been asked by Imbert Rubei to conduct both Helié and his apprentice to a place of safety. Whereupon Helié said, 'With a knife in your hand? I think not.'

The Dominican protested that it was necessary to defend oneself outside the walls at night. He seemed very angry. Helié addressed him a calm voice, saying that he was in possession of all the facts. 'You,' he said, 'were the true author of that summons from Bernard Gui. It was written after Sejan discovered that I was looking for Jacques Bonet. You were perhaps hoping that I would come to the priory gate, as requested, from whence you could conduct me to a quiet place and kill me there. Do you think me a fool? I know everything. *Everything*. Except the fate of Jacques Bonet.'

The Dominican started to bluster, and shake his head. He was trembling, either with fear or fury. He said that Helié was mad; no one was intending to kill him! Helié replied that it was pointless to protest any further. He knew about Loup, and the bones, and the letter. All he wanted to know now was what had befallen Jacques.

'Let me assure you that *I* do not intend to inform on you,' he added. 'It is my intention to flee from Narbonne, and go into hiding—as I have already told Na Berengaria. So neither you nor the Beguins have anything to fear from me. But I think that, if we are to help each other in outwitting the inquisitors, we must be truthful. I myself have thrown aside all pretence, Brother Henri. You should perhaps do the same.' Looking up into the Dominican's face, Helié's own expression became strangely subtle. 'You will find that I am well acquainted with the methods employed by inquisitors of heretical depravity,' he said. 'It is clear to me that you must fear, above all, any sort of inquiry into the fate of Pierre Olivi's bones. Now—if the subject ever *should* come to the notice of Jean de Beaune, there are certain things that can be done in your defence. One need not bribe an inquisitor, you know. It is much cheaper to bribe a notary. Or a nuncio. If the registers are incomplete, there can be no conviction.'

By this I judged Helié to mean that he could give the Dominican advice on corrupting or defacing the inquisitorial records. And I thought at the time that I should very much like to share this information, which would be useful both to me and to my brothers in Christ. But I said nothing. For Helié had instructed me not to speak.

The Dominican hesitated. He seemed to be in two minds. Helié then proceeded to explain how he had identified the letter of summons as a forgery. Though I cannot remember exactly what he said, I do recall being impressed by the sharpness of his intellect. Still, however, the Dominican remained silent. So Helié adopted another tactic.

'Perhaps you distrust my motives,' he said. 'Perhaps you believe that I am trying to entrap you all. If that is the case, then let me explain why I am here—and not in Toulouse, making my report to Bernard Gui.' He pointed at Martin. 'This boy is my apprentice, and my heir. He has been infected with heretical opinions. If any one of the Beguins is ever interrogated, then his name will be mentioned. Whereupon Martin, too, will be arrested. I cannot allow that to happen, Brother. I will do everything in my power to prevent it.'

No doubt Helié was lying, for he was a good liar—as I have since learned. But at the time, I was persuaded. So was the boy, who gazed at him with frank adoration. That admiring look must have been all the Dominican needed, by way of proof.

He said, 'And now you have told *me* about him.'

'Exactly.' Helié nodded. 'You know as much as the Beguins do. I have entrusted you with a shield to use against me. How can I seek to inform on you, when to do so would condemn this boy? His safety is my sole concern. Therefore I *must* ensure that neither you—nor the Beguins—ever come to the notice of Jean de Beaune.' Helié cocked his head, and edged closer to the Dominican. 'If Jacques Bonet is dead,' he murmured, 'then there is nothing to fear from that quarter. If he is alive, then he could be a threat. I must know where he is. I must know what he might reveal. And knowing this—' his voice dropped even lower, '—knowing this, I shall make my arrangements. You understand?'

It was at this moment that I was assailed by grave misgivings. I realised that my fate was in the hands of two ravening heretics—a Dominican and an agent of Bernard Gui. These men had more in common with each other than they did with me. I suddenly felt that they understood each other, and was appalled at the realisation.

'Of course, you may choose to walk away from here without revealing anything,' Helié concluded. 'But where will that leave you? No better off. Worse, if anything. A wise man, Brother Henri, would not scorn my help.'

Then the Dominican spoke at last. In his gruff way he said, 'Jacques is no threat. Not any more.'

'But he was?' Helié asked.

'I panicked,' the Dominican replied, shifting about. His manner was at the same time impatient, angry and defensive. 'The fool believed that I could perform miracles. He discovered the truth about Olivi's bones—what they were, and who had stolen them. Imbert Rubei had revealed my name; that simpleton has been a burden to me all along. It was he who invited Jacques Bonet into his home, without consulting wiser heads. It was he who allowed himself to be tricked into divulging my secret. Then Jacques came to me, and asked me to help him in exchange for his silence. He wanted to escape the clutches of Jean de Beaune by disappearing into a priory. A priory! He said that he would never be found, if he disguised himself as a Dominican lay brother.' Brother Henri shook his head at this. 'He wanted robes, and a letter from the Prior, and all manner of things. It was impossible. He thought that he could find refuge in some priory far from Carcassonne. He would not listen to reason. He said that if I refused to help, he would report me to my superiors—and by this means, perhaps, might win some kind of pardon for his sins. He was mad.'

'So you killed him to protect yourself?' Helié proposed.

'I lost my temper,' the Dominican confessed. 'I hit him with a mattock. We were in the priory grounds.'

'And then?'

'I cut him up with a saw and burned him.' Martin gasped, and so did I, but Helié remained calm as the Dominican continued. 'I burned him in the bread ovens, while joints were being roasted. I gave his clothes to the almoner, saying that they had been donated to the priory. And what was left after that, I interred.' Brother Henri folded his arms. 'He was an unrepentant heretic, and would have gone to the stake in the end—taking many others with him. Though I killed him in error, without stopping to reflect on the consequences, I am not sorry for it. You would have done the same.'

I remember thinking: He may be right, at that. No doubt Helié *would* have done the same. Then Helié asked where Jacques's remains had been hidden. But the Dominican would not say.

'Because you do not trust me?' said Helié.

'Because I do not trust *them*.' Brother Henri jerked his thumb in my direction. 'The less they learn about me, the better.'

'Does Berengar Blanchi know your name, or the full story of your crime?'

'No.'

'Just Sejan and Imbert?'

'Yes.'

'And now—Martin? And Blaise, here? Not so many.'

'But Berengar Blanchi knows Sejan. And others know Berengar. The arrest of one will mean the arrest of all, as you must understand.' This time it was the Dominican who drew closer to Helié, stooping down to address him. 'Something has to be done. Can you offer no solution?' His tone became oily. 'You are a clever and experienced man. You know how inquisitors think. Tell me where to go, and what to do, for I can gain entry to many secret places. With my help, perhaps you can find an answer to our predicament?'

'Yes,' said Helié. 'I believe I can.'

And then he plunged his knife into the side of the Dominican's neck.

Thinking back, I realise that he must have opened up the man's entire throat with a single, slicing jerk when he pulled the blade out again. At the time, I saw only the blood, which sprayed out in a great gush. With his windpipe cut, the Dominican could not even groan, let alone scream. He sank to the ground, gurgling, and died at my feet.

Helié had stepped back, but he was still covered in blood. First he wiped his blade on the hem of his cloak. Then he said to me, 'It had to be done. He would have killed you all, without qualm, just as he killed Jacques Bonet.'

I simply stared. Words cannot convey my shock and horror. Though I have seen men die, it was never so brutally. *No* man should have to die thus.

'Make no mistake, we could not trust him.' Though Helié spoke quietly, I sensed that he was not as calm as he appeared. 'Having got away from here, he would have worked to destroy us all. Though it might not appear so, this is the best solution—for you, at least. And I have taken the sin upon myself.' Helié next turned to his apprentice. He said, 'It was for your own protection. Sometimes one must attack to defend. You have to learn that, Martin, or we shall never be safe.'

But the boy rejected this lesson. I saw it in his eyes: he abominated both the man and his bloody act. He began to retreat, step by step, his mouth crumpling.

Helié watched him for a moment. I do not know if he was pleased or dismayed that his apprentice should have disowned him. His face told me nothing.

When he spoke, it was only after a long pause. He said to me: 'Take him back over the wall with you. Send him home. I shall see to matters down here.'

And that, essentially, is what happened. I climbed back over the wall, behind Martin. Helié remained. Whatever he did with the corpse, he was thorough; no trace of Brother Henri the Dominican was ever found. If he sliced up the body and burned it, I would not be surprised. It became my opinion, and the opinion of Na Berengaria also, that he was demonically possessed. The Devil stared out of his eyes that night. I saw it. The boy saw it. Martin was shaking so badly when he climbed the wall, I was afraid for him.

That was the last time I met the man who called himself Helié Seguier. He left Narbonne the following day. I have heard tell that his affairs were settled by a notary whose name I forget; the apprentice inherited his house. I saw this boy once or twice afterwards, in the street, though not recently. He never again appeared at the Donas shop. When his eyes met mine, he looked away.

I believe that he has repudiated the doctrine of Holy Poverty.

I do not know where Helié might have gone. I made no inquiries about him. Though he once professed to be a follower of Pierre Olivi, I do not now think that he ever was, despite the fact that he failed to inform on us. Do not ask me what his motives were. I have never understood them. May God preserve me from such an understanding, for Helié Seguier was a strange, unholy man, beset by evil thoughts.

You should know this. He was your creature.

The apple does not fall far from the tree.

Author's note

This book is based on true events, involving many real people. Their stories are partly told in contemporary inquisitorial records.

Blaise Bouer and Berengar Blanchi, for instance, were tried before the Inquisition in 1325. Blaise earned a pardon by going to Sicily to ferret out other heretics; in 1328 he was absolved and set free.

Berengaria Donas was tried in 1326—the same year as Guillaume Adhemar and Pierre Espere-en-Dius. Imbert Rubei faced the Inquisition in 1328, as did Guillelma Roger, who was imprisoned as a penitent heretic.

The fate of Pierre Olivi's bones has never been discovered. In his work *Practica Inquisitionis Heretice Pravitatis* (*The Conduct of the Inquisition of Heretical Depravity*), which was finished in 1323–24, Bernard Gui wrote, 'His [Olivi's] body was exhumed, carried away, and hidden in the year of our Lord 1318. There is much doubt as to where it may be, and different tales are told by different people about it.'

There is no record of a Helié Bernier (alias Seguier) ever being tried before the Inquisition. A note scribbled in the margin of his journal states that it was given to Martin Moresi 'for his protection against calumny'.